ADAM TS CONLON

Wolves Of War: The Threat

PRIVATE DRAGON
Publishing

First edition

ISBN: 978-1-951405-09-0

Editing by Theo L Parsons
Advisor: Jake Lueckler
Typesetting by Samantha Knight

This book was professionally typeset on Reedsy.
Find out more at reedsy.com

Contents

Acknowledgement

special thanks:

Alice Conlon

Rebecca Luo

Garrick Davis

&

M. B. Whitlock

Wolves of War

ACT I

THE THREAT

BY

ADAM T. S. CONLON

"What are the most necessary qualities of an officer in time of war? Answer: courage, and a contempt of death."
—*Aleksandr Kuprin* The Duel *(1905)*

I: War Is Coming

ORRICK LOOKED AROUND THE SMALL barracks, inhaling the musty smell of old wood. Though he had spent these last eight years away, the scent conjured old memories of breaking curfew to whisper tales of knights long dead with other pages, fueled by the thrill that a patrolling knight could enter at any moment. He would soon realize his boyhood dreams of grandeur.

His hand, calloused and riddled with pale scars, gripped an iron bedframe. This room held twelve beds spaced evenly apart and sheeted with stiff, white linen. A mannequin stood next to each bed, all wearing the chainmail hauberks and sword-belts of their respective squires. At the far end, a bookshelf was laden with dog-eared combat manuals.

He closed his eyes and thought of the past fourteen years. He came to Akademia Palatæ just a boy of seven, from Newtown in the Brzeg Voivodship. His instructors taught him reading, writing and sums, as well as how to sharpen swords and scour mail.

At ten, he began swordplay and archery. At thirteen, Wilhelm pan Atrax, Count of Eastern Nin, furthered his instruction, coaching him in riding and military tactics. Orrick found the sea-hardened man a font of knowledge, but hardly the kindest. Whenever Orrick erred—and oft did Orrick err—his master beat him thoroughly.

The memory made him grip the post harder. Every thrashing was a lesson, every scar a reminder. But never did he make twice the same mistake.

It seemed not so long ago that he scoured mail until his hands were raw or cut himself while sharpening or poorly drawing swords.

Am I truly ready? Have I truly earned the right to be a knight, to be addressed as "pan?"

He smelled the sea air of the Newport wharves, a hundred leagues south. Weight on his shoulder broke his reverie—a hand. He turned, saw the face of Anton Dasher, another knight apprentice.

"Thought you'd be here," he said, smiling.

It always shocked Orrick how white and straight his teeth were. His cheeks and the corners of his eyes dimpled. With a pointed chin and silky chestnut hair, he was oft surrounded by gaggles of giggling girls.

Once his friend's initial dazzle wore off, Orrick sighed. "I'm reflecting."

Anton shook his head, relinquished Orrick's shoulder. "'Tis difficult to conceive sometimes. We're both boys from Newtown, sent to the academy fourteen years past. Now we've but a sennight before we surrender ourselves to duty."

"We've waited so long, hard to believe the time's arrived. I, for one, cannot wait to serve." He hoped Anton saw not through the falsehood.

Happily, he didn't. "Know your rank?"

"None of us do until the ceremony."

Anton ran his fingers through his hair, chuckling. "Well, is there aught you hope for?"

"We've all desires. I'd like some adventure. Pan Atrax would address the captains of incoming vessels. We apprehended smugglers more than once."

Orrick smiled at the memory. His teeth were nowhere near as straight as Anton's. All Pallatons grew two sets of incisors, one over the other. He closed his mouth and ran his tongue over the right fang, liking the feel of its point.

A massive frame darkened the garret, blocking the torchlight.

In stepped Rupert Sedgwick, with coppery hair and a barrel chest. He was quite jovial, and his gut shook every time he showed it. This time was no different: he swung a bottle of wine, sloshing it around. He stank of the stuff, eyes only slits, he laughed loud. "There's me boys!"

"Celebrating, are you?" asked Anton, closing the barracks door.

"E'ryone is! Shite, I'm surprised y'all ain't!"

Orrick frowned, bemused. "Is that kitchen wine?"

Rupert belched. "Wazzit t' yeh, 'Rick?"

"The wine's for next week's ceremony," Orrick answered. "Should Pan Tuttle catch you—"

"Oh, fie on 'im! The Ole Turtle ain't gonna know 'bout this! 'E's too busy—" Rupert hiccoughed "—gettin' ready fer the cer'mony!"

"It matters not if the headmaster catches you," replied Orrick. "Any knight 'round the grounds may turn you over to him. If he's too busy to discipline you, the task will go to them."

"B'aw, y' worry too much!" The large squire hiccoughed again. His mouth curved into a sleepy grin. "Some people went 'round t' Albion's bars. They're gon' be too crowded! 'Sides, I only had that Ianth shite! I didn't touch the Flavès!"

4

Orrick chuckled. Tourm had two winemaking regions: Ianth and Flavès. The former offered sour, bitter reds. The latter produced sweeter and bolder whites, much more preferred throughout the nation.

"The bars can't be that crowded," Anton said. "Only three-and-twenty graduate."

Rupert seemed not to hear him. He continued bellowing his tale. "... So, I went an' found the bottlery—an' the *bottles*!" He snorted at his own jape. "So, I decided—"

The door opened, and they all stiffened toward it. Rupert hid the bottle behind his back.

Indeed, a knight entered—with blood-red hair and olive skin. His square jaw clenched when he laid his eyes upon them.

Maxim pan Ausma!

Orrick and Anton's fists went to their hearts, the customary greeting between soldiers. Rupert's fist went to his as well, sluggish and off-mark.

Maxim seemed not to notice. "Good ... I was told you three would be here."

Terror gripped Orrick's heart. Pan Ausma was a Knight Valiant, a general. His word held sway over even Tuttle's. What did he want with three squires?

Rupert. The stench of wine was all he could smell. He worried he might drown in it. *He came looking for us …*

"I wonder why three pupils would remain here whilst the others celebrated." He eyed Rupert. "But … I am glad for it."

"Pan?"

Ausma looked at Orrick, his face stern. "A sennight past, three armsmen of Newtown deserted their posts with weapons belonging to your father. Tonight, someone saw them in an Albion tavern, bragging of their misdeeds."

Orrick frowned. *Why would they want to steal my father's weapons?* Stealing weapons from the house that hired you was a terrible thing, punishable by loss of hand. Deserting your post, however, meant death. "Are the men apprehended?"

"No. 'Tis why I came to you."

Anton ran his fingers through his hair, smile faltering. "Us?"

"Aye," said Ausma, smirking. "Seeing as you and Orrick are the only students hailing from Newtown, I thought it best to send you."

Orrick furrowed his brow. "Lacking a knight's company?"

"I've spoken already with Tuttle. He agrees. Besides, you're not mere squires but knights' apprentice. Think of this as your final test. If unable are you to fell three deserters, unworthy are you of Szczerbieç's touch."

"Only the two of us?" asked Orrick.

Squiring, Orrick had apprehended many a smuggler, but each of those times had been with Count Atrax and a slew of other soldiers. Never faced he traitors alone. That they armed themselves with Newtown steel made it personal. Orrick wanted to go. These men dishonored his House.

"Rupert must come with us," said Anton.

"*Must* he?" asked Ausma. His blood-red eyebrows rose, plainly shocked. "Figuring how?"

"We've all fought together in the yard," said Orrick. "Know we his capabilities."

"Besides," added Anton, "'twill be three against three, pan. Evens the odds for the deserters."

"Do you concern yourself more with justice or fairness?"

Anton stammered for an answer, but Orrick jumped in. "With all due respect, pan, you've given us a mission and we need to see it done—before the deserters decide to leave for places unknown."

Ausma looked the drunk squire up and down and up again. His lips curled. "If you wish, although you may rescind your request because of his ... state."

7

"Nah!" Rupert bellowed. Clearing his throat nervously, he added, "I mean—no, lord knight! I'll—uh—I'll manage."

Ausma's face became stony once more. "As you like it. The deserters alight in the Black Horseman alehouse." He turned on his heel and left, cape rippling behind him.

"Right," said Rupert, surprisingly sober. "Let's get ready."

Normally squires wore gambesons, jackets of thick material. But Orrick, Rupert, and Anton were no mere squires. Just short of six moons passed, they each attained the title of knight apprentice. It was a small, private ceremony, but held great weight. In their masters' eyes, they did well enough to earn voices amongst knights. Whereas knights would shush normal squires, they considered apprentices equals, valuing their input.

But a knight apprentice did more than just parley with knights. Their masters expected them to fight well, always considering tactics. Because of that, the three had their own chainmail hauberks, steel grieves, and goodly made swords, offering better protection in combat.

They equipped the grieves and chainmail shirts, going over padded gambesons. Last came the sword-belts that held their weapons: a Rhabdolian-style longsword, a dirk, and a dagger.

Anton offered his pleasant smile. "Feeling knightly, Orrick?"

Orrick looked to his hands, gloved in thick leather. "I ..." He shook his head. Why these armsmen deserted their posts was beyond him, but he knew he must stop them. His hands became fists. "Even if I don't feel as one, I'll make them believe I am!"

Anton's grin widened. "Well said! Let's make haste."

They left Akademia Palatæ, marching through the hallowed halls of stone and torches. Squires and pages, awake and about even past curfew, littered the way. They slunk to the shadows as the three graduates passed, as though they could melt into the walls and save themselves from sight. If Orrick were not on a mission, he would turn them in. Instead, they continued.

Outside, the chilly night awaited. Wróżka's Moon came in a sennight's time, the first day of spring with it. For now, winter clung tight. A blanket of clouds choked the sky, sprinkling snow gently down. Orrick hardened himself against the cold.

Rupert guffawed. "Forgot we our cloaks!"

Anton shivered. "Should we—?"

Orrick shook his head. "I'd prefer not to go back."

"Fair 'nough. On then!"

The guardsmen stopped them at the gate, questioning them differently than Orrick expected. "Finally getting some drink, eh? Joining your fellow squires for a bit o' Ianth's finest?"

"We've a task from Hetman Ausma himself," Orrick answered, frowning.

The guardsmen looked at one another, shrugged, and allowed them onward.

They walked through the cobblestone streets that parted the rows of houses, each with an oil streetlamp burning in front, moonlight shining on the smooth white rooves. They turned at Steelers' Row. In the day, the doors were open and the forges hot. Smiths crafted everything from weapons and armor to gates and cutlery to jewelry. But now, all was dark and quiet.

And cold. Very cold.

Further south lay the slums. Streetlamps came fewer here, and so too the businesses. Crumbling little houses stood peppered with holes. Thatched rooves moldered away to wide black patches. Many a beggar found surcease upon the stoop of shops long closed.

The Black Horseman maintained a reputation for bringing in brigands, rotters, tempters dealing in illegal philters, and the occasional deserter. They found it by the noise. Inside, men half in their cups shouted out a bawdy tune.

Orrick swallowed hard. Anton smirked and nodded. Rupert's glazed eyes shined with determination. Orrick put his hand on the door and pushed it open.

Drunken singing hit Orrick like a punch, loud and not as sweet as the bards that played in the square. And if the singing was a punch, the smell was a cleaver to the face. Wine, ale, sweat, and urine stung his eyes.

The patrons seemed not to notice them. Orrick scanned the room and saw nothing out of place. Men stinking drunk, whores in their laps, barmaids serving them tankards.

Orrick walked to the back and saw them half hidden in the shadows, gripping flagons of ale, boots scuffed and muddily caked. The patrons' eyes were glazed even more than Rupert's. Their faces were streaked black with sweat and grime.

Orrick kept his surprise, for each deserter looked barely older than him. Perhaps that youthfulness added to their disregard. Their laughing faces—laughing despite their treachery—burned in Orrick's mind. They thought they could get away with their theft. *Whatever they plot, it ends here.*

Orrick drew his sword. "Lay down your arms!"

Anton and Rupert drew as well. The sight of naked steel spread silence throughout the tavern. Men stopped mid-drink. Barmaids ceased their services. Whores clung frightened to their patrons.

The face of the center deserter matched the others in the bar, but soon contorted into a stained smile. "How'm I gonna lay down me arms, lad? They's on m' body!"

Orrick's eyes narrowed. "Meant I the arms you stole from my

11

father!"

The sneer widened. The man to his left chuckled. "A man needs arms t' work, lad. Ain't you know that? Pity 'bout your papa. Hope 'e finds'm." He shrugged and nodded to the whores. "Otherwise your mum'd end up like these ladies 'ere!"

Now all of them laughed.

"Relinquish at once the weapons you took from Newtown or face a Pallaton wroth!"

The lackey on the left could take no more. He pounded his fist on the table. "'Im an' 'is—ah, ha, ha, ha!"

"Now, now, 'old on lads!" said the central rogue. "This moppet claims 'e's the son o' Voivod Pallaton." He stood, and Orrick saw the weapon at his hip: a single-edged saber with a delicate arch. The others followed suit, also wearing ornate blades.

Orrick looked to the patrons. None of them had moved. All eyes were upon them. He met the leader's gaze.

"'Tis a right pity ... see, you've got it backwards!" He smiled again. Orrick could practically smell the rot. He wanted to smash his pommel into that incessant sneer until it was nothing but blood and splintered teeth. "These swords're *ours*, milord! Lord Pallaton gave'm t'us, 'e did! 'Twere for a job well done, said 'e!"

The other two deserters agreed, stupidly bouncing their heads.

"*Silence!*" Orrick cut the air with his sword. "Return the weapons *now!*"

The laughter stopped. The central deserter put his mud-caked boot on the table. "The moppet wants the swords, lads. Best *give'm!*"

He kicked the table, sending ale and half-eaten food clattering to the floor. The three criminals bared their steel and leapt over the mess. The entire tavern lurched as patrons and employees alike scrambled to exit. The leader clashed with Orrick, blade meeting blade.

Anton and Rupert dashed forward. Rupert was large, but not slow. He slashed at the lackey's sword hand and plunged his sword through his chest. He seized, and Rupert let him fall to the ground.

Using his hips to his advantage, Orrick drove the leader back, slamming him into the wall, shakily pressing his sword closer and closer to the deserter's pockmarked face. *This is over*, thought Orrick. Yet, as he struggled with the leader, he found he could not make good on his promise. The lead deserter struggled free, slashed wildly. Orrick parried and dashed away.

Fire in his eyes, Orrick rounded on the youth, no match for the knight apprentice. But even with the deserter backed into a corner, Orrick could not strike true even when presented with an opening. Something stayed his hand, uncertain what.

The leader drew back, and Orrick pursued. The saber swiped.

Orrick doubled back—but not before the tip sliced his cheek. He shouted out and touched the wound, saw blood on his hand.

Then he knew.

Fear stayed his hand.

He remembered the wharves of Newport, where the seafaring Order of the Black Dog had captured pirates with several crates of illicit molomak. Orrick had cornered the fled captain in an alleyway. Pan Atrax arrived, said the kill was Orrick's. He would forever hear the dead man's taunt.

"Aye, lad! Kill me! I's dead anyway!"

But Orrick had faltered. Even if he was the captain of a drug-smuggling ship, did he truly deserve death? His harm was indirect. Wouldn't the dungeons better fit his crimes?

The captain attempted to flee, knocking Orrick to the ground. Pan Atrax finished the captain with an axe-blow. Afterward, he stammered on about being unable to finish him, thinking about the man's life. Pan Atrax told Orrick something important, something he needed to know: "On the field o' battle, 'tis kill or be killed."

The frantic clash of metal brought him back. One sword beat down upon the other. Anton cried out, "Help me! Help me, Rupert!"

Orrick had a request of his own, a question he wanted answered.

"Why fled you your post?"

The lead rogue smiled his black-toothed grin. "Bugger the moppet an' 'is questions!"

Someone screamed in pain and horror. Orrick felt hot blood spray on his neck. He heard the booming guffaw that could only be Rupert. "Finish'm, Orrick! These cur ain't naught t' a Pallaton!"

"I'm surprised this *craven* is a Pallaton! Seems you're no good, lad!"

Orrick cared not for his taunts. When their swords next met, he drew close, locking the blades together. "Tell me why deserted you your post!"

"Bugger Newtown!" the rogue spat. "War's a-comin'!"

Orrick's eyes widened. "Tourm's seen peace for fifty years. What war—?"

"Y' can't make me!"

The rogue drew back, breaking the lockup. He lunged forward in a wild dash, swinging too wide. Orrick sidestepped and Rupert caught the man between the ribs.

The sight was horrible. The deserter dropped his blade as blood dribbled from his mouth. The point of Rupert's sword stuck out of his back.

15

After, Rupert took a discarded bar rag and wiped clean his blade. He inspected it, found it good, and sheathed it. He turned his gaze to Orrick and Anton, disappointed.

"What's the matter wit' y' both? That's three kills for me and none for the people *from* Newtown." He took a step backward, as if in fear of some contagion. "Y' ain't ... *cravens*, are y'?"

"I'm *not* a craven!" argued Anton.

He might have said so, but Orrick saw different. His usually placid eyes were wide, and his voice wavered.

"It's just that the armsman I faced was very skilled. You ought know, Rupert!" He pointed to the corpse. "You fought him yourself!"

Orrick looked at it and gasped. It was the first time he'd laid eyes on anything so gruesome. The deserter had been cleaved from his collarbone to the base of his ribcage.

Rupert stroked his stubbly chin and nodded knowingly. "Aye, aye; 'e put up a good fight." He eyed Orrick. "Now what 'bout *you*?"

Orrick ran his tongue over his right fang, looking for an answer. His mind kept returning to the alleyway, to Pan Atrax's warning. His mentor had tutored him in many aspects of fighting. He displayed great skill with swordplay and tactics. He was fair with the spear and maul, and only slightly better with archery. Despite all his efforts, Orrick could not kill then

... and he could not kill now.

When he lunged, he was open ... He practically delivered his soul to the void. I could finish him not. But I mustn't lose face.

He looked Rupert in the eye. He thought of a lie—a half-truth, really. "These deserters disgraced mine House. I'd know why." He was sure his voice was stronger than Anton's had been.

"Sometimes 'tis better to judge without deliberation," Rupert grunted. He was a year older than Orrick; taller, as well. No doubt he had spent more time with his knighted master than Orrick had with Pan Atrax. Orrick eyed the corpses, certain these kills were not Rupert's first.

No matter. Orrick looked at his own sword, free of blood. Rupert was right. If he continued hesitating, he'd be lying in pool of blood with them. *Am I that cowardly?*

"Orrick?" He blinked. Anton asked, "Are you well? You became quiet."

"Lost in thought, I suppose."

Anton's dimples slackened. "Where those deserters were going matters not, Orrick. Nor why they fled. What matters is, they flee no longer."

"Aye, you're right." He looked to the door. The Black Horseman was trashed: overturned tables and broken flagons littered the ground. "Come, we'd best alert Pan Ausma."

But his mind was not truly on the deserters. Not any longer, at least. Frowning, he again steeled himself for the cold, but felt worse than any facial expression could convey.

How will I ever be a knight proper if I cannot kill mine enemies?

II: Blustery Meetings

Armitage Pardwy, the Crown Prince of Tourm, set down his pewter chalice. He had a promise to keep. If he did not dress now, he'd be late.

He would meet Orrick Pallaton at Lamplighter Inn, a nice tavern at the northern entrance of Travelers' Way, where pubs and inns lined all down the lane.

He'll be Orrick pan Pallaton come the morrow. Armitage smiled at the thought. *Certainly, a feast will follow the ceremony. But why celebrate then when we can celebrate now?*

Armitage turned away from his gilt vanity mirror and entered his walk-in closet, nostrils welcoming the fabric's flowery scents. There was nothing he enjoyed more than high fashion. He ran his fingers over each garment he passed: the finest velvets, the smoothest silk, velour deep and rich. He stopped at his newest accruement, a half-cape from Pinberry, the nation to the north. The outside was black velvet, and inside was gold-cloth, the fabric woven of golden filé that shined like no other. Still, before his eyes all his clothes shimmered like jewels.

They were wonderful, true enough, but these staples of finery were not his aim. He found two garments and parted them. Behind the line of clothes sat a simple wooden chest, its iron hinges black and bumpy. He found a key hidden inside a coat pocket, unlocked the chest, and opened the lid.

He lifted these simplest of clothes as though they were the finest treasure: a sackcloth tunic, leather jerkin, and coarse, rough-spun woolen britches. He put all of these on, then donned the boots of peeling leather underneath. At the very bottom was a heavy cloak, brown and hooded.

He wore these garments more than any other, even though they were common, ugly, and quite frankly unfit for a prince. But they were comfortable and, most importantly, provided anonymity.

Smiling still, Armitage closed the chest, returned the key, and left the closet for the vanity mirror. There, he soured.

He was a prince, true. Nowhere near as strapping as his younger brother. His hair sprung from his scalp all wiry and bright orange; Mother's color and his Father's type. He thought it hideous, especially with his square jaw yet oddly pointed chin. Looking upon it always spoiled his mood. The freckles dotting his pale face like stars on a clear night sky held no such beauty in his eyes. He rubbed his pointed jaw. The coppery bristles irritated his soft skin. The beard came patchy, but he would be glad to cover those freckles even if he only grew wisps.

I look a sporing mushroom, grumped Armitage, and drank from his cup. Once he returned the pewter chalice to the table, he stood in front of the mirror and straightened his back. With the jerkin and the cloak, one could hardly make out his stick-thin frame. He hunched his back and stiffened his right leg, dragging it as he walked.

Straightening again, Armitage smiled at his reflection.

Now ... should I do a Nin accent, or Newtown?

He thought about his last trip to Pinberry with his father. The people of Dactide City spoke very much like Tourmians. But the people of the Ásmo region spoke with rolled tongues and exotic flavors.

Yes, I could be a merchant from Ás—

A knock on his door disrupted his thoughts. He went to it but remembered the horrible brown cloak enshrouding his body. He gasped. *Not good, not good! Should my parents catch me, they'll not even let me attend the ceremony!*

His parents—especially his father, King Biel—approved not of Armitage's tavern-going. Armitage only tried to get in touch with the people of Albion City. They would one day be his subjects, and he did not believe a king should hide himself away in his palace. Father thought differently. He only saw it as Armitage drinking himself into a stupor, without the safety of his sworn sentries.

"Gamboling with peasants," he calls it.

His lips sneered and the rap came again, sharper this time.

Damn, I cannot wait!

He feigned tiredness, making his voice sound sleepy. "Who is it?"

"Ozella," the hard answer came. "You aren't truly sleeping, Armitage."

His betrothed was the only daughter of House Altgeld, sovereign of the Rhabdolia Duchy to the west. Once, Tourm and Rhabdolia were two separate kingdoms, and bitter rivals. Fifty years ago, Tourm finally claimed the land. The kingdom had been peaceful ever since.

But the longstanding peace was not without its repercussions. Rumors spread that Rhadbolia sought independence from Tourm. The only way to appease them was a marriage between the Crown Prince of Tourm and House Altgeld. Right outside the door was the culmination of that deal.

I doubt any father was prouder to have a girl.

Politics between Tourm and Rhabdolia mattered not. What

mattered was that she had caught him. Armitage sighed and unbolted the door, allowing her to slip inside his chambers.

She was beautiful, he supposed. Even at night, without her rouge, her milk-colored skin was radiant. From her nightcap spilled auburn hair, long, soft, and straight. And her sleeping gown was of the thinnest silk, leaving her pointed breasts exposed to whoever happened upon her as she walked down the hall. But she liked it that way. She was Armitage's by right, by oath between the Houses Pardwy and Altgeld. That did not stop her from using her natural charms and wiles to entice looks from guardsmen.

Her thin eyebrows rose as she looked Armitage up and down. "You mean to go out tonight?"

She, too, knew his secret. Like Father, she cared not for it. But if his future wife could walk the corridors in such an immodest state, then surely he could enjoy some drinks with his good friend.

"I do," said he. "Mean I to celebrate with Orrick. After tomorrow, he'll go away to wherever his knightly duties take him."

"He could be a guardsman in Castle Albicant, you know. This needn't be goodbye."

"Most likely he'll be a knight-errant for Brzeg," Armitage sighed. "Most Pallaton sons return to Newtown when their training is over. Why wouldn't Orrick be the same? You've

23

met Voivod Pallaton, haven't you? You know how *traditional* he can be."

Ozella wrinkled her nose at the thought.

The Rhabdolians hated the Pallatons, hated Brzeg. After all, it was a Pallaton—Orrick's grandfather—who broke their defenses fifty years past and won the war for Tourm. More than that, they could not accept the ancient traditions. Savages, they called the Brzegu, and the Pallatons were their lords. Why, the last time the Voivod met with King Biel in Albion, he came without a baggage train.

Ozella went to the pitcher of mulled wine and poured herself a cup. She sipped, staring at Armitage. "Very well, go. I'll tell His Majesty not. But hark well upon my words, Armitage: news of war comes on travelers' lips. One day you'll be caught, and I don't wish to think of the unsavory alehouse you'll inhabit when that happens."

Armitage waved his hand dismissively. "You and Father worry too much! Besides, I'll have Orrick protecting me." He investigated his own cup and chuckled. "Although I *could* be less conspicuous." He thought of an outing three moons past and rubbed the back of his neck. "Ordering a glass of nineteen-sixty-two *Pałac xe Triumfu* was not my finest moment."

"Only a lord would dare order a wine so rare, let alone one seventeen years his senior." Ozella shook her head, wagging her copper locks. She took another sip of wine. "Honestly, what were you thinking?"

Armitage barked a laugh, silenced himself. "I—" staring into his cup, the smile would not leave his face. "I was thinking it was one of Flavès's best and that I'd like to drink it."

"'Tisn't only you, Armitage," she continued, ignoring him. "You drag *Orrick* into your gallivanting as well. He needs to be awake tomorrow—fully awake for his vows, and not crapulent."

"It'll be fine. There's naught different this time than there is any other time. Besides, however am I to lead them—knights and peasants—if know I naught their faiths, faults, hopes, and causes?"

Armitage had once asked Orrick that same thing, and he gave no answer. However, he knew he would not have the same luck with her.

Ozella replaced the cup on the table. When she turned to face Armitage again, she scowled. "There are other ways. This gets out of hand—this time, gamboling with the peasants could cost your friend his knighthood!"

She walked to his heavy door and opened it only a crack. Before she left, she turned to say one thing more. "Is he even your friend, I wonder? Or do you just use him as a scapegoat for your drunken capering?"

With that she closed the door behind her.

Armitage placed his own cup on the table. Suddenly he was

not very thirsty, and yet all he wanted to do was drink—drink and forget.

He scoffed. *Of course is Orrick my friend.*

He remembered their meeting as though it was yesterday. If truth be told, it was only six moons past. But their meetings became so regular that he felt they'd been friends for years.

Orrick had only just returned with all the other squires to prepare for their final examinations. There was a welcoming feast, like every year. The King met with Headmaster Tuttle, the instructors, and the returning cadets proud to call themselves knights apprentice.

Armitage remembered the others squires as haughty, smirking, laughing, bragging ... but Orrick had picked at his food, looking like a failure—something to which Armitage could relate.

He looked out the window. Dark purple sky, the moon a single, silver eye. It reminded him of Ozella. Always watching, always scrutinizing, passing judgment, and never blinking.

Damn her.

Why did *he* have to marry her?

He wondered if his younger brother would have fared better against her sharp tongue. It mattered nothing now. Alabaster was taller and stronger, handsomer as well. But Armitage was firstborn. The contract was signed and sealed; the oath spoken by king and prince, duke and daughter.

He looked at the winecup. *It might as well be ashes.* Surely Lamplighter Inn would offer better company than what he received in his chambers.

Armitage pulled the hood over his head and slipped from the room. The hardest part, always, was sneaking out. Guards patrolled the palace halls. Half a dozen knights watched the gatehouse, warding off anyone that might approach the castle. And these were not mere foot soldiers, but White Knights, overseen by Paladin Ladd pan Winchell. The knights themselves claimed they knew every inch of the palace, even those the royal family had long forgotten. It was necessary to protect the king.

While the Prince did not disagree, he trusted these "forgotten places" would be unguarded. If the royal family knew nothing about them, why would a thief or assassin?

Armitage slunk from his room, careful to remain against the walls. Though torches burned in their sconces, casting a dim light on marble halls, the darkness provided enough cover to creep around.

He found the place two moons past, and he used it as often as he could. Before, the night watchmen would catch him each time he tried to sneak off. So, Armitage spent many a night and day searching for one of these "forgotten places."

27

Finally, he found one: a small room with a hearth perhaps used as a solar for visiting barons. Though it might have seemed an ordinary room at first glance, he had noticed that the hearth was without soot. He found that the stones at the bottom could be removed, leaving a black tunnel in their wake. He called it the sneak thief's crawl.

And to think, he chuckled to himself, *I never would have discovered it if those knights hadn't mentioned it.*

He came to the room and slipped inside. Happily, soldiers rarely came down its corridors. If they did, however, the cloak allowed him to blend into the shadows the moment he saw a far-off white glint.

Immediately he went to the hearth and removed the stones. He wondered if those White Knight braggarts even knew of this place. He wished not to ask them, though. That would ruin any plans for future excursions.

Finished at last, the Prince looked at the sprawling darkness in front of him. He crouched on his hands and knees—thankful he came without his finer frock—and crawled through. Only blackness lay ahead and around. His fingers slid along the ground, touching smooth pebbles. Once or twice, he felt something like blades of grass. He prayed no spiders hid inside the lightless tunnel.

That would be terrible if they found me a corpse, halfway inside a tunnel, on my way to gambol with peasants ...

But no spiders came. Or, if they did, they bit not.

Armitage sighed as he neared the end, exasperated.

A pinprick of light and the air grew cold. Tomorrow was the first day of Wróżka's Moon—the vernal equinox. But it seemed as though she took her time. *Then again, the Goddess of Wind could very well prefer the air be cold.*

Armitage crawled through the tunnel as he approached it. A burst of chilling air slid invisible fingers around him. Shivering, he retreated into the folds of his cloak.

As he exited, he found himself pressed against the castle wall. The moat circled around the structure and remained frozen. Part of him wanted to slip-slide across the glassy surface, but that would be too dangerous. A sardonic thought crossed his mind: *The only thing worse than a prince found dead in a secret passage is a prince found dead in his own moat.* He wondered if it was a quote he'd read somewhere.

Without further ado, he shimmied along the edge until he found the bridge leading to the gatehouse, where travelers would deliver their horses to grooms before entering the castle. The drawbridge had been closed for the night, as he knew it would be. Again, that was not his goal. Instead, he sought the small stone near it. He rolled it aside and entered the hole, again crawling on all fours.

He followed the path, which curved from north to south. Whatever the strange, moist grass he felt on the tunnel down was, it now covered the area completely. He prayed gramercy his knees had some cushion as he crawled.

Finally, he reached the end. There was a small latch, broken long ago. He pushed his way through and into a small fireplace in a shack of brick and mortar. The second passage took him under the moat and the retaining wall of the castle to this little shack somewhere near the northern edge of town. Armitage knew not what it was before, only that it was secretly connected to the castle.

Bodies littered the ground: beggars looking for warmth and surcease. None stirred, even when Armitage exited the fireplace and put back the stones.

Again, he straightened his cloak, bundled himself up, and headed into the cold. A layer of snow lay upon the ground. Perhaps somewhere in the After Realms, Wróżka laughed at Tourm's people.

Armitage shivered, teeth chittering in his head. *It seems winter was the season ruled by four gods—not the standard three.* Or perhaps somewhere beyond the all-encompassing void, Tur—God of Ice—refused to relinquish his hold.

This is no time to wax philosophic. I must find the tavern.

He made his way to the first tavern on Travelers' Way. Outside it was cold, but a streetlamp lit each establishment, bleeding yellow light onto the snow-covered roads. The frosted windows glowed from within. Promises of light, warmth and merriment from which Armitage could not turn away. The ingredients might be of lesser quality than what was in Albicant's bottlery, but the laughter made the stews heartier, the ales tarter, and the wines sweeter. He could not keep the smile from his face as he pushed open the door.

The place was alive with mirth and the smell of strong drink. Cloaks hung upon racks. They—and the patrons' boots—darkened the wooden floorboards with melting snow. Old knights and lords, come for tomorrow's knighting ceremony, spoke loudly to one another, telling tales concerning their lands. In one corner, several younger knights played a game of dice. Armitage wanted to join them—would have if he hadn't promised Orrick.

He found him sitting by the bar, knowing him by the thick black hair crawling past his slump-backed shoulders. Orrick never did have the best posture. A large hand wrapped around a tankard.

Armitage smiled and pushed past the revelers, sometimes even turning to his side to avoid running into a barmaid or a boisterous table. Finally reaching Orrick, he took the vacant seat next to him.

"Glad you're come," his friend said without looking up. He certainly didn't sound it.

"I trust you received my message?"

"I'm here, am I not?" He looked at Armitage, offered a small smile. Then he went back to his drink.

Armitage plunked a copper mite onto the bar and grunted, "One o' what 'e's got." When the barkeep turned to fetch the drink, he dropped his voice. "I heard there were deserters from Newtown a few nights past. You killed them and reclaimed your weapons ... but you look not at all happy about it."

Orrick took a swig from the tankard and dropped it back down with a liquid thud. "'Twas Rupert Sedgwick did the killing. I only watched, helpless—"

"Helpless? *You*? That's a laugh!"

"Aye, but it's true."

Armitage looked at him disapprovingly. In the lingering silence, Orrick looked back to him, noticed the glare, and sighed.

"It *isn't* true," he admitted. "They deserted their posts, made off with master-forged weapons. When I asked why, the leader said—"

"War is coming."

Orrick looked at Armitage, confused.

In the silence, the barkeep delivered the tankard of ale: strong, dark, a sweet start and a bitter finish that dawdled in the throat. It was a good drink, and strong—just what Armitage needed after Ozella's tirade and the reminder of the threat.

Orrick took a drink himself: several gulps, in fact. When the tankard hit the wooden countertop, he asked, "Heard it from someone, did you?"

"Aye ... 'eard the knights talkin'."

Orrick nodded. "Precisely so. I tried to ask what he meant, but he lunged—and Rupert ran him through."

Armitage stared into the amber foam in his cup. "A pity, that. Those men hurt Newtown, slighted House Pallaton. We'll never know what their aim with your weapons was, nor where they intended go with them ..."

"Aye. And neither shall we know the meaning of their words." He looked at Armitage and noticed the uneasy look on his face. Orrick scowled. "What do you know of it?"

"I ... we only received word from Tourm's Gate a fortnight ago. Father ordered it to remain secret."

"Secrets never stay secret long." Orrick took a drink. "Out with it, Ninnishman."

Armitage gasped. He'd forgotten his accent. He'd wanted an accent of Ásmo, but apparently used the harsher drawl of the southern duchy. He summoned the drawl again.

"Oh, a-yar. Turns out people's sayin' rumors 'bout the nation t' the west ... Kendala."

Orrick arched an eyebrow. "What rumors?"

"Borderland skirmishes," growled Armitage. "Some people say they mean t' break through." He shook his head and took a drink. "Don' know wha' they want, though. Don' know why King Archibald don' jus' send a' invitation."

Orrick's voice dropped to a whisper. His eyes were the color of thunderclouds. Lightning seemed to surge behind them. "Are they a threat?"

"Hard t' say."

Orrick stared at Armitage. The Prince couldn't look away, even if he wanted to. "Are you certain it's even safe for you to be out here?"

Armitage scoffed. "Are y' me father now?"

Orrick shook his head. He straightened his back and drank long from the tankard.

Armitage smiled. "'Sides, we ain't got naught t' worry 'bout! 'Snot every fishmonger's friendly wit' a knighted man!"

Orrick sighed and shook his head. Something was troubling him, something deeper than the deserters and the threat of war. He watched his friend tilt his head back, swallowing the rest of the ale. His tankard thudded on the counter.

Orrick looked beaten when he said, "I could kill him not."

"Kill …" Armitage dropped his voice, this time not losing the accent. "The deserter, y' mean?"

"Aye, the deserter. I've never killed before. When I was six-and-ten, I was with Count Atrax, finding smugglers in Nin. I'd cornered their captain, and he pleaded for death. 'Twas the first I thought about it … but the thought's plagued me since."

"Y' mean, the first time y' thought 'bout death? 'Bout killin'?" Armitage barked a laugh and slapped his knee. "You're jus' sendin' yer foes t' the Under Realms, 'at's all!"

"'Tis more than that." Orrick gave Armitage a hard look. "A man has hopes and dreams and a family. Then …"

"Naught."

"Not merely naught. There's a difference between an old man dying in bed and a young man dying unfulfilled."

"What do you care? They're foemen."

Orrick shook his head. The frown on his face seemed permanent. "I care because that's me."

Armitage fell silent, peering into the tankard of pewter and horn, tried to see the nut-brown ale past the amber foam.

"Though other men may say otherwise, I'll not find the answer in that cup." Orrick put a hand on Armitage's shoulder. "'Tis late, and tomorrow requires us both ready. Goodnight."

"'Night, mate."

The Prince watched Orrick find his cloak amongst the others on the rack. He wrapped it around himself and left the tavern. As a burst of cold wind caused the patrons to shudder, Armitage shook for different reasons. He was unable to keep the worry from his mind.

If Orrick doubts, the knightly oath is forfeit. I suppose that's his burden.

He, on the other hand, would not return just yet. Grinning, he took his tankard and approached the young men tumbling dice.

III: The Knighting Ceremony

Orrick stood in the throne room of Castle Albicant. He, along with twenty-two other cadets, waited to receive Szczerbieç's touch. All of them were dressed in academy finery: leather britches, blue woolen doublets, white sashes filigreed with gold-cloth.

Along the eastern wall sat their families, as well as the knights they had squired with for the past seven years. The crowd buzzed like a hornets' nest. In line, however, everyone stood nervously quiet.

Orrick's parents had made the trip from Newtown. He'd be happy to see them again' it nigh came on ten-and-five years since he last had their company. For now, he could not find their faces.

The chatter silenced. All the cadets turned to the dais where King Biel now stood, tall, wide, imposing. He raised his strong arms to garner quiescence. Unruly blond hair covered his face. The velvet tunic stretched over his wide paunch did nothing to hide the fact that he looked more like a forest-dwelling freeman than a king.

Behind him sat the royal family. Queen Jeneve with her beaky nose, wispy frame, pale skin, and orange hair—all traits inherited by Armitage. The only thing he did not receive from her was the slight breasts, poking inside her white samite gown.

Seated next to her were her children, Alabaster and Armitage. Alabaster was one year younger than Armitage, but looked more like his father with broader shoulders, blond hair but fine like his mother's, and a stronger, squarer jaw.

"Prince Alabaster looks as though he'd fit with us," said a soft voice beside him. Chelsea Wingate, sea-green eyes and smile bright. The sunlight spilling in from the windows caught in her curly hair, making it shine like spun gold. Orrick blushed, and so did she.

"Well ... everyone knows House Pardwy came from warriors. It surprises me not he looks like us."

"Yet no one in House Pardwy has seen battle since they ascended as kings."

Her hand slid into his as she stood beside him. Years ago, as they graduated from pages to squires, they spent many a day together until knights selected them as squires. Chelsea remained in Albion City, and Orrick went to Nin. They met again six months past, when the knights apprentice returned to the academy to prepare for their final examinations. He remembered her as a good friend, a companion, though not one so near as Anton or Rupert, or even Armitage.

Despite their longtime severance, she smiled whenever she saw him. He tried to think why, and Rupert summed it up one evening when he said, "She remembers y' from childhood, me lad—an' she enjoys how yeh've grown."

There was something else Orrick could not place. That last day, just before they departed for squireship, he and Chelsea had kissed. Simply an innocent geasture from a young maiden who would miss her friend. But her hand in his defied the promises made between Houses Wingate and Kerwin.

'Tisn't right, he thought bitterly, and hissed, "Do you forget you're promised to someone else?"

Face impassive, she slipped from his palm and stood at attention—along with everyone else—when King Biel cleared his throat.

Orrick looked again to the royal family and their sworn sentries. Beside the King was Ladd pan Winchell, wearing the white cape and white-enameled armor of his station. At his side was a sword unlike any other, with white gold guard and a hilt wrapped in white leather. An egg-sized diamond gleamed from the pommel. He was both Paladin of Tourm and Defender of the King.

What excited Orrick even more was the sword he held in his hands: a greatsword, guard and disk-shaped pommel made of red gold.

"*Szczerbieç*," whispered Chelsea, thrilled as he was.

Orrick felt awed to be in the presence of such a blade, and it had yet to leave its sheath.

"My lords and ladies, happy parents come to see their children into adulthood, the knights that raised them as squires, the masters that taught them in Akademia's hallowed halls, and finally to the squires themselves, I bid you welcome, not just to my throne room, but to a new spring and a new year."

The audience applauded politely, but the cadets remained silent. Before the ceremony, Lord Headmaster Patrick pan Tuttle bade every graduate remain silent throughout. He stood now in front of all the squires and masters. At that moment, the King summoned him up to stand with him.

With a narrow neck, bald head, thin spade-shaped lips, and beaky nose, the joke amongst the cadets was that Lord Headmaster Tuttle looked like a tortoise, which happened to be the sigil emblazoned upon his grass-green surcoat. That his skin was leathery brown only added to the illusion. He peered at the students before him, contemplating, and then faced the King.

"You've assessed these cadets since childhood," said Biel. "You and your masters trained them, brought them up as warriors knowledgeable and strong. Do you give these youths to adulthood and deem them worthy of Szczerbieç's touch?"

Tuttle looked again to the students, scrutinizing. His mouth curved into a smile. Voice as dry and crumbly as old parchment paper, he said, "I do, Your Majesty."

"Have you the scroll of names?"

Tuttle pulled a small scroll from his surcoat.

Biel nodded his approval. He looked to Winchell, who dropped to his knee and extended the hilt toward him. The King took the golden grip in both hands and pulled it free from the sheath. The crowd—knights, squires, and families—gasped in unison. Everyone in Tourm knew its story.

Tourm's first king was said to have an affinity for the color white. The high walls guarding Albion were white stone and marble, and the towers of Castle Albicant were made of ivory from boarwhales, hunted nearly to extinction for their four thirty-foot-long tusks. Most of the buildings were named accordingly: Castle Albicant, the Ivory Tower where royal family slept, and the Whitehall for feasting.

But architecture was not enough.

Gorill, the Great White King, promised a handsome payment and a lordship to anyone able to craft a blade of that was as white and cold as frost. Many bladesmiths tried, but only one succeeded: a smith taught by the dwarves of Ojcakask folded the steel with calcite and diamonds to replace the carbon. He gave the blade a hilt of red gold. The guard arched toward the blade, studded with balls of yellow gold. Lastly, he lined the coin-shaped pommel with seven diamonds, and one opal in the center.

It never had seen battle. Instead, the realm's rulers wielded it as a sword of justice.

"Dasher!"

Orrick watched his friend walk to the dais, chestnut hair shimmering. Orrick tried to smile, but he recalled the deserters in the alehouse. Last night, nightmares plagued his sleep. The rogue laughing and joking ... the table ... the beer ... the blood ... Now everything was at the fore of his mind.

"Are you unwell?" asked Chelsea, breathing hotly into his ear.

"Nay ..."

She relented not. "You sweat and clench your fists."

Orrick shook his head, dismissing her questions. He barely saw Anton stand as Pan Dasher.

"You'll take a place at Durwyn's Pass, guarding Tourm's Gate."

"Thank you, Your Majesty," Anton said, then stood along the wall to watch the rest of the ceremony.

Orrick should have been happy.

Am I ready? Am I truly ready?

"Pallaton!"

Orrick snapped his head up. He was next in line. Twelve knights stood against the wall. Ten more remained behind him. He approached the dais, bowed his waist to his former headmaster. They clasped forearms.

"I've seen you come into academy as a page, received reports on your squiring and when you became a knight apprentice. Never forget what you've learned in school, in the yard, or from your comrades. Neither shall they forget you."

"My thanks for all you've taught me," he answered.

He faced King Biel. Though he and Armitage were fast friends, he spent not much time with His Majesty. He knew him to be a good king, fair and just. But he knew not the man beyond his speeches.

"Ready to take your vows?"

Orrick's mind returned to the pub, the bodies of the deserters, the smell of blood and ordure. *Knighthood means killing.* The litany cycled: *Am I ready? Knights must kill …*

No. A new thought came to mind. *Knights must protect.*

43

Orrick swallowed hard. "I am, Your Majesty."

"Kneel then."

As Orrick knelt before the King, he felt a red flush creep up his neck. Now more than ever, he felt the eyes of the audience upon him. His parents were among them. He hoped to make them proud.

"Orrick of House Pallaton, heir to Brzeg Voivodship, do you pledge to protect this kingdom with all of your strength and heart?"

"I do, Your Majesty."

"And do you swear fealty to the throne of Tourm and whoever sits upon it should it be passed from me to my son?"

"I do, Your Majesty."

"Yours is Tourm," Biel said, and Orrick felt the weight of Szczerbiec upon his shoulders. "Rise, Orrick *pan* Pallaton! Name thee I, Knight-Errant xe Brzeg!"

Orrick stood a knighted man. He received his duties, to be a knight-errant of Brzeg, traditionally what became of House Pallaton knights. He stood next to Anton and the others. Among those that followed were Rupert Sedgwick, named Knight-Errant of Orghent; and Chelsea pani Wingate, the last one knighted, whose skill with the shortbow made her lieutenant in the Order of the White Falcon.

The King sighed deeply, pleased, as he cast his gaze to the row of newly knighted men and women. "'Twas Virgil xu Lac wrote, ''Tis neither money nor faith the round world revolves; the oil is blood, in my resolve; should desiccate our reserve run; only half the world shall face the sun.' You are the blood that pumps the heart of our nation. Yours is Tourm."

Even the new knights applauded this time. Biel spread his hands and the room quieted. "To celebrate the graduates of nineteen-ninety-five, I welcome all to Whitehall."

Whitehall was Castle Albicant's great hall, meant for entertaining many guests. Bards plucked their lyres, singing merrily as conversation rumbled through the air. Flavès wine, Miellish mead, and Brzeg ale flowed like waterfalls. The twenty-six tables comfortably sat twenty people, ten on either side.

The servants had laid food that Orrick could only describe as gorgeous: lamprey pie and buttery lemon-drenched bloodfish from Nin, each as long as a man; capons dripping spicy sauce made from dragonbells and honey; mountains of buttery mashed turnips and honey-glazed carrots.

Orrick could not stop smiling. He spied the lords' table, where sat the royal family and guests of honor, seeking Armitage. He saw his sworn sentries—Tartus, Callows and Grimm—but no sign of the Prince. He shrugged and sipped from a tankard of sweet, golden ale, smooth as it ran down his gullet. A hard slap on the back nearly brought it up again.

"You swore fealty to me," said a noxious voice.

Orrick turned and looked Armitage in the eye, smirking. "*After* you ascend the throne. Neither am I your squire, your servant, nor your protector. Make I for Newtown tomorrow as knight-errant."

Armitage frowned and dropped his voice low. "Then your time in Albion nigh ends ..."

Surprised, Orrick furrowed his brow. The Prince sounded forlorn. Still, Orrick's smirk returned. "Come now, Your Highness—" Armitage scowled at the word. Orrick knew he hated being called 'highness.' "Would you see me the fly, hanging on some wall? Albion is a good city, but my place is beyond these white walls."

"Please sound not so noble!" Armitage protested. "A knight-errant is for killing jadwilki, scimitigers, and vampire cats when one can afford more than an armsman! You're naught more than a royal rotter!"

Orrick peered into his cup. "If my duty is to protect Tourm against wild animals, then I mind it not at all. 'Twas the oath I swore."

Armitage pursed his lips. He had no answer. It was his betrothed that stopped him from disgracing himself.

Beautiful, with a pale and clear complexion and auburn hair that shined like red gold, Lady Ozella Altgeld appeared in a silken gown the color of goldenrods, edged in silvery lace. The fragrance of honey and flowers wafted from her neck.

"Congratulations, *Pan* Pallaton," she tittered, voice giddy from wine. Her eyes shone playfully.

Orrick bowed, taking in her radiance. He never could understand why Armitage complained of her so often. "Thank you, my lady."

She glanced at Armitage. "You might learn from him."

Armitage barked a laugh and slapped his knee, but quieted when he saw his father glaring at him from the lords' table. "Right, right," he said, dismissively waving his hand. He shook Orrick's shoulder. "Women, aye?"

Ozella cast a dark glance at him. "Speaking of which, when might you settle down, Pan Pallaton?"

This again! Orrick maintained his composure. "I know not. As you know, Pallaton sons choose their own wives, and I've no maiden's promised hand. There will come a time when I might settle down. But not now in my youth."

Armitage and Ozella exchanged glances.

"Well ..." said the Prince with a lopsided smirk "... mayhap you might choose my cousin, Chelsea?"

Orrick coughed on his ale, eyes wide. *Did she put him up to this?*

"You know her," said Armitage. "She mentioned you and she were in academy together. Also ... she's not taken her eyes

47

from you this entire time."

"I know." *I've been trying to avoid her gaze.*

"You do!" Armitage exclaimed, clapping his hands. "Then why not court her? Ozella and I know of a lovely spot in Rhabdolia, near Astoria. 'Tis a small grove where seasons never change. I'm unsure what ancient spell tethers it."

"Oh yes," Ozella agreed. "The flowers and trees blossom as if forever in springtime, and animals gently slake their thirsts in the cleanest pools you ever saw."

"All this even when winter has killed all other woods around it."

Orrick eyed them sideways. "What has this to do with aught?"

"'Tis a wonderful place to woo a maiden like my—"

Orrick barked a laugh, silencing him. "Forgiveness, but firstly, Chelsea is betrothed already."

"Oh, yes ..." muttered Armitage.

"And secondly," continued Orrick, "why would I want to take a maiden all the way across Tourm in the middle of winter to see a forest for a few hours? I can likely find a place closer to Newtown in actual springtime."

Armitage blushed and Ozella puckered her lips. She was about to speak her mind, but Armitage intervened. "Never mind him, lady mine. My lad is merely not a romantic." He offered a smile to console her.

Orrick crossed his arms over his chest, eyes cool. "And should I be? 'Tis true, wish I for mine House to thrive, but there is yet more to explore. Let me spend my years killing jadwilki and vampire cats. Mayhap a rescued maid might I find to charm. Until then, can't Tourm be my maiden?"

"I'd expect as much from you," said Armitage. "House Pallaton are warriors, if naught else. I hear your mother and father made their journey without baggage train or guard."

Ozella gasped. "*How*?"

"They dislike an entourage," Orrick answered, shrugging. "In fact, I believe most Pallatons have gone without since Aileron received the voivodship."

"Whether your family is lords or knights, it matters not," said Ozella. "Traveling without a train is so uncouth."

"Both Nigel and Fiona are knights, aren't they?" asked Armitage.

"Aye," said Orrick.

"And all knights were once squires. They would know how to pack, how to fight, and how to care for themselves and their horses."

Orrick smiled. "'Tis as you said, Armitage: House Pallaton is naught if not warriors."

"*Savages* if you ask me," Ozella said, frowning.

Seconds slipped by in silence. Orrick realized it was not a joke.

Armitage laughed, again intervening. "My lady, did you know there'd be no Tourm were it not for the Pallatons? Aileron was a rotter that killed two thousand goblins in a single battle, earning him the title Slayer."

"Aye," said Orrick, "and then there was Terzo, who ..." He stopped, remembering his grandfather's hand in Rhabdolia's capture fifty years past.

"Yes," said Ozella, eyes flashing. "Precisely as I said: *Savages*."

Armitage frowned. Orrick knew he disliked the Altgelds' attitude, but he knew as well that he could not say anything about it. Still, he pressed. "Legends say Aileron felled undergods larger even than your lord brother. Elsewise Tourm would've been crushed five hundred years ago."

Orrick expected Ozella to give a poisonous look. However, her eyes became greedy. "Undergods?"

"Yes, undergods," Armitage said with finality. He appeared not to notice the curl in Ozella's voice.

Orrick himself was sure he only imagined it. "How strange

you know not the history of House Pallaton."

"Quite right," said Armitage, nodding. "After all, Aileron's history is Tourm's history."

"I find it strange not at all," answered Ozella. She sipped from her wineglass. "House Altgeld is the sovereign of all Rhabdolia, a place of beautiful green meadows and forests, studded by lakes. What has Brzeg but salty steppes and homely hills?"

Armitage's coppery eyebrows furrowed. "You're being quite rude today, you know."

Orrick waved his hand, smiling. "Now, now, if it's all the same, I'm unbothered. Certainly, our regions differ, but what's of import is both Houses benefit Tourm. Is that not right, my lady?"

"Indeed, it is," Ozella grumbled, glowering.

"Good!" roared Armitage, clapping Orrick's back. "Speaking of Brzeg, now that you're knighted and no longer confined to the academy, I'm certain we can ride out there together."

Orrick blinked, surprised. "*We?*"

"I've slaked myself all I care to on Domoż's wines. I've grown tired of Ianth's hippocras and Flavès's whites. The miners' drink would remedy that."

Orrick soured at the thought. He had never tasted the white

whiskey distilled in his hometown. Known as the miners' drink, the big, burly men from the mountains and hills drank it after a long week's work. The thought of the Prince entering these establishments—the thought that Orrick would be his only defender—frightened him. He tried to intervene.

"Newtown's taverns are harsher than Albion's—"

"It matters not!" Armitage exclaimed. He winced when he caught his father's glare and quieted again. "I'm ... in need of a change of scenery; away from scrutinizing eyes. I'm certain Father would protest not if I accompanied you to Newtown."

A new voice, deep and booming, rumbled above them like thunder. "And what could his highness possibly want there?"

Orrick turned, looking to find the new speaker. However, his eyes only met with cold plate mail. His gaze climbed higher—he even had to lean back—until he found the giant's face.

"Oh," said Ozella, sweet as syrup, "hello, Erasmus."

The knight before them was indeed Erasmus pan Altgeld, Ozella's elder brother and heir to the Rhabdolia Duchy. Packed with hard muscle and standing eight-feet-tall, he was the largest man in the kingdom, and certainly the largest man Orrick had ever seen. His face was long, his chin square and stubble-free. He always wore plate armor no matter the occasion. Today 'twas bronze with white, triangular filigree, reminding Orrick of a never-ending row of teeth. He wore no surcoat but a sash the color of lavender. Upon his breast was pinned a golden brooch fashioned like a bull's head.

Orrick gulped when he saw him—how could he not? *It is good luck Tourm won Rhabdolia fifty years past. I'd hate to meet the likes of him in combat.*

"Oh … Erasmus …" Armitage said, as if greeting a stray cat. As frightened as Orrick was, the Prince seemed not to worry. "We were discussing a spell to Newtown. Never have I been, you know. I'd like very much to try their famed white whiskey."

Altgeld folded his arms across his massive chest. "And my sister comes with you, does she?"

"She may accompany us if she'd like," Armitage said. "Have you ever been?"

"I've never had the displeasure." The giant knight snorted at his own joke. "But I've heard talk. Hinterlands surround it on all sides, wild places where hide rotters and highwaymen, savages steal infants, rape women, and cut the throats of aught nobly born. Why, the place is practically hell itself! No, Newtown is a place for drunken miners and scavenging animals. 'Tis no place for ladies—or princelings, for that matter."

Armitage waved him off. "Orrick has spent most of his life in Albion or Nin. I'd like to see him back to his hometown. Besides, my mother is from Brzeg, you know." He offered Orrick a small smile. Out of politeness, Orrick raised the corners of his mouth.

"A pitiful place to be born, but to inherit it! Feel I sorry for the Queen and nearly for him—*nearly*. Now come, dear sister. Lord Father wants a word."

Orrick watched as Erasmus led Ozella away. Before, he had wondered why Armitage complained. Now he need not even to ask. She seemed demure and beautiful, but somewhere deep inside she was more malicious than her brother. He took several long gulps of ale.

Armitage slouched next to him. "Well, *that* was depressing."

Orrick passed him the tankard and he drank too.

"My thanks," said the Prince, handing the empty cup back. "Now, to ask Father for permission to sojourn in Newtown. You're due to find your own parents as well."

Orrick's eyes widened. He had not met with his parents yet, who sat at the lords' table as esteemed guests, right next to Duke Ezarl Altgeld. Still, the Duke's children's quips hindered not his courage. He followed the Prince in hopes of convincing their parents.

IV: Squires Selected

The barracks hummed with excitement. Chattering heads, gossiping, bright smiles. The pages' enthusiasm was palpable—for all except Brandt. He was of squiring age—as were all the others present, fourteen springs.

The knighting ceremony ended not long ago. The graduates feasted, and the King met with the knights and lords from the visiting regions. Soon, those selfsame knights and lords would come and look for squires. Important though it is, squiring for a knight made Brandt jitter. Certainly, he had prepared for his time among those warriors ordained by Szczerbieç, but there was something else.

All the friends made these past seven years in Akademia Palatæ would be torn apart, separated, sent to live in different regions. Some would squire for guardsmen. Others for knights-errant. Others yet for a military order. True indeed, Brandt had spent less time making friends and more time focusing on himself.

His recent growth spurt unbalanced him, and he felt all that time in the yard had been wasted. So, sat he on a bed, watching the other pages babble.

No, he had made no friends his seven springs here, but there *was* someone he wished to see.

Then she appeared. Brown skin, thin neck, and spaded lips made her look as much the tortoise as her other relatives. But her big, bright hazel eyes and the dark ringlets that fell about her face had captured his imagination since first they were introduced. She was a knitter. Oft did her parents send her dyed wool, and always would she turn the stringy bundles into colorful accessories shared amongst her friends. Even now, she wore a beige sweater of heavy wool, made by her own hands, perfect for early spring's blustery weather. What Brandt wouldn't do to receive a gift from her!

Wąda Tuttle—he could never forget her name; he said it to himself before he slept—fluttered into the room, laughing, and chatting, and smiling with the other squires. She looked just as hopeful as the rest of them. And shouldn't she be? She was a good bowwoman—perfect for a White Falcon archer.

She spotted him and approached. The sight of her made him sit up a little straighter. Tall for his age, last autumn Brandt shot up like a weed, his arms and legs just as wiry.

"'Lo, Brandt," she said.

"'Lo," he honked, deathly aware how much his voice sounded

like a goose's.

She seemed not to mind, but instead giggled. She swept her hand to the place beside him. "May I?"

Don't trip over yourself! You're sitting down now, but by Sibilia, you're clumsy enough to trip over yourself sitting down!

"Are you well, Brandt? Look you thunderstruck."

His voice made something of a squeak, and he cleared his throat. "Please, Wąda, please sit."

She bowed and obliged. The mattress deflated under her frame. Brandt struggled for composure. Long had he eyed Wąda. They had spoken several times and he considered her more friend than acquaintance ... but never was he in her close circle. Now here she sat upon his bed—well, they were not alone, and this was not *his* bed, and they were no more romantically involved than when she smiled at him minutes ago—

"Are you *certain* you're well? Look you feverish."

"I'm certain," he squawked.

"Whenever I've a fever, Mother sends feverfew cakes and ice-mint crème. Better tasting, 'tis, than what the herbalists serve."

Brandt smiled, feeling slightly more comfortable. "That sounds really good, actually."

"A pity I never let you try one. My friends—"

Her big eyes wandered to them, scattered about the barracks. Squat and bushy Antonina, lanky Lera, and gaping and gawking Esme. All of them, including Wąda, wore bright scarves.

Brandt looked confused. "Why then sit you with me?"

"Ah—I wanted to."

"You did?"

"We've had so little time to talk. Oft are you by yourself, or working with instructors. You hope for a good knight. I feel we could have been friends ... but little did I feel you wanted friends."

"It felt foolish to me, making friends with whom I'd part come fourteen springs." She smiled at him and his mouth went dry. "'Twas I the fool all along."

Quickly—perhaps sensing his tentativeness—she changed the subject. "What do you hope for?"

A marriage pact between our Houses, he almost said. "For what?"

"Your *knight*. Hope you for a military order? Or a knight-errant? Or a sentry or guard?"

"I—" In truth, whenever Brandt trained in the yard, he imag-

58

ined himself an infantryman. If luck found him, a lieutenant in the Silver Wolves' heavy infantry would recruit him. But in that moment, it saddened him to think that he would go far away from her, so he said, "Aught will do."

She looked surprised. "*Aught*?"

"Aught," he said, uncertain.

"And I—"

"The White Falcons, right? You've a good eye—your aim is impeccable."

She blushed and looked down at her hands. "I don't know about *impeccable* ... mostly the arrow hits the rim and never the hub."

"See?" said Brandt, smiling. "No one else in our year can manage even that. Impeccable!"

Wąda giggled. "Thanks," she said. "You always make me laugh. That's why I wanted to come say goodbye to you. I really wish we could have been friends."

"We are friends," said Brandt. Nervously he rubbed his thumbs. "Seven springs a page, seven springs a squire. Grace we again the Academy's halls when we're one-and-twenty. This needn't be 'goodbye,' but merely 'see you again in se'—"

He could not finish the sentence for fear of choking up. It

seemed she thought the same; she nodded solemnly and said, "Wanted I not for this to be so sad."

"We are luckier than most, you know," said Brandt.

"How so?" she asked, dabbing her eyes.

"Your uncle is headmaster, and my sister is Countess Ozella's lady-in-waiting. Many of the pages here haven't seen their families in years, and neither shall they until their graduation."

"You're right. Imagine I that many pages shall travel to places hitherto unknown to them. Domożians will go to Nin, Ninnians to Rhabdolia. A Pallaton graduated this year, you know."

"*Brzeg?*" The westernmost territory. Legends abound about the tough men and strange creatures inhabiting harsh territories of steppe, hills, marshes, mountains, and quarries. The drama of Tourm's infancy unfolded in Brzeg, with goblin hordes and undergods. Rhabdolia thought itself more civilized—but this was because Brzeg and House Pallaton had, time and again, thwarted their attempts to move into Domoż.

"I can't imagine any page wants to squire in Brzeg," said Wąda. "Who do you think he'll choose?"

"I cannot know. There aren't any pages hailing from Brzeg."

"Either way, nigh comes our time. So soon shall a knight

gather us into the training yard, where knights new and old will assess our skill. Before ... wish I to give you, well—" Wąda rummaged through her sweater and withdrew small woolen bundle. Brandt received it, awestruck. He furled the two gray socks.

"What?"

"You dislike them?" asked Wąda.

"No, but ... the ones you and your friends wear are *brighter*."

"Ah!" Wąda pointed to Antonina, "Purple for Naga-Bissa's Moon." To Lera, "Icy blue because she was born in Tur's Moon." And then to Esme, "Orange for Pix-Złota's Moon. I was born in Wróżka's Moon, so mine are light green."

He understood. "Mine are gray for I was born under Ged-Srebro's Moon."

"Yes! So ... do you like them?"

"I do. Thank you ..."

Wąda pushed her hair behind her ears, and Brandt saw how her eyes shined. He wanted to say something, but he was unsure of what. He wanted to be bold and kiss her or—*something.* He knew not what, but he knew time ran short. He clasped her hand and she gasped. Whether 'twas a noise good or bad, he never found out, for a young, pockmarked instructress entered and said, "All pages follow me to the training yard!"

Wąda let go of his hand and rejoined her three friends. Brandt stuffed his new socks into his gambeson and tailed the back of the line, fraught with worry. Why in the name of sweet Sibilia did he go and do *that*? How quickly she left him to be with her friends, how abrupt their time together ended. Damn his awkward eagerness; he scared her away.

It's for the best, he told himself. He had entered Academy without friends, and it seemed he would leave without them.

Akademia Palatæ's expansive training yard unfolded before him. Spending so much time in the dim barracks made the sunlight blinding. He shielded his eyes with his forearm until the garish glare eased. On the west side, targets lined for archers' target practice. On the east side, blunted weapons for mêlée practice.

Brandt looked to the west and saw the hopefuls and a line of White Falcons. Wąda already stood in line. A blond man who looked awfully impressive stood near a short girl with curly blond hair. Brandt recognized the man as Count of Waldsee, Cuthbert pan Draque, Lord Commander of the White Falcons. The woman, Chelsea pani Wingate, was his newest lieutenant.

He knew not what he did—knew with every fiber of his being he should go eastward to the mêlée—but went he to the row of archers. He wanted to apologize to her, to wish her luck. Wąda's eyes focused as she strung her bow, face stony. That was one of the tests, too. She paid no attention to the pages already lined at the targets, shooting, and mostly missing.

Wąda finished stringing her bow and looked around. Chelsea and Count Draque both seemed impassive, as if nothing they saw impressed them. Looking at the arrows littering the ground near the bare targets, Brandt surmised no one showed them anything impressive.

"How long have you studied archery?" asked Chelsea.

"Five years," said Wąda, biting her lip. "Well, I mean, pani, I strung bows for five. I've only shot for three."

"I've remarks that you're the best in your year. Is this true?"

"Our archery instructress has ripped her hair out by the handful, pani."

"Has she?" asked Chelsea.

"From frustration, pani. Seems I'm the only one who can purposefully hit the target."

For the first time, Chelsea moved to stroke her squarish chin. At least, the chin she would have if it did not disappear into her neckline. "You like archery, don't you?"

"Oh yes. There is something almost relaxing about it—releasing the tension in body and bow."

"Releasing the tension in body and bow ..." For the first time, Chelsea smiled. Even Count Draque smirked. "I like it. Whenever you're ready, take your place on the field. You get three arrows."

"Good luck, Wąda," said Brandt.

Wąda stopped her march and looked at him, blushing. "P-please go away. I need to concentrate."

"I merely wanted to apologize—"

"*Page!*" snapped Chelsea. "Either string your bow or leave the field."

"But I haven't a bow!"

Chelsea raised her blond eyebrows. "Therefore—?"

"Leave the field ..."

Brandt skulked away. Words crammed in his throat. He turned back to see Wąda loose her third and final arrow. The other two hit the rim, but the third landed closer to the hub. Grinning, Chelsea nodded her approval. "Congratulations, Wąda Tuttle. You're my squire."

Wąda smiled gummily and looked back to Brandt, whose smile held more sadness. He turned away and let Wąda bask in her victory. For him, the mêlée yard held his destiny. Indeed, there were a few Silver Wolves watching.

Infantrymen.

This was it—time for Brandt to impress them the way Wąda had impressed Chelsea. It need not be perfect, merely better than everyone else. How hard could that be? He picked a blunted short sword and round shield. All around him, steel clanged against steel as hopeful pages charged one another. Brandt took his place in line, looking at all the knights, hoping to catch the eye of some Silver Wolf. Among those watching was a young man with long black hair and bad posture. Something about the way he carried himself—the stony glint of his eyes, his scowl—drew Brandt's attention. If Chelsea looked unimpressed, this knight appeared utterly wroth.

The instructor cried out, "Next is Brandt of House Hargrove, of the Maycoast! He shall fight against Thom of House Lewcz of the Szalet!"

Brandt stepped into the circle and put his guard up. One hit, one kill. In tournaments, best out of ten hits would be a match, but this way the knights could better assess a page's skill. Thom Lewcz was a shorter fighter, skilled, but he had never learned how to overcome reach. He pounded Brandt's shield, neither sidestepping nor maneuvering but tiring himself out all the while. When the blows came fewer and weaker, Brandt reached. Even with his short sword, he delivered a good cut to Thom's shoulder and won the point. Several knights—Silver Wolves included—clapped. But the stony knight's scowl deepened.

Brandt returned to the line. The applause was half-hearted, he knew. *I must need be faster*, thought he. Silver Wolves wore

65

plate mail and used heavy weapons. But even with additional weight, they must not get caught up on the battlefield. Dispatch and move on.

Each fighter had two rounds. Before long, Brandt faced Thom again, who swapped his arming sword for a longsword—better reach, but unwieldly to the inexperienced. Thom carried no shield this time.

The two circled each other. Brandt must be faster this time, show the Silver Wolves he could quickly dispatch his opponent. He used his reach, lunging with his long legs, thrusting with his long arm. But he overshot his mark. Thom turned on his right, Brandt's left, heavy sword high.

Panicking, Brandt dropped to his knee and held the shield high. Thom rained down blows like a hammer. The vibrations made Brandt's arm go numb. But again, Thom was all power and no finesse, chopping like a woodsman. Brandt felt the shield crack, but Thom was slow on the rise—

Now!

One more blow would shatter the wooden shield. As Thom raised his sword overhead, Brandt moved all at once, stepping out with the opposite foot, thrusting. Longsword poised overhead, Thom looked surprised—just as surprised as Brandt—when the tip of the short sword poked his sternum.

The instructor said, "The winner of both rounds—Brandt Hargrove of Maycoast!"

More light applause from the Silver Wolves, but the black-haired knight, scowling still, raised an eyebrow.

As the Silver Wolves scrutinized and squabbled over their decision, Brandt approached them. "Lords, what thought you of my performance?" He tried to give his most confident, most sympathetic smile.

The Silver Wolves looked at one another. "Sorry, lad," said one, "you're too slow."

"Aye," said the other, a Ninnishman. "Y' shoulda struck out sooner in the first fight, caught him with your shield and moved around."

Brandt looked disheartened. "And the second?"

"Y' overshot your first strike. Get y' one chance on the battlefield, elsewise another foeman can get y' from behind." To his comrade he asked, "What about that Thom Lewcz? Guts there, aye?"

They would not pick him, Brandt knew. *But I won.* He sighed, walked away, stopping when the black-haired knight stood before him. No longer did the man scowl but smirked, almost pleasantly.

"My lord?"

"Good stuff there," said the knight.

67

Brandt blinked, confused. "But the Silver Wolves said—"

"Hark not on their words. Saw I the bouts entirely. You're new to your length, are you not?"

"Aye, my lord."

"I knew it." The knight chuckled, revealing four incisors. "But neither were you reckless. You waited, knowing Thom would tire and striking when the risk was less. Fighters like him are all muscle. Important tools are speed and power—but a duel is more than how hard one hits."

"I don't understand, my lord."

"Tactics win duels as much as they do battles. Used you your opponent's shortcomings and your own limitations to your advantage. Congratulations, Brandt Hargrove, you'll squire for me."

Brandt shuffled his feet, confused by the compliments and even more so at being chosen. This knight belonged to no order, but ... "Forgiveness, my lord, but who *are* you?"

The knight chuckled. "And I thought everyone knew me. Orrick pan Pallaton, Brzegu Knight-Errant."

Brandt's throat went dry and he felt the blood drain from his face.

Brzeg ... blessed Sibilia, the knight is Marquis of Brzeg. I could refuse, but—but do I want to?

Rhabdolians squiring for Brzegu never happened, nor the other way 'round. Brzeg's historic thwarting of Rhabdolia's invasions made certain their rivalry remained bitter. Rhabdolians, Brandt included, learned nothing of Brzeg except what the academy instructors taught.

Yet Orrick offered Brandt compliments. He came with praise and a promise of betterment. Perhaps his deepening scowl meant he wrestled with mentoring Brandt. But mayhap behind them laid those days of rivalry. Rhabdolia's Revolt ended fifty years ago, after all. And an Altgeld soon marries into the family royal.

"You're silent," said Orrick, concerned.

"I—" What else could he say? He looked around at those chosen and those unchosen. Wąda, still smiling, talked excitedly with Pani Wingate. "—am happy to be your squire, Orrick pan Pallaton."

V: Wolves In The Wild

The company had been riding for hours over the undulating meadows and rounded tops of the Homey Hills, colored saffron in the waning sunlight. Trees came sparse in this region. Only a few bare pines dotted the land. Beyond the Homey Hills were the hazy peaks of Starter Mountains. Valleys dipped into rock quarries. The way to Newtown was lonely indeed. Southward, the loam lay flat, brown from winter's dry air.

From atop Xły, his green-eyed, crème-colored charger, Nigel pan Pallaton noted, "Unlikely we'll by nightfall make Newtown." He looked very much like his son, the differences subtle: both were black of hair, gray of eyes, and bore brows heavy with concern. But Nigel had a broader nose, sun-darkened skin, and a beard as black and thick as the hair from his head.

Beside him rode Fiona, his wife, Orrick's mother. Her face was fierce, and so was she—fiercer than all the academy women and most academy men, as well. Tall, long legs and arms, and hair the same color and texture as straw. A long scar trailed from her hairline down to her tight, thin lips. Her eyes were as hard and colorless as a frozen lake.

"So, *this* is Brzeg," said Armitage. "Mother hailed from House Berwyn in Felmond, you know. How far to Felmond?"

"Southward and along the Milkmoon's banks," answered Orrick, who rode a black horse with silver eyes, borrowed from House Pardwy's stables.

"Ah, then 'tis out of the way from Newtown. I've not choice but to take a detour on my ride back to Albion." He craned his neck behind him. "What say you, my sworn sentries?"

"Dislike I the wilderness," sniffed Pan Tartus, leader of Armitage's sworn sentries. Small, dark eyes gleamed in hollow pits. His skin was dry as parchment. Clearly, he was not a man who enjoyed long sleep.

Armitage sneered. "Then we must need quicken our pace."

The others in the caravan—knights, squires, and servants—grumbled disapprovingly.

"Perish the thought, then ..." the Prince muttered.

"We can make camp here if no one minds starlight as shelter," Orrick offered.

"'Tis no shelter at all!"

Orrick frowned. "Know I the Homey Hills want for canopies. Alas, the only we may offer are of Turnip Marsh." He pointed south, toward a distant tree line of uncharted wilderness.

Pan Tartus stiffened at the suggestion.

"Are y' serious?" asked Pan Grimm, another sentry. "There are skinmiller bears an' highwaymen—"

Orrick and Armitage chuckled. Those strange, uncharted forests called the hinterlands never ceased to instill fear in foreign travelers. As Grimm said: they held many dangers. Many that entered never returned, killed by the very things mentioned by the older knight.

"'Tis fine," said Nigel, halting their laughter. "We packed tents. Might as well use them."

Hearing the news to make camp, squires and servants dismounted and tended their knights. Brandt shuffled over, a gangly lad of fourteen years, with a head that looked too large for his body. His mop of brown hair only added to the illusion. When Orrick first saw him, he wondered how his skinny neck could even support such a thing. Then he saw the lad spar with sword and shield and knew the lad was something special.

But Orrick did not base his selection on skills alone. The lad was the second son of House Hargrove, Barons of Maycoast, a seaside fortress. Though not heir, he could still become an influential figure.

If I might show one Rhabdolian that not all in Brzeg are savage, perhaps others shall believe as well.

As the lad helped him down, Orrick said, "Thank you, Brandt."

"Thank *you*, my lord." Then he went to help the other squires, leading Orrick's borrowed black rouncey to the group.

Indeed, their union was at first tumultuous. Brandt was uncertain, and even Orrick struggled with the idea of a Rhabdolian squire. Lord Father and Lady Mother had been against it, but 'twas Orrick's decision. He offered Brandt encouragement and courtesy. Brzeg culture clashed with Rhabdolian culture as much as their armies had. Orrick silently promised to be as accommodating as possible.

"Does it feel good to return home?"

Orrick saw his father's smile and returned it. "Aye, 'tis the same feeling I had returning from Nin."

"Doubtlessly so," said Nigel. "Welcome back. Care to aid me with the fire?"

They gathered kindling from felled branches, and soon Nigel had a small campfire roaring. Armitage swaggered over, clasping a deep green bottle. When he opened it, the air became perforated with the sickly-sweet smell of elderberries and juniper.

73

"Got this from Pałac's bottlery," said the Prince, grinning. "A good year, too. Trust me when I say, Lord Dickens relinquished this not without a fight."

Orrick raised his eyebrows. "Oh?"

"I spent more than it's worth …" Armitage shrugged and put the bottle to his lips. After several gulps, he pulled the bottle away with a wet *pop*. Refreshed he sighed, "But 'twas worth it."

Orrick barked a laugh. "Would you like a chalice?"

"I thought not to bring stemware and there's no use drinking fine wine from tin cups. Want some?" He held the bottle out to Orrick, who conceded and drank with sips more reserved.

"A good year indeed," he agreed.

Armitage hiccoughed his approval and took the bottle back. "Flavès whites are always better than Ianth reds. Bitter things, they are, Orrick. Don't ask me to stand them—I cannot!"

"I'll not," Orrick answered, grinning. Before he knew it, his laughter mingled with the flame-snapped bramble and his shoulders bobbed with the flames.

"What?" asked Armitage, eyes searching.

It does no good to hide things from him. "You can't handle the Ianth's bitter reds, yet you're come for white whiskey."

"I hadn't thought about it like—" He paused, drank from the bottle once more. His face had soured when he pulled it away. "Bah! Damn you, Orrick!"

Orrick snorted his laughter.

Armitage could not contain himself. His face was almost as red as his hair. Suddenly, the Prince's face became serious, even dour.

"I ... uh, want to apologize ..."

"About?" asked Orrick, concerned.

"About everything: Ozella, Father, and ... *this*." He gestured to the baggage train tended by knights and squires. Not only had King Biel insisted that Armitage bring his three sworn sentries, but also a baggage train with servants, clothes, food, and even wine.

The last item proved unnecessary, however, because the large group had found surcease in Pałac xe Triumf, a famous vineyard in the Flavès region. Orrick had not slept that night. Instead, Armitage bade him tour the cellars with Lord Dickens to taste from different casks. Tall and chubby, with no hair and wind-burnt cheeks, Dickens spoke with such flair. His passion for making and drinking wine was beyond anything Orrick had experienced before, compared even to Armitage.

Orrick shook his head. "Think naught of it. You're a prince, and your father only wishes you don't fall prey to—" *Savages,* he almost said.

While Armitage insisted on joining the Pallatons to their manse, Ozella and her brother remained behind in Albion, much to Orrick's relief. The girl was radiant, well-bred, a thing of beauty, but also of jealousy. In her mind, Armitage was hers alone, not something she was willing to share.

What petty creature would refuse her beloved to ride out with her friend? Unless that friend was a savage ...

The word rang in his head like a church bell. Certainly, her speech held no evil; she merely used it to dissuade her betrothed about gamboling with peasants. If possible, she was less fond of Armitage's cavorting than even the King.

Still, they were words carelessly chosen, he decided.

Armitage eyed him, waiting for him to finish. When he did not, the Prince shrugged, took another swig, and said, "'Tis right Father would be concerned. Not all are friends to the royal family." He sighed. "'Twould've been nice to experience things as Pallatons do—naught but you, your horse, the open skies ... Speaking of which, how fares your horse?"

Orrick smiled at the black rouncey. Like most warhorses, it came from drákoń descent. Bred and magically imbued by elves, they resembled normal horses, but their eyes bore different colors, and their hooves sparkled metallically, made of a material that required no shoeing. "Cień is a fine horse. The marshal chose well."

"Well, he certainly *matches*."

There was something in the way Armitage said it. Orrick bit.

"Matches? I suppose he's a fitting choice. Strong, swith—a knight's horse, doubtless, though young still. May I share a secret?"

"Of course." The Prince's grin was impetuous.

"I've always wanted a drákoń—the dragon-horses that rarely tire. Did you know? Before drákonie, cavalrymen must needed switch their horses between each charge."

"Really?"

"Yes, but they're expensive, and thus uncommon amongst farmers. Packhorses and squires' sumpters are not drákonie. Rarely are they found outside of Tourm."

"That *is* interesting," said Armitage. Then, he grabbed a handful of Orrick's shaggy black hair and tugged. "But I mean the marshal was good enough to lend you a horse matching *you*!"

Orrick pulled away, laughing. Armitage laughed, too, and Orrick was glad for it. He always worried when the Prince brooded.

"So, *Pan* Pallaton," he said between gasps. "Ever did you think your first task would be escorting your prince to your hometown?"

Orrick pointed at the bottle. "First answer me if you really had enough, as you said."

Armitage stopped laughing and glared at Orrick. "Shut up," he replied, which only made Orrick laugh harder, barking and hollering into dusk's gilded blush.

"Please, my prince, Pan Orrick," said Grimm. "Keep low your voices!"

As Orrick and Armitage made merry, the squires made camp. Upon the flat, dry land, mingled with the trees, new structures popped up: tents of rich purple or green canvas. Chill wind made shiver both people and pine needles. Nigel had built two more campfires, room enough for the knights, squires, and servants to huddle around for warmth.

"We should aid them with the food," said Orrick.

Armitage took another swig. "*Must* we?"

Orrick smiled and patted his friend's shoulder. "'Tis good of you to visit the lowborn, but even better to strive alongside your servants and soldiers."

"A point well made," he relented. "To the stores!"

Merrily, Orrick led him there.

Armitage was many things: a drinker, a gambler, a reveler. However, Orrick believed he would be a just king, and that he would keep his heart open—tolerant, and merciful. He would be glad to one day swear fealty to him.

Not that the Prince needed to know that, at least not right now. *The void knows how pompous he can get.*

Orrick and Armitage collected mutton and spits to roast them on, as well as turnips and fava beans to boil over the flames in a black pot. The servants filled the pots with boiled river water. Each person took a spit with mutton, the larger pieces for the lords and heirs, and smaller pieces for the knights, squires, and servants. In silence they ate beans and turnips upon tin plates, finishing shortly after the mutton had finished roasting.

Night fell. The distant mountains were a purple haze, and Turnip Marsh's tree-line as black and jagged as a dragon's maw. The knights from Albion, superstitious, turned their gazes to the stars.

Brandt pointed his mutton toward a five-star constellation, two low between three high. "The Crown!"

"Aye," said Orrick, "and on such a clear night."

"A good omen to lords," Nigel concurred.

The meal finished, they basked in the campfire's orange warmth. Winter had passed, but the nights remained cold. Nigel pan Pallaton drew his sword, Żmija, and ran an oilstone over its serpentine length. Fiona did the same with her prized weapon: a beautiful, thin saber of master-forged steel called Xąb.

"You did well, son," said Nigel.

"Yes," said Fiona. She held her saber up, examining it by firelight. "You felled the deserters and retrieved our weapons." She lowered the blade, punctuating the thought with a smile.

Orrick shook his head, worried. "Not all is well. The deserters said war comes to Newtown."

Fiona continued sharpening her saber, but her eyes watched the dancing flames. "I admit hearing troubling rumors from Nin. But I don't believe we north of them should worry."

Orrick nodded and watched the flames. His lips and chin felt greasy from the mutton, but there was an uneasy feeling in his stomach that had nothing to do with the meal.

If Lady Mother says there's naught to fear, then fear I shan't.

Both his parents had graduated from Akademia Palatæ. Orrick remembered his father telling him how they had separated after knighthood. She became a guardswoman in some fort, he a Knight-Errant of Brzeg. On his journeys across the harsh voivodship, Nigel realized how much he missed Fiona. When he asked for her hand in marriage, she would only consent if he bested her in a duel. Her skill at that time was with an arming sword, but Nigel's was with saber. Apparently, she could not withstand his high moulinets.

Orrick smiled at the thought.

No wonder Nigel took to her. *Alas, there was no one in Akademia Palatæ like that for me.*

His mind went to Chelsea, her golden curls, her strong back, her skill with archery, proficient enough that the Order of the White Falcon recruited her immediately after graduation. He remembered her sheepish smile, her soft voice, and the way she had stared at him across Whitehall. Before they separated for squiring, they spent many a day together. But he never thought of her as anything more than a friend.

Does Armitage jape? Or does truly he think Chelsea the woman for me?

Orrick always imagined wedding a warrior over a lady. That was the blood of House Pallaton. Chelsea was both, a fine archer and cousin of the royal family, born from one of King Biel's sisters.

Thoughtful, his tongue flicked over the sharp edge of his incisor. She was betrothed, he knew, and thus 'twas unmeet to pursue her.

"Come," said Nigel, standing. He examined his serpentine blade once more and slid it back into the scabbard. "We must sleep, for come morn make we for Newtown. Knights—"

Tartus, Grimm, and Callows snapped to attention.

"Choose who among you takes first watch. I warn you: things oft come down from the mountains."

Whilst everyone went to their tents, the Pallatons prepared their sleeping sacks and blankets of rough-spun wool upon the reedy ground. The squires had tethered the horses to trees before supper and made sure they had water to drink during the night, as well as apples and oats to eat.

Orrick bundled a blanket into a makeshift pillow and lay his head upon it. His fingers curled around the grip of his longsword, a relic of his days as a squire, now the good but plain weapon of a knight.

Or, at least, a man knighted.

He imagined that one day he would have a better station than knight-errant, and a sword forged by the manse's bladesmith to accompany that position. He shut his eyes and thought of something even better—a white steel sword that burned with fire when he swung it.

Sleep came not long thereafter. With it, terrible nightmares.

Men, faces caked with gore, bayed at the moon.

He could hear them in the distance, but they came closer. Panic seized his heart as he ran wild through forsaken forests long uncharted, said to hold numerous dangers both natural and magical.

'Twas neither highwaymen nor witches he feared but the insane men, drunk on rotten blood and graveworms. They followed him wherever he fled. He knew not where everyone else was—his mother and father, his squire, the Prince!

Naught mattered. These madmen, more animal than human, followed him. Somehow their senses tracked him, like wolves—like—

"*Wolves!*"

Orrick was up in an instant, sword free. Stealing a quick glance behind him, he saw the squires attempting to calm the horses.

"Not merely wolves," said another voice. "Jadwilki—poison wolves!"

Orrick swallowed hard.

The goblins had made the jadwilki during the Days of Devils. Before Aileron fought the goblins, they bred them to hunt and kill humans. Now long gone from Tourm, the goblins had left their beasts.

Armitage poked his head from his tent, surrounded by Grimm, Callows and Tartus. Each of them guarded him with swords drawn.

"Are you well, Armitage?"

"Oh aye—*save for the scumpin' wolves*!"

Good, the Prince is safe ... "Fear not; we'll have them routed!"

"I'd rather them *dead*!"

"Dead, then!"

He returned his gaze to the jadwilki surrounding them. A pack of five, large enough that their ears were level with a man's shoulders, coats the colors of dusk: hues of red, orange, purple. Their backs arched, shoulders hunched, legs strong with muscle.

Orrick gritted his teeth. *I could not kill the deserters, but these are not men, and I've a prince to protect*!

Closest to them, Orrick thought to draw the wolves' attention. Armitage's sworn sentries remained near him. He charged the nearest wolf. It reared to strike but Orrick lashed out faster, burying his sword between its eyes. He wrenched the blade free from the jadwilk's skull and whirled to face another, stepping away from its jaws.

The other wolves had grown aware. The remaining four encircled him, hackles raised, frothy muzzles growling, rippling. One lunged, but Orrick turned away and caught its flank with a backslash. It landed, bleeding but alive. Orrick roared and lashed out again, unaware of another leaping jadwilk until its fangs sank deep into his left forearm.

84

"Shite!" he cried. Light filled his mind, red and hot and flowing as blood. Another wolf came right behind him, two more close by.

Feel pain later, he thought, and smashed the poisonous wolf's snout with his pommel. He pulled his arm free, but it fell, useless. At least his sword-arm remained intact.

Another wolf lunged. Fiona appeared beside him, Xąb a dancing line of quicksilver. Her blade sliced the beast's underbelly and spilled its bowels onto the dusty ground. The stench of blood and ordure rose like steam.

A low growl drew Orrick's attention to the first jadwilk he had targeted. With barely a warning, legs silent as shadows, it attacked again, but Orrick held his blade horizontally and its bite found only iron. Fiona killed the jadwilk that held his blade, as Nigel appeared and dispatched another.

The final jadwilk growled low and howled wildly. Alone, it turned tail and fled into the night. Fiona made to run after it, but Nigel shouted and brought her back.

"Orrick's wounded!"

"Dammit!" She sheathed her sword with a silvery squeal.

"'Tis ... no trouble ..." Orrick said, brain shrouded in mist. "We ... can—"

With that, he collapsed to his knees.

85

VI: Manse Of The Mages

F iona tore a strip from her tunic.

Brain foggy, Orrick saw the bite. The jadwilk's teeth had punctured deep, and torn out flesh when he smashed its muzzle. Angry purple ripples circled the bite marks, difficult to see under the night-blackened blood.

"This will staunch the flow," Fiona told him, taking his arm.

He tried not to scream as his mother applied the makeshift bandage, but the pain in his arm and the fog in his head turned everything black.

"I—" The flatlands spun around and around. He tried to steady himself, fell forward—but his mother caught him.

Fiona snapped her head to the others. "He needs an herbalist. No doubt he's poisoned by the wolf's bite."

"We must onward to Newtown," said Tartus.

"We haven't time," said Nigel, frowning. "But there is one closer. Northward lies a small cottage surrounded by twelve sycamores. An enchanter dwells within."

Fiona bristled. "Know I of whom you speak. An odd man who experiments with herbalism and wardspells. Strange lights and sounds come from there." She put her hand on her saber. "No, I'd rather start for Newtown and be there by morn."

"We haven't time!" said Grimm. "Jad poison quickly spreads."

Fiona's eyes became icy. Still, she relented. "I'd sooner not trust a man of his ilk. Alas, it seems we've no choice ..."

Brandt took Orrick's sword and replaced it within the scabbard. Then he and Nigel hefted Orrick up. The bandage Fiona supplied was a boon: the blood flowed not as freely now. However, he felt his arm quickly numbing and voiced his concern.

"Surely jad poison," grunted Grimm.

"Nonsense, 'tis merely the bandage is too tight," Fiona argued, glaring. "As it must be for his survival, I'll remind you."

"I'll have none of your tears when the rot seeps into his brain," scoffed Grimm. "A knight you may be, but a woman still ... and you'll always know a woman's weakness."

She freed Xąb and aimed it at Grimm's throat. The other sworn sentries jumped back, hands on their swords, ensnared by indecision.

"Pay for your words like a *man* then!"

"Desist, Fiona," said Nigel, patting her elbow. "We've as much time for a duel as we do the trip to Newtown."

Eyes smoldering, still locked on Grimm, Fiona withdrew.

"I'd take care were I you, Grimm," said Armitage, grinning. "We can always escort Orrick to the enchanter whilst you and she remain behind to settle your differences."

"I'll not give him the satisfaction of my blade," sneered Fiona. "He'll remain to unmake camp with the squires. We'll head to the enchanter's house now."

"What?!"

Armitage chuckled. "As Her Grace wishes."

Orrick's head dipped until his chin touched his chest. He wanted to say something, but no words came. His face felt clammy and dripped sweat despite the cool night air. He wanted help, wanted his lady mother to argue with Armitage's sworn sentry no longer. But he was grateful Brandt took his sword and that his chainmail shirt restricted him not. He could not bear any more weight.

Nigel and Brandt supported Orrick as they walked, led by Fiona. Even with their aid, Orrick struggled. The ground was flat, but they walked north to the Homey Hills. Pines and sycamores hundreds of years old surrounded them. Roots thicker than human legs jutted from the ground. Orrick tripped more than once.

They scaled a hill, something Orrick protested. Legs dragging, he felt a tiresome wretch. Choking bile rose in his throat. He was unsure how long they walked—minutes, hours, days? Whatever the time, felt he relieved when Fiona cried, "There!"

Ahead, albeit distant shadows, grew a small grove of trees, pointed and twisted with leaves few. There seemed to be nothing but darkness … and then Orrick saw. Flashes of lights—red, yellow, blue, green, white, and pink—punctuated the darkness like distant thunder glancing from a cloud.

"I mislike this place," said Fiona. Orrick could not see her face, but knew she scowled.

"We haven't time to return," said Nigel.

Fiona sighed. "Onward, if we must."

"Yes," said Armitage, "I'd like to meet this … enchanter." Orrick did not even know he had come with them. Then again, 'twas foolish to think the Prince would remain at the campsite.

Further into the grove, the flashing lights brightened. Even Orrick wanted to turn back. The path to Newtown was long, even on horseback, but at least he would be away from whatever awaited him here. The mage could continue his work and Orrick could seek aid from healers friendlier. He might die before truly living as a knight, but in the pit of his overworking stomach he feared whatever lay ahead was something even more terrifying.

The group walked through the circle of sycamores, a homely path. Wind roared in their ears like a savage beast. In the clearing's center was a brick manse with a blue roof. A thirteen-point star emblazoned the front door.

Windows shone with soundless lightning. Armitage shouted above the din, "I see them—Grimm and the squires are not far behind! Best try the door now!"

Brandt struggled under Orrick's weight when Nigel parted to wrap his meaty hand around the bronze handle.

"Of course, 'tis locked!"

"I've a hard time believing no one's home," japed Armitage. It was no time for jokes; no one laughed, but no one shushed him.

Swearing loudly, Nigel pounded the door with both fists. The winds died away; the windows, so alive before, blackened. New lights replaced them, small and yellow and soundless. Candles.

The door opened, and in the threshold stood a boy no older than Brandt. Thick, flaxen hair shrouded his face, thin and gaunt like the rest of him. Yellow eyes darted to each of them, ablaze behind silver-framed spectacles.

"Why call you at this hour?" he asked.

He looks the commoner ... but has a noblemen's mouth. It was an odd thought, and amongst all else Orrick knew not why it came to him.

"Seek we the mage residing within," said Tartus, stepping in front of the Prince.

The boy looked him up and down, scowling. "What business does a knight of Castle Albicant have so far from the capital?"

"He travels with me," said Armitage, stepping to the front. "I demand visitation with this manse's master. Comply not, and you'll find yourself feeding jadwilki before the night's end."

The lad was unmoved. Still with only his head outside the door, he looked at the Crown Prince, eyes venomous. "And what's *your* business here?"

"For the love of—" Armitage shoved Tartus forward. "Kill the urchin for a traitor!"

"There shan't be need of *that*," said a deeper voice. The enchanter arrived from the darkness, body angled under his large, gray cloak, just as malnourished as the urchin. Young of face, but his long, limp hair was stark white. Even stranger, his eyes burned red as coals, a gaze mysterious but not unkind.

"So!" huffed Armitage. "The master finally arrives!"

The enchanter's eyes widened with concern. "Why comes a royal envoy to my home so late in the—" he paused, looked behind him, then back to the group "—so early in the morn? We've done naught wrong."

The sullen youth nodded, smirking.

"We're not come for you," said Armitage. He looked taken aback by his own words. "Well ... we *did* come for you—but—"

Orrick squeezed his way to the front, holding out his bleeding arm. "Forgive me, but if my prince continues stammering, I fear I may pass out ..."

The grey-robed mage clicked his tongue. "A jadwilk's bite. I suspected mine ears heard their howls. Alas, I thought not to look."

How the mage could hear anything above the awful din was beyond Orrick. He felt it better not to question him—didn't think he could if he wanted to.

The enchanter set his burning eyes to Orrick's. "You were right to come here. I apologize for mine apprentice's impertinence. We are ... wary of visitors. Make way, Nero, and allow them inside. I'll check for slime-root potion in the stores."

"We'll not need everyone with us," said Fiona, glaring at Grimm. "Tend to the horses. It shall be I, my lord husband,

Brandt, and Prince Armitage that enter."

Grimm succumbed to Fiona's ferocity and sighed. "Aye, my lady ..."

The manse was larger than Orrick expected, larger than it seemed on the outside. Every corridor they walked through contained ambries of books, shelves of folios and assorted papers. Each door bore the same thirteen-pointed star.

"I wonder if we'd find such furnishings in the kitchens and privy," Armitage joked.

Orrick could not even smile out of politeness.

Nero guided Orrick into the solar and sat him upon the most hideous couch he had ever seen. Swirls of maroon, gray, and blue rolled and waved in a mottled pattern. It hurt his eyes just looking at it, but he was thankful for so many cushions. Alas, they were just as ugly as the couch that held them. For a strange second, he thought himself a frog sat upon giant waterlilies.

Before Orrick could drift into darkness, his eyes jumped open at a bang. The gray-robed mage entered from a porthole where once had stood a wall. He carried a jar containing grass-green jelly, and his face looked as sour as the slime-root potion he held. "Tea, Nero," he softly commanded.

When Nero left the room, the enchanter removed Orrick's bandage. At once, blood flowed over Orrick's wrist and dripped

93

onto the floor. The wound stung as though the very air gnawed it.

The enchanter opened the jar. With a knife procured from the folds of his robe, he scooped a lump of green ooze and smeared it on Orrick's wounds. The jelly stopped the flow immediately. He wrapped another bandage of clean linen tightly around his arm.

"'Tis but a salve," laughed Armitage. "I thought you called it a potion."

The enchanter smiled, lidded the bottle tightly, and turned it upside-down. Through weary eyes, Orrick saw that the bottom contained another lid. The enchanter opened it and asked, "What is your name?"

It was a strange and sudden request, but he obliged. "Orrick pan Pallaton. Yours?"

"Nib Blackpool," answered the enchanter. "If you are Pan Pallaton, am I to believe these two are your lord father and lady mother, Nigel and Fiona, Voivod and Voivodina xe Brzeg?"

"Correct," said Fiona, her voice as taut as a bowstring.

"Then I must apologize for my lack of grace," replied Nib. "However, I believe tending to patients more important than formal gestures. I extend mine apology to you also, Your Highness."

"Think naught of it," answered Armitage. "We're of the same beliefs."

"We also, considering the one you heal is our son," said Nigel.

A wry curve parted Nib's lip. "Good to know, my lords—ah, Nero returns."

Nero stood in the doorway—the true doorway—holding a teapot in one hand and a mug in the other. Using the knife, Nib scooped the dregs from the slime-root potion and plopped them into the bottom of the mug. Nero gingerly poured the hot tea with it and Nib stirred the contents with the knife. Once done, he handed it to Orrick.

"Drink while it's hot," said Nib, smiling. "Foul of taste, yes; but fouler still if cool."

Orrick nodded and tilted the steaming mug to his mouth. The smell was noxious, like a sour fruit rotting in the sun. Still, he drank several mouthfuls before pulling the mug away. His tongue and throat burned.

Nib raised his white eyebrows. "Drink *all* of it."

"Must I?" asked Orrick. He wanted to hang his tongue out of his mouth like a sweating dog.

Nib held aloft the jar of green jelly. "To phrase it for a soldier, slime-root is a pincer attack. The salve is for the wound directly but cannot be used alone. A potion is made from the dregs and drunk whilst hot. This provides a quicker way into the bloodstream, and thus better healing. The liquid is not enough. One must drink the *dregs*, at the bottom of the cup, for the full effect. Understand?"

"I do," Orrick affirmed, and downed the mugful without further ado.

When Orrick finished, he wanted to scrub his tongue free from the bitter taste. Nero collected the mug, the teapot, and the jar, and headed into the basement from the porthole in the false wall.

Armitage sat next to Orrick, arms folded over his chest, eyes following the lad out. His attention returned to the enchanter. "You're indeed skilled, Nib, but why do you work so far into the wilderness?"

"Does Your Highness suggest I work in Castle Albicant?"

Armitage shifted uncomfortably.

"Alas, I've little heart for the people of Albion. Content though I am to live nearby, eat the food, drink the wine, and admire the land, my place is out here." He stood, smiling pleasantly. "With Pan Pallaton now bandaged and medicated, I believe formal introductions are in order. I'm Nib Blackpool, Enchanter of the Order of the Grand Star, at your service."

"The Order of the Grand Star?" asked Armitage.

Nib nodded. "An order that strives to see the powers of old returned."

Armitage snorted as if told a joke. "And what, pray tell, are the *powers of old*?"

Nib inhaled, and then looked at Orrick. Brandt stood near him, ghostly white with concern. Nigel and Fiona waited, breath bated and eyes distrusting. Ignoring Armitage's inquiry, he spoke to them.

"Nero is my wizard apprentice, recently graduated from Akademia Magia. Are you not recently released from Akademia Palatæ, Pan Pallaton?"

"I was," Orrick answered, confused. "But Nero looks too young to be a graduate. You called him a wizard apprentice. If Nero graduated, why is he with you?"

Armitage scoffed and folded his arms across his chest. "Before he answers you, he must answer me."

Nib licked his lips thoughtfully. "I shall answer you shortly, Your Highness. For now, I speak to Pan Pallaton and 'tis rude to interrupt. Now, where was I?"

Orrick looked at Armitage. The Prince was tactful enough to control his anger despite Nib baiting him. "Oh, go ahead!"

"Yes," said Orrick. "Nero is still your apprentice even though he's graduated."

"Magicians and knights are so vastly different, and yet so re-markably similar. When a knight graduates from academy, he joins his brethren. Whether he is knight-errant, guardsman, or soldier, he still has others he must learn from. Knights-errant answer to the sovereigns of his realm—dukes, counts, barons, lord mayors. Sentries and soldiers have captains and commanders, Knights Ardent and Valiant.

"Nevertheless, a knight is thrust into his position never with but a sword and whispers of good tidings. So 'tis the same for magicians."

"How so?" asked Orrick.

"Knights swear into servitude and pursue strength. Magicians swear into servitude and pursue knowledge. When the magi-cian graduates, 'tis based on deeds and knowledge accrued. A magician must then learn all he can from his mentor. And there are so many things about magic, known and unknown. Alas, most of it has been lost."

"Lost?" asked Orrick and Armitage, together.

"Lost," repeated Nib, solemnly. "What remains of magic is thus: Illusionists create wards by manipulating light and aerial moisture. Herbalists make medicine from natural ingredients. Seers use dreams to see the future. Tempters make mind-altering stimulants such as love potions, hallucinogens, truth serums, and poisons."

Armitage harrumphed. "Magic sounds not very lost to me."

He only feigned his displeasure, though. Orrick noticed the appeased, even curious, glint in his eyes.

"Well, Your Highness, of the four branches I mentioned to exist, only two require innate magical ability. While a boon for herbalists and tempters, only seers and illusionists are truly gifted."

Armitage smiled. "Would that I'd been born with that gift ..."

"So you say, but the cost of a magician is high. We come to academy, whether highborn or low, to spend our days and nights pursuing knowledge, proffering ourselves unto the mysteries of ages long past and gods long gone. Even now do dwindle our powers."

"Dwindle?"

Nib chuckled sadly. "Long ago, before the world was as we now know it, humans could weave spells so grand that they commanded the very elements. Alas, soon there might not even *exist* magicians."

"Ah, you speak of the Tide-turners in the faerie stories."

Nib tented his hands and looked at the Prince beyond his fingertips. "The Tide-turners' power came from magical stones. They are *not* faerie stories. The Sundering of the Stones is historical fact, one that came before the Days of Devils. What I speak of was intrinsic. For instance, recall I an old tome stating that some magicians could rend a man's soul from his bones with a single utterance. It makes an illusionist's vanishing ward look a mere parlor trick! Alas, 'tis no longer ... "

Armitage scratched his wiry hair. "And the Order of the Grand Star seeks to revive these powers?"

"Revive is a word too strong. Then again, that may be what some seek. I prefer to know what happened to it all. If humans could truly command the elements and even death, then where did that power go? What was the reason for its coming, and what was the reason for its going? These are the answers we seek."

For the second time, Armitage folded his arms over his chest and scoffed. "'Twas a longwinded explanation for such a simple question."

"One of the marks of a magician—an oath if you'd like—is never to opt for the simple. Seek we the grandiose. Even after a magician apprentice becomes a magician unto himself, he must continue learning, working, and, most importantly, searching."

Armitage yawned. "For those lost powers of old."

"The very same," Nib answered with a patient smile.

"Master," said Nero, leaning against the wall, "bore us no longer with tales of powerful magic. Those powers are gone with the overgods. Never may we know where, but they're gone just the same."

"I refuse to believe they are." Nib looked to Armitage. "Some believe elemental magic came from the overgods, that they took the power with them when they fled Xiemia."

Nero stood straight and tall. "Does this idea make little sense to you? The overgods have left and took their gifts with them."

"You've seen the Summering Glade with your own eyes!" said Nib.

"The Summering Glade?" asked Armitage. "I've been as well."

"Good, you know it then."

"Aye," said Fiona, "but we've not."

Nib examined her. "In that acre, winter comes never. Why not? Even you are curious, Nero. 'Tis a magician's nature to be curious—'tis what we strive for."

"Forgive me master, but our goal as magicians should be finding answers—not merely being curious."

"Ah, Nero ... you've still a lot to learn."

"As luck would have it, I agree." The lad turned to the door. "Now if we're done with your experiments and the visitors, I would seek some rest long needed. Is that well with you?"

"Go. Rest." With Nero gone, Nib sighed and said, "A lad exceptionally smart and careful ... 'tis a shame his arrogance is ill-matched with his skills. You all must be tired as well."

"We are," answered Orrick.

Indeed, he felt drained from the arduous night behind him. The dusty road, the dance with wolves and the strange mysteries of the manse of mages weighed heavily on his mind. He welcomed sleep, and the cushions rocked him like a boat on the sea.

The last thing he heard before drifting off was Nib saying to Brandt, "The horses may graze my grasses. Find my well and some buckets behind the manse that the beasts might be watered. Tell the other knights to come inside."

Hours later, Orrick opened his eyes to the strange sights and smells that permeated the magician's solar. Brandt, his skinny, brown-haired squire, slept comfortably on the floor with an ugly cushion from a different couch. The other knights—Tartus, Grimm and Callows—and their squires lay there as well.

Lord Father and Lady Mother must be elsewhere, thought Orrick. *Nib must have given Armitage a room as*—"Ugh!"

As soon as he sat up, his head exploded like a war drum, beating and screaming bloody murder. He felt brained by a battle-axe and somehow lived to tell the tale. Eyes shut tight, vision red and broken.

A hot mug forced its way into his clenched fists. He looked up and saw many eyes, but all were the hot-coal red borne only by Nib.

"Drink this," he said. "Fireberry tea spiced with firestick. 'Twill aid your aching head."

"Why do I—?"

"Headache means the slime-root worked," said Nib, undoing Orrick's bandage.

To his surprise, the bite marks had puckered into little scars, and the angry purple bruises had lightened to acidic yellow. *'Tis truly working*, he marveled, flexing his fingers. Stiff, but better.

Nib's eyes were torches as he searched Orrick's. "Experiencing any lightheadedness or delirium?"

"No ..."

Nib cocked an eyebrow. "Repressing, are you, the will to do wanton destruction to people or objects?"

Orrick shook his head, which he regretted. "N-no ..."

"What about a fear of water or drinking?"

Despite the pain, Orrick scoffed. "A fear of *drinking*?"

Nib frowned. "You've not touched your tea."

Orrick examined the cup. It was without cream and perhaps without honey, things he would have preferred after such a bitter potion. Still, he drank the sun-red liquid to appease the mage. It was cooler than the slime-root potion; sweeter, too.

"Good, good," said Nib. "Naught is as bitter as slime-root."

Orrick was thankful for that. He finished the fireberry tea in only a few gulps. He remembered to drink the dregs as well, without Nib reminding him. Strangely and most wonderfully, his headache receded.

"Fear of drinking or swallowing is a side-effect of jad poisoning just the same as the other symptoms I've named. Peculiarly, and I know not why, swallowing becomes most difficult, and the inflicted cannot seem to do it without great pain."

Orrick sighed; happily, he had that problem not.

The white-haired wizard offered Orrick a pleasant smile. "It seems the poisoning is just as cured as your wounds. Gone, soon, should your headache also be. You may leave my manse whenever you feel able. But first ..." he stood, and Orrick realized he had been kneeling "... I must speak to your lord father concerning my recompense."

"How much do we owe you?" asked Nigel. He stood in the doorway, armored in black leather, Żmija at his side.

Nib smiled. "Not a question of *how much*, my lord, but *what*."

Nigel folded his arms, gaze unwavering. "Blackmail?"

But if Nigel frightened Nib, he showed it not. "You come quickly to that conclusion. Are you worried?"

"As Voivod xe Brzeg, I feel it in my best interest to know where mine enemies stand."

"Enemies?" gasped Nib. Then, as a surprise to both father and son, he laughed raspy. "Perish the thought, my lord. Expect I neither your purse nor your firstborn son. Merely ask I that no one disturb me. My work is precious to me and work I cannot without solitude."

Nigel raised his thick eyebrows. "Your work?"

"Aye, my lord. While they may only seem as colorful lights and strange sounds in the night, I assure you 'tis work. I'd prefer to remain undisturbed whilst conducting it."

Nigel stroked his black beard and eyed the man with bladelike eyes. "People fear what they understand not, and I indeed count you as one misunderstood." He sighed. "But only the gods know where we'd be without your skills. As you like it. No one of Brzeg shall disturb you."

"The gods have naught to do with it," said Nib.

Orrick looked confused. "What mean you?"

"As I see it, there are two otherworldly forces: the overgods and the undergods. The overgods remain elusive—uncaring of mankind. Aught that happens in the world, good or bad, 'tis the undergods' doing. Of that, above all else, I'm certain."

"Do you worship them?" asked Orrick.

Nib raised his eyebrows. "The undergods?"

Orrick nodded, and the master scoffed.

"Of course not; merely I state facts. The gods' realms lie behind the veil of reality, deeper than any star—mayhap even than the void or the After Realms. 'Tis known that mankind has not interacted with them for eons."

"Who were these overgods?"

Nib sighed. "Would that I had tea of mine own—long tales are oft in need of it."

"Mine apologies, I only—"

"No, lad, 'tis important you know."

Orrick listened intently.

"From the oldest tomes, we can surmise there were twelve overgods. Each governed a natural aspect. And twelve of the Grand Star's thirteen points represent an overgod."

"I know them," said Orrick.

"And know you the Language Holy?"

"Only a few words."

Nib raised his eyebrows, apparently surprised by the answer. "How do you know the twelve overgods?"

"Limehouse has a shrine, and we've named moons for them."

"Quite right, and know you why?"

"Because created they our world."

"At the gathering of all twelve came Xiemia and all it holds. Know you them?"

"All do. The four most known are Wróżka, the Goddess of Wind, Wodniça, the Goddess of Water, Robak, the God of Stone, and Smok, the God of Fire, but there are others still—and not thirteen."

Nib nodded. "The twelve are believed to have made Xiemia, but 'tis believed also they created magic, the same magic I spoke of last night."

"Where humans wielded great power—"

"Even before the Tide-turners with their crystals came."

"But something happened to them," Orrick surmised. "Else-wise they would be here. What?"

Nib smiled. "Would *you* like to be a wizard, Orrick? We are not merely healers and crafters of illusions. We are historians."

"History?"

"Knowledge bequeaths itself only to those that seek it. Peas-ants know not where to find it and nobles care not to seek it. But we, born with the gift, are thrust into it. Alas, there are no tomes that would tell me true."

"No tomes ... but legends?"

"Legends ... perhaps, yes; if you know the legends of the Tide-turners."

"But you said they were—"

"They are *not* faerie stories, but the happenings around that period remain mysterious. We guess, we assume, we piece together the puzzle with the events that came before, not those that came after."

"So, what happened?"

"*Xa Magia Bóg* came and washed antiquity away."

"Antiquity?"

"*The Machine Empire*, as historians know it. The world was quite different. People have even found relics of this time in the Badlands."

Orrick frowned at Nib's rambling. "What made it different?"

"Magic and mechanicals were one."

Orrick shook his head. The enchanter no longer made sense. Never heard he that word before. "Mechanicals?"

"Consider the farmer's plow. Imagine if magic changed it. It could move on its own, faster than a horse could pull it, and could do an entire day's work in an hour."

"Did such a thing ever exist?"

"It most certainly did, and the world continued to grow with it. Eventually, it became too much. The people cured diseases, even stopped fearing death itself. Then came Xa Magia Bóg and washed it all away."

"So, what was it?"

"Some believe certain cultists longed for a purer world, believing they could become gods themselves. Summoned they Xa Magia Bóg. Or perhaps it was created by the overgods in answer to the cultists' prayers."

"Is that why?" asked Orrick. "Did humans make the overgods leave?"

"I believe it could have been enough to make them surcease to their own heavens far from the sights and sounds and destructions created by humankind. Alas—" he frowned "—would that the undergods went with them ..."

Orrick stared into his empty mug. Headache subsided, he thought, *Is Xa Magia Bóg the thirteenth point?*

"This is why magicians, when casting their spells or brewing their potions, pray in the Language Holy. We hope the over-gods will better hear us and answer in ways more dynamic."

Before he could ask anything further, Nigel interrupted.

"Stuff and nonsense."

Orrick looked at his lord father, questioning.

"If ever existed the overgods, they are gone—done with and deaf to humans—and never shall we know why."

"Mayhap your lord father speaks true. The will of the gods is not to be understood by the minds of men. Now," Nib looked to Nigel. "You're come to rouse your son, and he is roused."

Nigel nodded. "Prepared are the horses. We leave now."

"Well, my lord, my thanks for your patience."

Orrick set the mug on the table and bowed. "Thank you for your time, Nib. Whether 'twas by luck, the gods' grace, an undergod's trick, or aught else, I'd be the flies' feast were it not for you."

"Worry not, 'twas my pleasure. I recommend you see your own herbalist as soon as you reach Limehouse. It should heal without rotting, but I would you change your bandages for ones cleaner."

"Yes, Master Nib. I do not see Nero this morn. Is he—?"

"Apprenticeship with enchanters require late nights. No doubt he still sleeps. He'll have your regards."

Orrick stood, lightheaded but able to walk. As he crossed the threshold, Nib called out to him. He turned around.

"If you wish to know more, start with the Machine Empire and continue from there."

"Thank you," said Orrick. "I shall."

When he, Brandt and Nigel exited the manse, they saw their squires had helped Armitage's sworn sentries into their armor. Everyone waited upon his or her horse, all of which seemed healthy despite the night's unceremonious quarters. Brandt helped Orrick onto his black rouncey before climbing atop his own sumpter.

A strange place, but not a bad one, he decided, smiling at the black windows. Nigel called to depart, and the company rode off.

VII: White Whiskey

I t was noon when the horses approached Pallaton Manse, named Limehouse. Surrounded by two ponds, capped with black shingles, fortified with great slabs of limestone burned crimson, the high seat of Brzeg looked somehow simple yet imposing. Battlements flew the Tourm's flag: a white gyrfalcon soaring above two crossed silver swords on a sky checked blue and gold. Below them waved the banners of House Pallaton, an inverted red longsword on field of black.

The marshal met them inside the gatehouse to take their mounts to the stables. A knight in hide leather, chainmail, and orange cloak bowed to his liege lord and Prince Armitage before escorting them all inside.

"I would meet with Castellan Ogar," Nigel said to the knight. "And fetch Nona Strega to see to my son."

As Voivod Pallaton went to find the castellan, the knight

escorted them all to the sitting room before leaving to find the manse's herbalist. It was not long before she arrived, an elderly woman with a hooked nose and skin as rough and wrinkled as tree bark. She took Orrick's arm in an iron grip, surprising him, and unwrapped the bandage to inspect the wound.

"Goodly done," said she, and replaced the bandage with one of clean, white linen.

"Thank you, Madam Strega," said Fiona, who remained behind.

"Yes, thank you," muttered Orrick.

"Not 't all, not 't all," she mumbled, leaving the room with a dismissive wave.

She was good at her job, Orrick knew, but aloof, and preferred strangers and shadows to the family that employed and sheltered her.

Orrick flexed his left hand, glad that Madam Strega wrapped bandages not nearly as harshly as Fiona or Nib. So tight, in fact, that his arm had numbed as he rode, and only holding it straight out in front of him would relieve the deadness.

Moments later, Nigel pan Pallaton entered the sitting room and sat. He wore his finery: dark gray silken tunic, lambskin leggings, and black boots of the softest calfskin. Orrick sometimes had to wear such things but preferred the crunch of hard leather and jingling of mail to the swish of finer fabrics.

Would that I might buy some plate mail, he thought. *Alas, I cannot yet afford it.*

Young though he was, tales of valor instilled the grandeur of knighthood in his brain. He may grow to be a lord like his father, but he preferred to be a lord commander like his grandfather, Terzo. Undoubtedly knights, his mother and father were content to rule their lands.

But her challenge to Grimm in the Homey Hills means she longs still for adventure.

Orrick wished for that as well. He was so adamant about enjoying his time as a knight-errant rather than marrying and sitting aside, commanding other men.

"'Twas some fancy footwork out there, if I do say so," Callows laughed, pouring a Flavès white. The friendly-faced knight handed a cup to Orrick.

He accepted it with a nod and smelled. *Flowery.* It was indeed aromatic, but dry enough that he had to suck on his tongue to regain moisture in his mouth.

"Why, Grimm was saying 'twas reminiscent of the Blood Knights."

"Blood Knights?" asked Orrick, disbelieving of the comparison.

"An order of four-and-twenty knightly lords who govern the Republic of Pinberry in place of a king," said Callows.

"I know who they are. Palatæ's master-at-arms oft mentioned them. They're said to be the greatest swordsmen in the world: fleet of foot, sharp of wits, bold as the mountains that surround them." Orrick looked at the acidic yellow bruise creeping up his arm. "A Blood Knight true would have been bitten not. Sooth, I'd not last five seconds against one of them."

Callow's smiled faded. "None of us would, lad."

Armitage drank from his goblet. "Damn good that Pinberry and Tourm are allies, then."

Nigel raised his eyebrows pointedly. "Perhaps not allies, but both nations know not to frivolously make war."

"Their armies aren't as great as ours or Kendala's, but what they lack in size finds skill as recompense," said Fiona. She sipped her wine gracefully. "Whether they would oppress us on the battlefield or we them is unknown and untested."

"Anyway," said Callows, "'tis not the Blood Knights I fear but the Karnath Elite."

"The assassins?" asked Armitage, enthralled.

"Formed in the Days of Devils by a wood elf prince," said Grimm.

"That's a legend," said Tartus.

"Even so, I know the tales," said Grimm. "'Tis said there are six in the shadows for each one you can see."

"Aye," said Tartus, "but 'tisn't true *skill* that guides the Blood Knights' swords—nor the Karnath's knives—but alchemies strange!"

"Should ever Tourm war with Pinberry, no doubt the Karnath assassins would come as well," said Grimm.

"Nah, they're rotters!" said Tartus. "Tourm could buy'm an' make'm fight against the Blood Knights—"

"'Tis said one Blood Knight's sword is worth a hundred Karnath daggers," Callows argued.

"'Tis said one Karnath assassin carries one hundred daggers on his person," Grimm countered.

Fiona stood, drawing all eyes to her. "Pans, I'll have no more talk of these hypothetical battles. True, Tourm and Pinberry are not great friends but neither they nor we would risk this longstanding peace."

The arguing knights looked dejected. She leaned back in her chair, sipped from her chalice. "Besides, there are other things—things that are real—that matter now." She looked at Orrick, her icy eyes rippling with concern. "Where will your first mission take you?"

"I know not yet. Somewhere exciting, I hope."

It was not.

When Orrick learned of his task, they all sat in the dining hall.

Ramona Fields, the head cook, had set the white-wooded table with a feast of roast pheasant smothered in a sauce from dragonbell peppers and black cherries. Accompanying the meat were sliced turnips topped with melted goat cheese, roasted snowfoul eggs, and pears stewed with cucumber and figs. Orrick's father that brought the news. After all, the lord of the land was the one who addressed the knights-errant to their duties.

"Jadwilki have been seen in the Homey Hills," said Nigel, looking at Orrick.

"Yes." Orrick rubbed his bandaged arm. "I'm aware."

"Good," said Nigel, stiffening. "Then you know as well that we cannot have one so far from the mountains. As knight-errant, 'tis your duty to put it to the sword."

Orrick grimaced. He could not protest with the Prince and his sworn sentries present. "I accept."

"Your reward shall be thirty silver pecks for its death. You'll receive one gold dash providing the pelt is unscathed."

Reminded that knights received pay for their work, Orrick

perked up.

Armitage smiled. "A jadwilk was your first kill."

"A pity one shall be my next," said Orrick, halfheartedly.

"Wonder I if this has aught to do with the one that fled last night?"

Nigel chuckled. "In fact, my prince, it does."

Despite the japes, Orrick could not keep the disappointment from his face.

Callows—whose face was considerably fresh for being a seasoned soldier—swallowed his bite of pheasant and said, "Hunting wolves is a fine task for a green knight-errant."

"You seem unwell, Orrick." Fiona looked at him, eyes hard. "One was nearly the death of you. Are you afraid?"

"I've killed others that could not find recompense in my flesh," answered Orrick. "I fear them as any should but ... I know I can kill them."

"Ah, is that it?" asked gaunt Tartus, a smiling growing on his face.

Armitage looked his way. "What?"

"The Homey Hills are too near to home. He wanted to go

somewhere exciting!"

Nigel scoffed. "You didn't expect to be sent abroad so soon?"

"No," Orrick admitted. *Though I'd have liked to.*

His mother was more comforting. "Tourm needs knights like you. Worry not, son. Your time will come."

The cooks brought dessert: a mix of wild berries emboldened by local spices, with saffron wafers and clotted cream. The butler brought a bottle of sunberry brandy and poured a glass for each guest. Gold as the sun, and so aromatic that one whiff was a punch in the nose. Orrick took tentative sips from the small snifter, same as he saw everyone else do.

Glasses and plates empty, Orrick noticed Fiona eying him. "You'll do well to go right to bed," she said. "We mean to send you to task as soon as Prince Armitage leaves for Albion."

"Yes, Lady Mother."

"We'll send Madam Strega to your room to give your wounds another look. After that, to bed."

"Yes, Lady Mother."

Nigel stood as well. "Before adjourning, I ask you join me in my solar."

This caught Orrick off guard. Was he in trouble for taking a tone

119

with his father? Without a word, Orrick nodded and followed Nigel to a small room at the top of a battlement. There was a single desk upon a barren floor of stone tiles. Black curtains flanked the tall, rectangular windows, allowing in the last rays of the setting sun.

Kindling rested unlit in the hearth. Above the mantle hung a sword in a scabbard lacquered black, locket trimmed with white fur from a beast unknown. Nigel took it down, turning it over in his hands.

"*This* is Bógplaga."

Orrick eyed it curiously. Nigel had seldom allowed him in his solar when he was a boy, but the few times he ventured inside, the sword drew his eye. It looked a worthy weapon then, and even more so now that Nigel brought it down for closer inspection. Orrick eyed it for the treasure it was. Hilt and pommel wrought of dwarves' red gold. Black leather wrapped the grip, aged and cracking. He had always wanted to touch it, to draw it, but could never reach. More than that, his father had put a fear in him when first he saw him eyeing it.

"*If you touch the sword*," he'd said in his lordliest of voices, "*you will die*."

That was when Orrick was a child. Now he was a man grown, and a knight.

"Bógplaga," repeated Orrick. The word tasted funny in his mouth. Like all the other blades of Tourmian steel, this one had been named in the holy language, the same language magicians spoke to weave their spells. "What does it mean?"

Nigel smiled patiently. "First, I must tell you the tale, and the tradition besides."

"Tradition?"

"This was Aileron's sword. When his son was knighted, he showed him the blade and told him its tale. Since then, it has become tradition of father and son."

Orrick grinned, relieved he was not in any trouble and happy to be rewarded for attaining knighthood. "Tell the tale, Lord Father."

Nigel chuckled softly. "First, 'twas a sword of white steel. This is important to know, for Aileron was a young rotter, thus unable to afford such a qualified weapon and did naught to earn it."

"How came he by it?"

"Belike, he took it from the corpse of a commander during the goblin wars. Spoils of war are oft gained through death—remember that."

Orrick nodded.

"No one remembers the name of the sword, but Aileron named it Rtęć—quicksilver. 'Twas with Rtęć that Aileron

121

became Slayer, felling two thousand goblins in a single battle, including Drlnÿg the Goblin King."

"Slayer ..." Orrick reflected. "An uneasy task. None have since gained the title, and only a few before him."

"Precisely."

"What happened to him?"

"After slaying Drlnÿg and routing the goblins from Starter Mountains, Aileron traveled Fangaard in hopes of finding work. At least, this is the tale we're told. All that's known for true is he vanished from Tourm after being branded, returning to Oldtown five years later."

"Pancerz ..."

"The Engine Devil," Nigel confirmed. "'Twas said his hide was impenetrable, that he could not be slain. Somehow, Aileron destroyed a piece of armor large enough to put his sword through. The sword broke in two, covered with the undergod's corrosive blood."

"So Aileron *did* fight an undergod?" gasped Orrick. "Those aren't mere tales?"

Nigel smiled, but answered not. Instead, he continued the story. "Aileron was heartbroken by the loss of his blade. To others, 'twas Rtęć. To him, 'twas *Moja Pani*—'my lady.' So, collected he the broken pieces and sought a dwarven smith—the only one who might mend his blade."

"Because it came from Tourmian steel?"

"Partly," answered Nigel. "Do you know why Tourmian steel differs from regular steel?"

"'Tis made with diamonds and calcite. It takes half a year to forge a blade, and there is no metal that can better hold a blade."

"Well," Nigel said, "perhaps not. There is another, a metal called *gwiezstal*—starsilver. Aileron knew 'twas the only thing could save his sword, and only dwarves and elves can smith it. The result is *this*."

With a twist, Nigel drew the blade from the scabbard. Orrick could not imagine a sword more wondrous. The blade was matte white, but it had veins of metal, blue as lightning, streaking across the edge itself, filling the cracks. But that was not all. Reddish stains smeared the blade, glowing with unearthly light.

"Aileron continued to call it Moja Pani but quicksilver no longer described it. He renamed it Bógplaga: Bane of the Gods."

"Bane of the Gods," repeated Orrick. "Then that truly is an undergod's blood? There must not be another blade like it in the whole of Xiemia."

"Most fear it for an evil thing. Some still believe that the

123

undergods will come back. Seeking revenge for their fallen friends, yes, but also because a human dared use an undergod's blood for his own gain."

A thought occurred to Orrick, a question burning in the back of his mind long before Nigel had taken the sword out. "Lord Father, what did you mean when you said I'd die if I touched it?"

Nigel raised his eyebrows. "Remember that, do you?"

"Yes."

"You're aware the glowing stains are the undergod's blood, deadly to all who touch it. There have been several voivods foolish enough to draw the sword in battle, too unskilled to wield it. There exists no cure for devil's blood. Thankfully, those men had heirs to carry on the Pallaton name."

"And this happens with a mere touch?"

"Even if not a mortal wound, the rot comes, and the warrior dies in moments."

"No wonder people fear it," Orrick marveled.

Nigel withdrew the blade into the night-black scabbard. Orrick jumped at its snap. "Good," said Nigel, smiling, "you fear it still. Remember, when you are voivod, Bógplaga will belong to you. You'll share its history with your son upon his knighthood."

"I will. Fear it though I do, I shan't break tradition."

"Good," said Nigel, replacing the sword upon the mantle. "Now, to bed. Tomorrow holds work for you and Brandt."

Finding his room from the solar proved difficult. Large Limehouse contained many twists and turns. He stood outside the great hall, dismayed to find it empty. Embarrassing as it was, he had no choice but to ask a patrolling guardsman.

"Oh, of course, Pan Pallaton," he said, smiling wide. "I understand. Y' lived in Albion, y' lived in Newport, an' all the suddenly you're back 'ere without a clue where t' go—"

Orrick let the guard prattle on like that, grunting confirmation between pauses but concentrating on the surroundings. Once was embarrassing enough. He did not wish to be twice guided.

When the guardsman found Orrick's room, he said, "There y' are, pan. You'll find it clean as springtime. When we 'eard y' was comin' back, we made sure t' spruce it up for y'."

"My thanks," said Orrick, closing the door behind him and leaving the guardsman grinning still.

Now alone, Orrick breathed relief. He found the room clean, indeed: there was nothing but a small desk and chair, a bed, a small shelf carried his books, and a mannequin upon which to deposit his armor.

Nearby, the desk held a pitcher of purified well water and a single goblet. Orrick hung his shirt and sword-belt on the mannequin, poured himself some water. He looked around the room, taking everything in. Like the rest of the manse, the same drab stone tiled the floor, the walls crimson limestone, the curtains black and drawn.

Though dreary the surroundings, there was warmth that had nothing to do with the small brazier alive with fire. Being back here made him feel touched by time, as though the ghosts of his ancestors kept watch over the halls.

Orrick's chest swelling at the memories. Sighing, he thought, *I've no time to think such things. On the morrow I begin my first task.* He looked to the heavy oaken door. *'Tis a pity Armitage is only here the night. I suppose we shan't—*

A knock startled him, even though he knew who was behind it. He felt dismay, for he had hoped the Prince would drop his foolish desire for white whiskey. Orrick found no such luck but tried to hide his disappointment when he opened the door.

"Orrick!" Armitage whispered, but nonetheless sounded excited. Like a shadow, he slid into Orrick's chambers and bade him close the door.

The Prince came ready: like before the knighting ceremony, Armitage had forsaken his jewel-colored doublets, lambskin leggings and goldbeater boots for rough-spun and hide. Instead of oiled, he combed his wiry hair forward to hide his face. He looked no longer regal, nor was his gait: his shoulders slumped forward, and he leaned on his left leg.

126

"Ready for su' white whiskey, m' lad?" he asked, grinning foxily. He deepened his voice and again afflicted with the idioms of Nin.

"We cannot—not this night. I've a task on the morrow and—"

Armitage frowned. "We'll not be long," he said, dismissively waving his hand. "All we need do is find a pub, have but one glass, and return! There shall be plenty of time to rest well for our separate treks."

"I advise against it, Armitage. Lady Mother bade me sleep—"

"She bade you to *bed* and mentioned sleeping not!"

Orrick sighed. "We've both duties to uphold, promises to keep come morn. Wish I not to disappoint Mother and Father, nor wish I to slight King Biel and the good House Pardwy."

"Is *that* what this is about?" The coolness in his voice intensified, as did the coy look in his eyes. "When you resided in academy, you had no trouble sneaking away with me. Now you're knighted and suddenly spending time with your friend and prince is beneath you. Is that it?"

"I said no such thing!" gasped Orrick, trying and failing to keep his voice low.

Armitage smiled. "I relent: You did not say you were greater than me. What you *did* say was that we would have white whiskey. Would you allow your prince to go unaccompanied to a Newtown tavern?"

Orrick was at an impasse. "I—Your Highness, I—" Unfortunately, it was not what the Prince wanted.

"I'll have none of that *Highness* shite," he hissed. Orrick knew an angry prince was never good. "Came I to Newtown to drink white whiskey, and that is what *we're* doing. I no longer ask as your friend, Pan Pallaton, but command as your prince."

Orrick could make no other argument, and thus no other choice. He dressed similarly to Armitage, in unassuming woolen britches, a plain tunic, a jerkin of old hide. With calloused hands, he mussed his hair to cover his high forehead. Deciding that he should not be defenseless should anything go awry, he took the dagger from his sword-belt and slipped it into the simple leather rope he wore as a belt.

Their goal this night, as it was every night they gamboled with peasants, was to leave all lordly countenance behind. They were Orrick pan Pallaton and Prince Armitage Pardwy no longer. Instead, they were Lorry and Ari, two travelers up from Nin. Like Armitage, Orrick deepened his voice and assumed a Nin accent. Then there was nothing to do but wait until Limehouse's lights dimmed.

When they were as certain as they could be that the manse slept, slipped they from Orrick's bedchamber, crept past the guards, and made their way into Newtown proper. They wandered the streets, darkened by the night but kept alive still by glowing torches burning atop poles. Newtown had no cobbled roads, so they followed paths of beaten earth, spying houses, inns, taverns, shops, and smithies.

"What's wrong wit' those?" asked Orrick.

Armitage had stopped at every inn thus far, peering into the windows and shaking his head. This time was no different. "It needs t' be perfect." He eyed Orrick. "What'cha papa say?"

"Showed me Bógplaga."

Armitage's eyes widened, Ninnish accent forgotten. "Aileron's sword stained by devil blood?"

"'Tain't no myth," Orrick answered.

"Apparently not … Now come."

Lorry and Ari continued down the path, stopping in the middle of town square, a large opening with a wooden platform for speechmaking and executions, but also festivities.

Orrick smiled at the memories. Słońçem, the summer solstice, happened here. During the festival, the square had four large bonfires, and young lovers clasped hands to jump the flames. If the lovers landed on the other side still clasped, their families considered them soulmates and they were married that night. Orrick remembered the food, remembered the heat. He was just a little boy when last he saw the couples jump.

Funnily enough, he could recall a hand clasped in his—and

sudden, intense heat.

He shook his head. *Impossible. Children are not allowed to jump.*

"Here!" called Armitage.

The pub he eyed was a rectangle of wooden walls. A door of darker material swung on loose hinges. Peering through the windows, Orrick thought it looked dilapidated. Men large and hairy hunched over the bar, sullen, hands clutching tankards. Orrick could not even begin to fathom why Armitage chose this place, but the smile on his face meant he was serious.

"The Plaintive Hound!" exclaimed Armitage.

Orrick joined him in looking at the swinging sign: a silhouetted huntsman's hound begging to an unseen master. He shrugged and led the way in, finding two empty seats next to a burly man with thick black hair covering his face and arms. The barman sidled up to them, face as dour as the establishment.

"Two white whiskeys," said Orrick. The barkeep nodded and went to work.

As they waited, Orrick looked around. Other men sat at booths and tables, looking exactly as large, hairy, and dour as the one Orrick sat beside. He began to think the Plaintive Hound was an establishment for oversized dwarves. He would not have been far off.

The man beside Orrick leaned over. His nose protruded from

his dark beard, bulbous and red with broken veins. Cheap ale and uncooked onions wafted from his mouth as he spoke. "Y' don' look like you're from 'round 'ere," he hiccoughed.

The abrupt, confronting tone summoned images to Orrick's mind of overturned tables, spilled beer, blood, screaming patrons, the sour stench of fresh excrement.

Those deserters ... how many of their friends drank in this very pub? Then again, they cannot know I had a hand in their deaths.

Orrick made gruffer his voice. "We hail o' Southport."

"Nin, eh?" The drunken patron licked his chapped lips, tasting the word. "Then y' wouldn' know this place is for miners o' Starter Mountains. Even the minin' lords c'mere after the workin' day's done."

"Ain't fishermen jus' miners o' the sea?" asked Armitage.

The patron narrowed his beady eyes. Orrick looked away, fearing the man's drunken wobbling would put him in a daze. "No. They ain't. An' y' boys don' look *sunbaked* enough t' be fishermen."

"Because we ain't," grunted Orrick. He hoped the miner was drunk enough to see past his insecurity. "We be jus' two travelers o' Nin. As for this bein' a *miner's bar*, well, I 'ear on'y *bar*. Las' I checked, Southport's coinage be Newtown's coinage."

The miner sat quiet for a few moments, then roared laughter as he slapped Orrick's back with a hand as big and heavy as a shovel. He winced, thinking of the bruise that would surely appear.

"Yer awright!" barked the miner.

Unsure why he had a change of heart, Orrick felt glad for the compliment, nonetheless.

That moment, the barkeep set down two pewter tankards filled with strong-smelling swill. Disappointed, Orrick discovered that white whiskey was not white, but clear as water. He raised the tankard, sniffed, withdrew. It stung with the scent of disinfectant.

"Ne'er 'ad white whiskey afore, have y'?" the patron asked. "Some places serve it in a *dainty snifter*—" he grimaced, hocked, and spat brown saliva onto the sawdust floor "—in a miner's bar y' drink like a miner!" He took a big gulp for emphasis. "I remember me first white whiskey! Drank deep an' retched for days!" He guffawed. "Even though it's a big ole glass, slow sips'll do y'."

Orrick nodded and put the flagon to his lips.

"Hold a moment, Lorry!" exclaimed Armitage.

"Aye?" He thought—hoped—the Prince had changed his mind.

"T' our travels!" toasted Armitage, as if a black jest. Orrick soured while the Prince grinned stupidly.

"Our travels," he muttered, again put the flagon to his lips, and sipped gingerly. Armitage did the same.

Orrick pulled the flagon away, as if he licked a soured corpse. Strong, bittersweet, oily. It was a chore—a menial task—to raise the flagon and sip again.

When a quarter empty was the flagon, Orrick cared not if the contents were sweet-wine or rat piss. He swung the flagon and sang with the bard, who plucked his lute and belted a jaunty tune.

Quiet was the Plaintive Hound when they came. Now, it was filled with patrons, all of them drunk and singing. The Prince, just as drunk as the rest of them, laughed and flirted with the seldom portly, cross-eyed, and black-grinning barmaid.

The bar quieted as the night went on. They sat there for what seemed like hours, listening to the tunes and the miners' scrambled chatter. Eventually, many of them had gone back to their homes, and so too had the bard. Orrick's half-finished tankard weighed in his hands, and Armitage fared no better. Tired, dismayed, they stared into their tankards and eaves-dropped on a conversation between an armsman and a miner.

"'Ear ye th' news 'bout Kendala? King Archibald's looking t' reclaim land 'at Tourm took cent'ries ago."

"Yeah—who ain't 'eard? Tha' failed invasion o' Nin ..."

"'Tweren' no invasion but some emissary—false emissary. Tried t' poison Count Jarl ..."

"I heard 'twas a skirmish ... Kendalans came from the hinterlands, killed some Black Dogs ..."

"An' I thought Archibald was a nice ole king ..."

"Archibald wan' western Nin—"

"Archibald wan' *all* o' Nin. All o' Tourm, too. Don' think 'e'll get it, though."

"We got brave men 'ere. If'n we need, I'll bash some Kendalan brains in wit' m' shovel!"

"War's a-comin'. That almswoman said s'."

Orrick lifted his head. *Exactly as the deserter said.* Come to think of it, were those deserters not armsmen too?

"Bah!" yelled the other. "She also said jadwilki'll come into town wearing people clothes and hocking clovers for a mite!"

"Damned if she weren' right!" decreed a third patron, who fell on his face and snored loudly.

The conversation entranced Orrick so that he did not hear Armitage whisper into his ear. He turned to sip from the flagon and jumped back when saw he the Prince so close to his face.

"Relax, y' great craven," the Prince hiccoughed.

Orrick smiled stupidly. Something about that amused him, but he knew not what. Head swimming, he tilted the flagon to his lips. No longer did it burn like hot knives when it slithered down his gullet.

Armitage waved his left land whilst his right placed the flagon on the bar with a thump and a thick splash. "I's just thinking we shou' go …" he said, slow and sluggish.

"Catch we hell if we return like this," said Orrick, accent all but forgotten, replaced with a ravaged slur.

"No m' friend …" Armitage placed down a few copper mites. "Hell comes 'n the morn."

They left their flagons at the bar, still a quarter full, and stepped out into the night.

VIII: Hunting Wolves

Hell indeed came in the morning.

Whoever came to call pounded on the door. Then again, for all Orrick knew, they could've been rapping softly. Every sound seemed amplified to the point of painful reverberation. Even his bedsheets, which rustled every time he moved, set his head afire. His mouth felt as dry as the Salt Steppe, and his muscles ached as though whoever pounded the door pounded his body as well.

Suddenly, it was gone. The messenger gave up, left. Orrick thought he could use the peace to regain himself. As soon as he stood, he wished he hadn't. He wondered if he was poisoned, if this was his final moment before death.

Aching and tired, he lumbered over to the dressing table, knocking the jug of water to the floor, clanging on impact. The sounds and vibrations made him recoil as if a firebomb had exploded. Several seconds later, he recovered. Orrick found a small mirror and stared hard at his reflection. Instead of a spry, young knight, he found a ghastly old man, hair damp and stringy, skin clammy and pale, eyes bloodshot, cheeks swollen. The threat of vomit lingered in his throat like a coiled snake.

The twice-be-damned messenger returned. Each knock was a hammer-blow to his brain. He opened the door wide and fast. Callows, face fresh, smiled cheerily. He hated that face, which knew not the venom of white whiskey.

The knight's eyes grew concerned. "What—?"

"Fetch Nona," said Orrick, voice as ragged as a rake on stones. He shut the door carefully as he could, but the bolt's click brought another grimace.

I didn't even finish the damn flagon!

Even his thoughts made him recoil.

There came another knock, soft as feathers. The knob slowly turned and old Nona Strega entered his bedchambers. She gazed at him with rheumy eyes, and then thrust another flagon at him, contents sloshing. The sound made his throat lurch; his stomach pitched with the increasing promise of sickness.

"Drink an' listen," she whispered, never one for pleasantries.

Regardless of her manners, her admired her skills. Elsewise, she would not have been Limehouse's sole herbalist. Orrick did as she bade. He put his nose to the flagon and breathed in.

Grass, herbs ... weeds. When he drank, he found it bitter and

137

thick with pulp. He drained the flagon in large gulps as Nona spoke.

"I 'member m' firs' taste o' white whiskey. Strongest stuff they make 'round 'ere—strongest in all o' Tourm, tell y' true. 'Tis poison, y' know." Her white eyebrows rose to her receding hairline. "What're y' thinkin', drinkin' s' much?"

Orrick peered into the flagon. The bitter green swill was gone, but wet clumps caked the sides. Surprisingly, his headache dulled to a pulse mingling with his own heartbeat. "I hadn't but one flagon."

"*One damn flagon?*" she screeched. "Y' went t' a damn miner's bar, didn' y'? 'Ose gruff men take'r whiskey like a fishy take'r water! 'S why I made so much chasegrass potion—I known! 'At princely friend o' yours 'ad a roarin' 'eadache but didn' wanna see me! Now I *knows* why! Y' damn lucky if'r lord father don' 'ear o' this!"

Orrick's eyes widened at his father's mention. "Don't tell him, please! I promise never to do this again!"

Madam Strega huffed, but her blue eyes dulled to their usual spacy stare. "'Tain't no worry o' mine. You're the one huntin' t'day."

Orrick rubbed the back of his head, the jadwilk all but forgotten.

"Seems reality's more bitter'n any crapulence potion."

Orrick swallowed and nodded, but the old herbalist had already slipped from his room like a ghost. He rubbed his temples before dressing in his tunic and britches, donning leather boots, steel greaves, jerkin, chainmail shirt, and leather bracers. Lastly, as always, his sword-belt which held the dirk and iron longsword. The dagger was still with last night's clothes. He would need it not, he suspected.

Leaving the room in much better spirits than when he woke, Orrick gasped to find Brandt waiting outside, already wearing his quilted gambeson.

"Did you check your sword, my lord?" he asked, smiling.

"No," Orrick answered. His squire looked disheartened. To appease him, Orrick pulled the sword free right there in the corridor. "'Tis clean."

"Aye, my lord," said Brandt, beaming. "I used an oilstone."

Orrick examined the edge, nodded his approval, and withdrew it. "Well done, lad. Are you come to escort me downstairs?"

Brandt bit his bottom lip, looking nervous. "The other knights ..."

Dammit, Armitage. "What of them?"

"They're quite upset, my lord. Much to his highness's protests, they make ready to return to Albion. Wait they in the gatehouse ..."

For me.

He followed Brandt from the manse. Like most midmornings in Brzeg, the sun shone with little cloud coverage. Cool breezes blew, and Orrick shielded his eyes from the glare.

When his eyes adjusted, he saw Armitage flanked by his three sworn sentries and their squires, all of them mounted. There were also the servants that had come with the baggage train.

Orrick went to the Prince, who looked as though he had been beaten with a stick. He wanted to laugh about it, but the mere thought roused both his head and stomach.

"Well met," grumbled Armitage.

"I want never to do that again," Orrick whispered.

"My friend, 'tis not but you ..."

Orrick nodded, smirking. "Aren't you forgetting something?"

Armitage looked confused. "I don't believe so. I am dressed. I've my knights, servants, wine—"

"Mention not wine," hissed Orrick. He shook the thought from his head. "No, lack you two horses."

Armitage raised his coppery eyebrows. "Do I?"

"Yes. I count nine of you and nine horses. Did you not bring eleven?"

"Oh." Armitage sighed, waving dismissively. "Consider Cień and Nash gifts from House Pardwy. Congratulations on your knighthood."

Orrick's mouth trembled before he managed, "I cannot."

"You will and you'll like it," said Armitage. "Fine then, if you'll take them not as gifts, consider them recompense for completing the task of bringing your prince safely to Newtown."

Orrick nearly blushed. "What would King Biel say, learning he's lost two fine horses?"

"That his son is naught but a common horse thief, what else?" His eyes looked like a fish flailing on a bone-dry deck, but that wry, mischievous smile returned. Unable to argue, Orrick grinned in return.

"Send me a message," said Armitage. "I'd like to hear of your first excursion as a lordly rotter. I'd also like to talk about what we overheard."

"As you wish, my lord prince," said Orrick, with a flamboyant bow.

"Oh, shove your titles up your arse!" he said, and kicked his white gelding and took off east. The suddenness surprised the other riders in the entourage who followed, shouting.

Yellow dust sprayed out from the horses' powerful legs as they fled down the Salt Steppe's dry flatlands. Orrick watched them until they were no more than faraway comets nearing the horizon.

When Orrick returned to the great hall, found he a marvelous spread set upon the lords' table. Eggs, bacon, mashed turnips dripping with honey and butter, and fresh juice squeezed from fat, golden sunberries. There was also roasted bread slathered with sunberry compote.

"This looks wonderful," he said. He turned to his parents, saw disappointment. "What—?"

"You know damn well," growled Nigel. "The knights came to breakfast—their squires, too, and yours. Even Prince Armitage was kind enough to nibble some bacon."

Orrick looked back to the table. The smells were wonderful, but he recognized a greasy undertone. There were many empty places, the settings already cleared away.

Suddenly Orrick felt afraid.

"White whiskey?" Fiona's nostrils flared as her pupils shrank to pinpricks. This time it was not pain that made him recoil.

"And from a miners' tavern, no less," said Nigel.

Fiona scoffed. "Between the drink and the cur, I'm not sure which would kill you faster!"

"If it makes you feel better, I hadn't even one—"

"Silence, *boy!*"

Orrick averted his eyes. There was no dancing away from this.

"We're not angered that you drank white whiskey. Had we any aversion to that, we would not have allowed a stay at Pałac xe Triumf."

"No," said Nigel, glowering. "'Tis that you brought His Highness to a miners' bar and drank the miners' drink. Endangered you yourself and the Crown Prince!"

"Endangered—?"

"Do you know what they call white whiskey? The pint of white death!"

"I knew it not," admitted Orrick, ashamed.

"And you did so, knowing you'd a task the next morn."

"I—I—" Reasons and excuses rushed to Orrick's mind. He hoped Armitage had forgotten, tried to talk him out of it, was commanded by his prince—

He knew his parents would hear none of it.

"What was the name of this damned place, the Snuffed Canary?"

143

"The Plaintive Hound," answered Orrick. *Remember I that much. Everything after, though ...*

"It matters not," Fiona decided. "You've all day and perhaps all night to recover. You'll spend that time wandering Brzeg. Madam Strega was kind enough to give you chasegrass potion, but there's more to white whiskey than aching heads and roiling stomachs."

"Your mother speaks true, Orrick. Now go—and return *not* without that pelt."

Orrick looked at the table. "And what of—?"

"You'll eat what you find out there: apples, berries, nuts, seeds—or naught," said Nigel. "And you'll have not another meal within this manse until you've returned."

Orrick wanted to argue but thought better of it. He was an adult, true, but his parents still held sway over his tasks and payment. After a moment of silence, he bent his waist in a pleasant but informal bow and left for the stables.

Brandt stood silently as Orrick saddled the rouncey. To his own black-eyed sumpter, the squire packed bags of provisions and blankets should they spend the night in the wilderness, something entirely likely.

Upon leaving the stables, Orrick saw the sun already shone at high noon. Ashamed, he looked at his squire, who wore a grim face since the altercation in the dining hall.

"I apologize for mine actions this morn ... and last night. 'Twas unmeet to drink so late and forfeit breakfast. Normally, I act like that not. The Prince and I—" He paused, not wanting to incriminate Armitage further.

"What?" asked Brandt. "What about the Prince?"

Orrick sighed. True, he ought not speak ill of Armitage. But it was clear they went together, and he hoped it was clear it was not his idea. "You must promise never to tell another soul."

"I promise," said Brandt.

"The Prince and I have made mischief together on more than this occasion."

Brandt pondered that for a moment. "How did you come to know Prince Armitage so well, my lord?"

Orrick winced. Improper though it might be for his squire to address him otherwise, he disliked honorifics as much as Armitage. Besides, he felt more like a knight than a lord, anyway. "Pan will do—Orrick or Pallaton, the choice is yours."

"Mine apologies, pan."

Orrick smiled. "All's well. 'Twas six moons past when the cadets returned to the academy for graduation. King Biel held a feast, and 'tis customary for the royal family to attend. We all wore all the finery squires are made to wear. I'm sure you know that velvet doublet is stifling!"

Brandt snorted, failing to hide his laughter.

Pleased, Orrick continued. "Armitage had accompanied King Biel and looked positively bored. During the dance, I saw him sneak away, but no one else seemed to mind. Since I was wearing such uncomfortable trappings, I feigned a need to collect myself and found Armitage drinking a Flavès white in the Hall of Heroes, perusing portraits of notable knights long dead.

"'We ought return,' told I him, but said he, 'Prefer I to drink alone.' As I said, Brandt, the entire event was dull. So, remained I with him for a time, both of us silent until he offered me the goblet and said, 'Prefer I a friend when drink I alone.' I accepted. What else could I do? 'Twas a request from the Crown Prince." Orrick sighed. "We were fast friends hence."

"Those meetings *are* boring." He offered Orrick a small but genuine smile. "I'll admit I was relieved to be chosen. But never did I imagine 'twould be by a Pallaton, let alone a man of Brzeg."

"Brzeg takes hints from the Language Holy," said Orrick. "Men are Brzegk, women Brzegka, and people of Brzeg are Brzegu."

"Oh," said Brandt.

"Would that we'd better places to go than the Salt Steppe," said Orrick, waving his hand to the sunbaked yellow earth ahead of them. Weeds, tangled like veins, grew from cracks in the sand. Small oases blossomed from the ground. Far in the distance,

Turnip Marsh stretched a line of green across the horizon.

"What's so bad about this?" asked Brandt. "I've never been west of Domoż. 'Tis so hugely different from Rhabdolia—and not in a bad way! I admit I miss the smell of Maycoast and the Lilac Headland. During Driada's Moon, the lilac bushes bloom in full along the coast, making a sea of violet!"

"I'd like to see it someday."

Brandt beamed at him. "Mayhap you shall, pan. They only bloom during Driada's Moon. Everyone agrees there exists no sweeter smell when blooms the headland. But how exciting are *flowers* when Brzeg has goblin-wolves? We only get vampire cats when leave they the Whitewoods. But so *rarely* they do, and *never* to the headland. The closest forest we have is the Forest Maze, but vampire cats live there not. Did you know that, pan? Not that anyone *would* know, I suppose. Anyone that enters the Forest Maze never returns—and no one knows *why*—"

Brandt prattled on like that for a while, Orrick only half-listening. As dull as he thought riding through the Salt Steppe was, he was glad Brandt found joy in it.

An hour passed, and the sun was at its highest—and hottest—place in the sky. In the time that passed, Orrick decided to head east, toward rock quarries near the River Milkmoon separating Brzeg from Domoż.

In a small grove they found wild sunberries, fat, round, segmented, and golden.

"Dinner is served," said Orrick.

Ripe sunberries contained so much juice that people unaccustomed to eating them became surprised. Though these were not quite ripened to bursting, the berries nonetheless stained their chins orange.

"Pan Orrick?" asked Brandt, fidgeting. "Have you—? Are you—?"

"What are you trying to ask?"

"Women. Are you betrothed?"

Orrick deflated. *Women. Betrothal.* Already Chelsea's flirtations confused him—came they unbidden and despite *her* betrothal. Armitage and Ozella both chided him for his lack of romance. Now Brandt asked it of him.

"Betrothed, I am not. Traditionally, Brzegy—including members of House Pallaton—choose their own spouses. Dowries and properties come second to love."

"How odd," said Brandt, confused but intrigued. Doubtlessly, the lad had been taught—as had the rest of Tourm—that marriage is a transaction between two families. Both families, not necessarily the individuals, must acquire something. Brandt asked, "How are lands or possessions passed on?"

"These things are taken into consideration *before* the ceremony, but this is not a pact made by spouses prospective and parents shrewd. Both families must agree. Finances and living arrangements must be approved upon. Ultimately, 'tis the lovers' choice, and eloping happens."

"Eloping," mouthed Brandt.

"Why ask you? Are you betrothed?"

Brandt shook his head. "No, but I imagine one day I will be ..."

"But?"

"But there *is* one girl. Wąda Tuttle, Pani Wingate's squire."

Orrick winced at Chelsea's mention. Still, Orrick surmised, "Friendly, were you, as pages, and now you're separated. You miss her?"

"I do. She has the prettiest hazel eyes. And she is a knitting master."

"Knitting?" 'Twas a skill Orrick never grasped.

Brandt excitedly pulled off his boot and wiggled his toes, swathed in grey socks. "She knit me these before we departed."

Orrick laughed. "Put your boots back on. Ride we north."

149

Brandt did, and asked, "But you have no one like that?"

Shaking his head, Orrick thought a moment. "I've known many girls, but no romance. Pani Wingate and I shared a kiss as pages. But she's betrothed and I respect that."

Brandt eyed him curiously. "You're supposed to be my mentor. Never have you had these woes before?"

Shrugging, Orrick said, "Spent I my time practicing and studying. Really, had I no time for romantic entanglements."

"What about before?"

"Before?"

"Before academy."

Orrick pursed his lips. "When I was child?"

"Remember I, before academy, a stableboy pursued my sister Beatrice. He chased her 'round, pulled her hair, brought her crickets, all in affection's name. Of course, he was lowborn and thoroughly beaten ..."

"Come to your point, Brandt."

"My point, pan—my question—is, have you no first love? No childhood sweetheart? Spent you your first seven years in a monastery, never to lay eyes on a girl?"

"Of course not! I had childhood playmates such as my close friend, Sylvia."

"Sylvia?"

"A childhood friend, a freewoman of the forest. Know I not why, but oft came she to Limehouse. Scampered we about the manse, making mischief, demanding sweets from the kitchen."

"And you're in love with her?"

Orrick scoffed. "Brandt, I've not seen her since we were six springs old. Know I not why came she to Limehouse, but if I barely remember her, I'm doubtful she remembers me. Why ask you?"

"When Wąda gave me the socks, I ... grabbed her hand and she ... stopped talking to me. I've not seen her since Pani Wingate selected her."

"Well worry not," said Orrick, climbing atop Cień. "For once we become heroes of Brzeg both, doubtless Wąda Tuttle will take you."

Brandt smiled at the thought. "How do we become heroes?"

"'Twill a slow process be. First, we must needs kill a wolf."

Meal finished, rode they north. The flat, cracked loam of the Salt Steppe soon changed to land more fertile. Pines stared down at them like sentinels. Grassy knolls and hills topped with shrubs popped into view. Further in the distance, a mountain range sprawled. Snow-topped, orange-brown peaks ended just before the cloudland. While only a blur in the distance, those mountains traveled miles high and miles back, separating Brzeg from Pinberry.

"Starter Mountains," Brandt awed.

"Aye, our destination."

"Go we there? Why?"

"Jadwilki come down from Starter Mountains, looking for food in the Homey Hills. Newtown lies where the Homey Hills meet the Salt Steppe. Still, they come, even though they know it's dangerous ..."

"I don't think I understand, my lo—*pan*."

Orrick smiled but kept his eyes on the horizon. "Jadwilki prefer blackbuck, sand-rats, and the occasional journeyman. Come they into the Salt Steppe but prefer the Homey Hills—there are more places to hide and more water. If this is the same creature that attacked us, she's no doubt returned to ground familiar until she feels brave enough to again come down."

Brandt argued not. He rode in silence until Orrick said, "I want to show you something before we reach the mountain's base."

He found a patch of crumbling earth five miles from the

mountainside. Cień and Nash drank from a small nearby lake as Orrick moved about the place. Several patches of short grass and a couple small saplings grew between the tumbledown chunks of stone that once might have been a manse or fort.

"A beautiful hideaway in the hills," said Brandt.

"This is where stood Oldtown five-hundred years past."

The squire's eyes widened with reverence. "What happened to it? I mean, the legends ... are they ... *true*?"

"I've oft wondered, myself. Mayhap the town was destroyed by a goblin horde, or fire, or the people found better land further south. But Father showed me proof last night. Aileron fought an undergod ... and that undergod destroyed Oldtown."

"Is that an undergod's power?" asked Brandt, inspecting a sapling. "Five-hundred years and only now do plants grow? Is that why you came here? You wanted to stand where that happened, to appease your mind for its doubts?"

"I suppose so," sighed Orrick. "Thank you for accompanying me."

"I go where you go, Pan Orrick." Brandt hesitated a moment, then said, "Tell me of the goblin wars?"

Orrick nodded his head and smiled. "The northern mountains and western hinterlands hold many dangers. When Fangaard was young, both Tourm and the goblin tribes sought to claim this region for themselves. The mountains and hills were full of ore—iron, silver, gold."

Brandt looked to the mountains. "Is it true even men sided with the goblins?"

"Aye," said Orrick, "and Aileron among them."

"He was?"

"A rotter was he, but once his contract ended, Aileron killed their king and routed them. The goblins remained in caves somewhere in the hinterlands, attacking in the name of the goblin king's son. Even then, Aileron defended Brzeg, which defended Albion."

"Now the dangers aren't goblins, but *savages*."

The word erupted like a geyser. Orrick tried not to frown. Despite mentioning his childhood friend was a freewoman, Brandt still used the word.

"That must need change," said Orrick.

"What, pan?"

"I mislike the word 'savage'. Call them free folk. Live they in the forests and hinterlands of Whitewoods, Turnip Marsh, and the Sea of Trees. House Pallaton has had ties to them for a long time."

"But you know not what?"

Orrick shook his head. "Are they friends, allies? Mayhap only to House Pallaton. I know what others think—that they're enemies; that House Pallaton keeps them at bay, or perhaps conspires with them."

"Will you ever know?"

"One day, perhaps, should Lord Father confide it in me. House Pallaton runs deep with traditions. All born into it become knights and upon knighthood, our fathers show us Bóg-plaga—"

Brandt jumped back. "Aileron's *sword*? The one stained with devil blood? That's the proof your lord father showed?"

"Aye," Orrick said. But this time, Brandt's excitement amused him not.

"You're certain that one day Lord Pallaton will entrust you with your House's dealings with the savages?"

Orrick's fists squeezed. "Aye," Orrick answered again, then sighed.

"Sorry, my lo—*pan*. Meant I, free folk."

"Remaining here does no good. Make we for the mountains."

Orrick felt glad for their break from the trail. True, he came to

Oldtown's grounds to reflect on what he learned. Everyone in Tourm knew the tale. But they, like he, doubted it. Rhabdolians had their own hero of the Days of Devils: The Prophetess Sibilia. But just as people no longer believe the Tide-turners' controlled nature, some people believed that Aileron never fought undergods, that Sibilia was not a messiah the Church claimed, perhaps that undergods never existed.

But there was another reason Orrick went, one that had to do with that damnable word: savage.

"House Pallaton upholds a lot of responsibilities. I wonder—"

"Does House Hargrove hold a grudge?"

Brandt paused. Even Nash looked like he might halt his trot. "A grudge, my lo—*pan*?"

"House Altgeld does. That I know. Fifty years are gone since Tourm halted Rhabdolia. Though it remains unsaid by Erasmus and Ozella, I fear their behavior towards me has everything to do with it."

"Because a Pallaton broke their lines?" asked Brandt.

"Unspoken, thus unconfirmed, I fear there may be a secret feud between our Houses. Ask I not as a knight to his squire but as a Brzegu to a Rhabdolian: Is House Pallaton so frowned upon?"

"We all have our loyalties, pan. The war was before King Biel the Fifteenth and Duke Ezarl's reign. We are all of Tourm now, pan."

"Loyalties and opinions personal are two different things."

Brandt hesitated. "I admit your House's name has been slandered by nobles and commoners alike. Most are indifferent. Remember, pan, most that fought then are old or dead."

"Dead though they may be, enmity oft stands for generations."

Silent for a moment or two, Brandt asked, "Is that why you chose me as your squire? Because I'm Rhabdolian?"

"I chose you because you're a good fighter and received good marks in academy ... but I suppose I wanted to prove that Brzegu aren't savages."

"Well, *I* don't believe so," said Brandt, "and I don't think others do, either."

"I hope you speak true, Brandt. There *was* controversy."

"There was? From whom?"

"House Altgeld, as I said. Before we left, Pan Altgeld came to me and demanded I rescind my offer."

"Oh ..."

"Said I, no, of course. But suspect I detractions from House

Hargrove. Unless think you, your parents care not?"

"They know 'twas our decision, both," said Brandt, smiling. "As for the rest of Rhabdolia, when become we heroes of Brzeg, you must needs also become a hero of Rhabdolia."

Night fell as they reached the base of Starter Mountains. Chasms opened here and there, mineshafts deep and shallow, some fitted with windlasses, treadmills, drainage pumps. Nearer the Milkmoon and its branches stood waterwheels. Each mine was owned by a lord, taxed by the voivod, and operated by the hairy strongmen that guzzled white whiskey.

Orrick scanned the area, looking for any signs of the hunted wolf. Futile, he decided. The jadwilk could be anywhere: a cave, a mine, upon a cliff, even miles behind, roaming the Salt Steppe.

Or it stalks the hills. The thought made Orrick look in the direction they had come. Truly, they could not know where roamed the wolf due to Brzeg's expansivity.

Orrick looked to the mountaintops, squinting when the sun dripped gold into his eyes. *Would that I had a hound. But what could a hound do without a scent?*

They waited like that for several minutes, motionless, eyeing crags and hills. In the hours they spent roaming the hillside, the wolf had not shown her pointed, foaming muzzle. No reason to believe she would, Orrick dismounted and said, "Make we camp here."

The squire looked puzzled. "How will we find the jadwilk?"

"We must lure her. Let us find bramble for fire and roast good-smelling meats."

"Meats? But came we without food."

"Then we'll find some. Help me make camp."

Nash carried the tent and burlap sleeping sacks. Brandt took the supplies from the sumpter horse and Orrick helped. As Brandt gathered kindling, Orrick unsheathed his dirk and headed for the hills. He returned just as the sun touched the land's end, a fat groundhog slung over his shoulder.

Brandt relaxed near the campfire. Orrick sat beside him, skinned the groundhog, fashioned a spit from sticks, and roasted it over open flames. They ate, and dusk crept across the sky like wine-stained linen.

Within moments, they devoured most of the rodent, leaving the head and arms. Orrick took first watch. He loosened the dirk and longsword in their scabbards, threw on a cloak to hide in the darkness, and crouched low three yards from the laid-out carcass.

Jadwilki had an uncanny sense of smell. They could catch the scent of carrion from a mile away. Orrick hoped the rendered fat, juices, and marrow would do as well.

Brandt tucked himself into his sleeping sack but did not close his eyes. On the contrary, they shone in the moonlight like two distant stars.

Orrick smiled. "Know how the poisonous wolves came to be?"

Brandt remained motionless. For a moment, Orrick thought he fell asleep with his eyes open. Then he said, "Goblins bred them."

"Centuries ago, Starter Mountains were home to rock wolves. 'Tis rumored goblins laid with them and jadwilki were born. Lived they within the goblins' hovels, kept as hounds. Sometimes goblins rode them into battle, like horses."

"But that's just a legend, right?"

"Perhaps ..." Orrick's mind turned to Bógplaga and the ruins of Oldtown. "I'm unsure what legend is anymore."

"Why are they called *poisonous* wolves?"

"They're not like needle snakes, with their deadly bites. The jadwilki are called poisonous, but their mouths bear disease, not venom."

"If the goblins have gone, why do their wolves remain?"

"Goblins are *not* wild animals. Wolves, no matter how tame they seem, remain forever wild. With the goblins' retreat imminent, they released their wolves to the mountainside. That way, no matter what son-of-man ruled Tourm, the goblins' mark remained."

"I'll hear no more!" Brandt gulped. He rolled over, facing away from Orrick.

Content that Brandt would soon sleep, Orrick resumed his watch over the hills. Happily, the cloak provided more than just cover in the dark, but warmth. Nights near the mountain were the coldest. Chilly air wafted from them, like steam rolling off a roast.

Roast. His eyes went to the groundhog carcass. There was naught to do but wait and think.

He remembered eyes as green as the forest—Sylvia's eyes. Plants. She liked plants, he remembered, and he had once sat with her beneath a sycamore, helping her count its leaves. That was long ago, when he lived life simpler. Now he had responsibilities, a realm to patrol, reputations to uphold, traditions to abide by—all without worrying over prejudiced Rhadbolians.

Hours later, long after he should have woken Brandt, a massive shape formed from the blackness. There she was, shoulders hunched, purple fur matted, feet more like talons than paws. Orrick tensed when he saw her approach. The jadwilk lowered her nose to the bone. Embers glowed in the campfire, but Orrick could see her muzzle wrinkle with every sniff.

Orrick remained motionless, unbreathing. Still, the cold, mad eyes turned upward, stared at him. The last of the pack, reduced to a lowly scavenger.

She gripped the carcass in her mouth, turned, ran back into the darkness. Orrick threw the cloak from his shoulders and tossed the dirk, spinning point over pommel until it too disappeared. He heard a *thuck* followed by a whimper and a weighty drop to the ground.

Orrick smirked and unsheathed the longsword. The wolf lay near; the dirk buried in her ribcage. Eyes ice-blue and rabid stared wide open. when yanked he free the blade, gave she no sound or jerk.

Dead, he thought, relieved. He should rouse Brandt. Tired though they were, the stewards surely would welcome them back—

Onrushing weight slammed him. The dirk slipped from his fingers as whatever pounced threatened to crush him. Then the weight was gone, just as it came.

A yard away, the shape landed. Orrick scrambled to his feet, readying his sword—but nothing could prepare him for what he saw.

Larger than any wolf, blue fur covered in jagged white stripes. Needle-like teeth matched the sharpened daggers on either side, dripping saliva down black lips. Eyes red as blood stared at him, pupils mere slits.

"*Scimitiger!*"

Its long tail flicked impatiently. For seconds, it was the only thing that moved. The beast leapt again. Orrick hefted the sword, but the scimitiger was too fast. Breath left his body as his sword left his hand. The giant cat tackled, pinning him.

It reared its neck, yellow teeth glistening triangles save for the two incisors that looked so much like Xąb.

Orrick's right arm came free. He sought his sword-belt, the remaining dagger—but his fingers felt only leather.

"*Shite!*"

The 'tiger made to bite, stopped, yowled. Something pushed the weight from him. *What now beleaguers me, a skinmiller bear?*

He opened his eyes and breathed relief. Brandt stood over him, offering a hand. Orrick accepted, watching the scimitiger. His dirk, forced from his hand when it first pounced, stuck to the hilt in beast's neck.

"I owe you my life," panted Orrick.

The lad smiled. "I'm your squire, remember? 'Tis my duty to aid you."

Orrick smiled back. "I'm in your debt, whether you're well with it or not. You'll have your recompense."

Brandt nodded and averted his eyes, blushing. He said, "We've no need to remain out here."

Together they packed up camp and tied the carcasses to their horse's flanks—the scimitiger to Nash and the she-wolf to Cień. Neither horse was comfortable having these predators on them, even though the beasts were felled. But Orrick knew leaving the carcasses would only attract more scavengers, so they packed and mounted their horses, and returned to Newtown.

IX: Knight-Errant

They arrived at the manse at dawn. Servants and sentries both came to take the beasts from the horses, commenting, "These would make fine pelts!"

Orrick thought otherwise; he'd felled the wolf between the ribs, and Brandt had stabbed straight through the 'tiger's neck. After returning the horses to the stables, Orrick and Brandt expected to sleep.

Orrick was not that lucky.

"Y' wasn' bitten, was y'?"

Orrick jumped away from the old woman, worried that his heart might break through his chest. "Please, no more scares! I've had enough this night."

165

"Went ye lookin' for jadwilki ... an' met a scimitiger. Figured I come see y' meself."

Madam Strega never ceased to unnerve him, despite being half his height and looking about as healthy as a rotting log. "Off with'r tunic. I ask ag'in, was y' bitten?"

Orrick took off his sword-belt and leaned it against the wall. "No."

"Scratches can give y' jad poison, too. Off with'r tunic."

He sighed and acquiesced. A large bruise flared on his right side. She pressed an iron-tipped finger into its center, making him wince. She found another bruise on his back from where the miner had slapped him, but he was content with lumping that in with the scimitiger wounds.

"Show me yer left arm."

He did. She gripped it, and he gritted his teeth. "Y' favored this'n," she hissed through blackened gums. "Merely a sprain. Lots o' bruising. Naught's broken." She fixed her eyes to his. "Y' *sure* y' wasn' bit?"

"I promise I was not."

Madam Strega eyed him accusingly. She stepped toward his dressing table, and he saw there were two things upon it. The first was a baked clay pot, and the second was a steaming mug. Orrick's throat clenched at the sight.

"You'll've jadryba jelly for your wrist an' bruises, an' slime-root potion jus' in case."

Orrick lay on his bed as the old woman collected the pot. The closer it came, the more he could smell the pungent odor, like a thousand fish rotting in the sun.

"Stinks terrible, don' it?"

"It's made from jadryba, is it not?" asked Orrick.

"Aye, an' y' know jadryba means 'poison fish.' Takes a while for me t' get'm. Gotta catch'm in Xexioro Swale, then ferment'r flesh an' venom in vinegar—liquefy 'm for a moon."

"Is it not dangerous?"

"Only if'r eat it. An' y' ain't gon' eat it. Now lie still."

Orrick tried to remain as still as he could, but the unguent was frigid and greasy, uncomfortable overall. Still, it was far more pleasant than the bitter slime-root potion which he drank when she was done applying the jelly—dregs and all.

"'Coz I can't find a wound, I can't apply the salve," she explained. Then she left, closing the door behind her.

Sleep found him easily, and he did not know how long it had him. When he woke, he was surprised to find that the jadryba unguent had numbed his wrist and torso. A strange sensation, to say the least. He ran his good hand over his ribcage and wrist, making sure they were still attached to the rest of him. He breathed relief when he learned they were.

But now came the part he feared the most. The side-effect of the slime-root was a terrible headache. He braced himself, opened his eyes ... and saw the rheumy old herbalist waiting at his bedside with spiced tea. He winced as the ache exploded behind his eyes, and drank down the tea with ravenous gulps, not caring that it burned his mouth.

Madam Strega checked his wrist and nodded. "All's well there. Y' should be able t' move it. You'll be back t' nearly killin' 'rself soon enough." She took the empty mug and left, chuckling.

As soon as the door closed behind her, he slipped from the covers and held his head. The medicine worked, but he still felt fatigued. In search of clothes, he crossed over to his dressing table and found something more interesting. Thirty silver pecks and three gold dashes, one for the jadwilk pelt and two, presumably, for the scimitiger.

He weighed the gold coins in his hands, looking at the gyrfal-con stamped on one side. He turned them over and saw the crossed swords on the other.

"True gold," he said to himself. He closed his eyes and imagined what he might buy with it, full plate armor, or perhaps a sword of family-forged steel instead of brittle iron.

Before that, he thought, jingling the coins in his hand, *there's something else I ought do.*

Orrick found Brandt training in the yard, practicing with a dummy of cloth, straw, and wood; something only human-shaped at a passing glance. The squire spotted him, beamed, and wiped the sweat from his brow.

"Pan Pallaton!"

Orrick returned the smile. "Orrick is fine when we're not with company." He held out his hand, palm up.

Brandt awed at the coins—one gold dash and five silver pecks. "For me?"

"You felled the scimitiger and saved my life. I promised recompense, did I not?"

"Gold, though?"

"And to call me by my proper name," said Orrick.

Brandt swallowed hard. "An equal ... nearly, at the least."

"I say you're well on your way to become a hero of Brzeg. Care if I watch you practice?"

"You'll not join me?"

"The soreness in my middle yet hurts. I'll coach. Take your stance."

Brandt did so, parting his feet at hip-width and centering his weight. Orrick shoved him, but the lad did not budge. "Good. A swordsman's weakest point is when he steps."

"Keep your balance, keep your life," recited Brandt.

"Precisely so, but no battle was ever won remaining static."

"Unless you were a Blood Knight or Karnath assassin!"

"Are you either?"

Brandt looked abashed. "No ..."

"No. And doubt I tales of prowess 'less I see them myself. Now, keep moving as you strike the dummy; left and right, again and again."

Brandt did as Orrick commanded and listened when he asked him to change his striking pattern and maneuvers. Brandt continued until he dripped sweat, promising he could neither lift his arm nor dance another step.

Brandt returned the wooden sword to its stand. When he met Orrick again, he bit his lip.

"You've a question?" asked Orrick.

"Aye. Whither the chapel? I've not seen one. Mayhap I misjudge Limehouse's size."

Orrick looked at the lad, confused. "Brandt ... we have no

chapel."

Brandt looked shocked, but quickly rebounded. "No chapel in the manse, mean you." He smiled. "Whither in Newtown, then?"

Orrick shook his head, concerned. "You misunderstand. We've not a single House of the Branch in all of Brzeg."

Now Brandt's look of panic subsided not. "No-church-but-*how*?"

"Be calm," said Orrick. "Follow me."

True, Limehouse had no chapel, no room dedicated to the Church of the Branch or its teachings. But it held one place he might take Brandt. To the right of the throne room, where the voivod holds court, lay the small dining room. To the left and down a corridor, a small shrine.

Orrick took Brandt there, still so like the rest of manse and yet so different. Walls still crimson, an alter of ebony held candlesticks twelve, each a different size and colored for one of the overgods. But the true marvel lay within the walls, for twelve windows bore down on all sides, mullioned high with stained glass, each one depicting an overgod:

Smok the dragon, fiery red; Wodniça, the mermaid, blue and green; Robak the lindworm, brown and serpentine; Wróżka, the gossamer-winged faerie skating on a breeze; Driada, the tree-shaped maiden; Naga-Bissa, the woman-faced snake;

171

icy Tur, tusked and antlered; Duhk-Sylf, a warrior of shining lightning; Ged-Srebro, the silvery armored fish; Pix-Złota, a pixie flittering in moonlight; Ańioła, the goddess radiant; Majak, the midnight dragon whose roiling coils make the void.

"What *is* this place?" marveled Brandt.

"Limehouse's shine to the overgods. Light a candle to whomever you wish—or multiple—and pray."

"This is what has Brzeg, instead of Houses of the Branch?"

"Public shrines are found in towns. 'Tis less formal. No candle is necessary, even here. But if you do light one, 'twill melt, so replace it."

"I don't understand," said Brandt. "You pray—"

"To the overgods themselves. Gone are they, and deaf to people's desires. Mostly this is to appease and placate our own nerves."

"Pray you in the Language Holy?"

"Nay," he laughed, "naught so complicated. We are neither magicians nor priests, who attempt mediation between man and god. Rather, sometimes it goodly feels to speak and hope something higher than any person might listen." He put his hand on Brandt's shoulder. "And if naught does—which is most likely—at least our fears or desires are no longer in our hearts sequestered."

"This is not at all like Rhabdolia. We believe in Sibilia, gifted by the overgods to lead the people through the Days of Devils. Without her prophesies, never would Fangaard have known to fight the undergods."

Orrick crossed his arms. "Tell me of Sibilia."

"You know her not?"

Orrick shook his head. "I only know *of* her; that she is significant to Rhabdolia and little else. Never was it required of me to learn more."

"Ah, well, she prophesized and performed miracles. Her first miracle, born was she immaculately; the overgods gave her life. But that pales in comparison with her second miracle. At the moment of her birth, said she to her mother, 'Take me to Rwązy Strait'—a river in Mielle. When came they to the river, said she, 'Redden shall these waters with blood, and corpses piled shall dam its flow.'

"An undergod indeed came and attacked the village, and those who heeded her lived on. That was the first undergod prediction, but not the last. Taught she the Knights Arborescent—knights of the church—to fight undergods. Her last miracle saw her wounded in the Holy Lands. Spoke she to her disciples, 'Take me to Argineld, that I may lay where disappeared my makers.' And walked she into Argineld—which none have entered or left—and disappeared into the After Realms to be with the overgods."

173

"And Rhabdolians believe this?"

"This was after the Sundering of the Stones, and before Aileron was born. Without Sibilia's gospels, Fangaardians wouldn't have won the war against the undergods."

Orrick pondered a moment, eyes down. "Brzegu believe Sibilia was a normal person, goodly at what she did—warrior or seer or both. Like Aileron, she is not worshiped. Know you why Brzeg has no Houses of the Branch?"

Brandt shook his head.

"In those crusades, centuries ago, the Church of the Branch, backed by Rhabdolian coin and crown, attempted to try the rest of Tourm as heathens and heretics. Brzegu believe in the overgods, but our traditions would have seen us put to the sword. So, pushed we them back."

"Well, suppose I there's naught wrong with praying to the overgods themselves. That's what Sibilia was—the bridge between the overgods and the world." Though he said it, he sounded unsure.

Still, Orrick did not want to argue further. "Well enough," said he. "Now come; 'tis suppertime."

Orrick and Brandt entered the small stone dining room, not the great hall reserved for feasts. Twelve seats rounded the slab of a table, upon which a single candelabrum stood, dripping red wax.

Orrick liked it better here. It was less formal. A steward stood in a corner near the doorway. Only Nigel and Fiona sat, picking at the meal already on the table; goat cheese, crusty bread, and three bowls containing almonds, berries, and apple slices.

"Recovering well?" asked Nigel as Orrick and Brandt took their seats.

"As well as I can," answered Orrick. He reached for a slice of bread and smeared some goat cheese on it. "I fear I'm unable to hold a sword until tomorrow."

"Tomorrow is what we can hope for. You'll begin your patrol then."

The bread stopped on its way to Orrick's mouth. "My patrol?"

"A knight-errant must acquaint himself with his city and those within," said Fiona. "Seeks he not to police—your father and I have watchmen for that. Instead, the knight-errant aids his countrymen."

"Ah," said Orrick.

"By the way, have some fruit." Fiona pushed the berries bowl toward him. "Cheese and bread alone will seize your insides."

Orrick nodded, adding some berries and apple to his plate. Then he bit. The goat cheese was herbal and creamy, dripping with dragonbell jelly. It was a wonderful thing to have on bread as crusty as the bakers made. He followed the piece up with an

175

apple slice.

Fiona smiled and looked at Brandt. "How fare you? I imagine there's quite a difference between Newtown and Maycoast."

"Rhabdolia is called the land of lakes. There are so many rivers from the sea and straits from the Tetra Lake. But Brzeg ... Your Grace, never have I seen aught so dry! And yet there are trees and folwarks. How?"

"Wąłas," answered Nigel, "a great underground lake."

"Ah ..." said Brandt. "I suppose all this will take some getting used to, but I like it so far. Pan Pallaton showed me Oldtown's ruins."

"Did he now?" asked Fiona, but both his parents eyed him. "He's teaching you our history, is he?"

"He is," said Brandt, buttering a new piece of bread. "I know Tourm's history comes from Brzeg—the goblin wars, the undergods. And I thought they were all legends, tales told to make Brzeg seem stronger than it is."

Orrick held his breath, unsure of how his parents might answer. Calmer than he imagined, it seemed.

"A common belief of most, especially amongst Rhabdolians," said Nigel, slathering cheese on another slice of bread. "House Altgeld's grudge has not subsided since my father quelled their revolt—may the void keep him. Still, their slander, or at least their faithlessness, neither surprises nor bothers me."

Orrick's eyes opened wide. "It doesn't?"

"Should it? We're one and all of Tourm. Ever shall there be naysayers, but there needn't be malice. Should our nation be called to arms, the Houses Pallaton and Altgeld shall fight side-by-side. That is what we must remember, above all else."

"That allies are not friends?" asked Orrick.

"No," said Nigel. "'Tis allies and friends are two different things."

"I begin to understand," said Orrick.

"Good. Besides, Nin has forgiven Tourm for claiming them. Soon, so shall Rhabdolia. Forgive me, though, I must take my leave." Nigel stood and left the small dining hall. Fiona wiped her lips and followed, leaving Orrick and Brandt with the lone servant.

Exasperated, Orrick threw down his half-eaten apple.

"What's wrong?" asked Brandt.

"Lord Father is wrong! Kendala wished to claim Tourm's portion of Nin, and we liberated each side, creating the duchy and routing Kendala from this side of Fangaard."

"The War of the Wharves," said Brandt. "You don't think—Pan

177

Pallaton, think you ill of Rhabdolia?"

"No," said Orrick. He picked up his fruit and took another bite. "Merely of House Altgeld. I've no qualm with the other Houses."

"But you only know mine."

"And Sedgwick," he said, thinking of pompous Rupert. "Is that not all I need? Tell me, how many Houses does Rhabdolia have?"

Brandt looked to the ceiling, thinking. "A great many ..."

"A great many," Orrick repeated. "Whether I'll know them all personally is yet to be known. I'll make judgments only for those I am acquainted with."

He stood, much to Brandt's surprise.

"Where are you going?"

"I feel unwell. Early though it is, I must need sleep."

Brandt nodded. "Rest well, my—*pan*."

He did indeed. He belonged to sleep as soon as his head touched the pillow.

When he woke, it was at the cockerel's cry, and he remembered no dreams. Never had he felt such a complete rest.

He slipped from his room with fresh clothes under his arm. The only ones yet awake were patrolling sentries and Madam Strega, who strolled the corridor like a ghost. She paused for a moment to glance at Orrick. "Feeling better are y'?"

"Yes." He flexed his arm and stretched his back to demonstrate. "I mean to bathe."

The herbalist pressed her mouth into a white scar. "An' y' need it—y' smell like a dead whale."

"Routinely do you cover me in fermented fish vinegar, so ..."

Madam Strega stared at him a while longer, her mouth still a line. Finally, she turned. "I'll draw your bath, let y' know when it's done."

"I'll come with you. Naught else I might do. And there's no need to heat it up."

He followed her to the bathhouse chambers, a small square room of stones with a basin in the middle. Pipes led to the outside wells, supplied by the great underground lake.

"'Twill be colder'n Tur's tusk," said the herbalist. "Y' gonna wan' it hot t' get'r unguent off."

Orrick relented. Curt though she was, Madam Strega knew her medicine. Orrick followed her to a second set of pipes connected to stoves. After stoking a fire, she pumped water into the basin. Within minutes, steam fogged the bathhouse.

Orrick stripped down and slid into the basin, relaxing as he did.

She's right, warmer is better.

The unguent, which clung to his skin in sickly brown patches, melted away in the heat.

When he was out, he dried and dressed and returned to his room and dressed for his patrol. After breaking fast with Brandt and his parents, he left.

Despite gray skies, Orrick and Brandt left the manse in high spirits. Their horses' hooves clopped in shallow puddles as rain pattered down upon the dirt paths. But a golden glow glimmered in the south, a sign that the storm would soon pass.

"Is this what a knight-errant does then?"

"I suppose," Orrick answered. "I've heard tales of them traveling to other lands, journeys, adventures—but mostly they remain in their town lest specifically summoned."

"Think that'll ever happen?"

"One can hope."

The two of them turned down an alleyway, hoping to find something. Alas, no one in sight. The weather kept most people indoors, which surprised Orrick not in the least.

"There are some folwarks we might check," sighed Orrick.

"Are we knights or farmhands?" asked Brandt.

"Knights-errant are servants of the realm. We go where we're needed."

"Truly are you so selfless? Haven't we, as highborn, better things to do with our time?"

"Lowborn and high aren't so separated in Brzeg. Sooth have we our place in court, but never do we forget Aileron was a peasant, too."

Brandt clenched his jaw, thinking.

"Besides," said Orrick, "I'd rather we did our duties than return and face Lord Father's wrath."

At that, Brandt smiled.

They found themselves in the town square, empty as anything else they came across—a shadow emerged from one of the paths. Moments later, a small girl scampered across, arm upheld against the rain.

"Halt!" called Orrick, and the girl stopped. She looked at him, terrified. *That bodes not well.* "Why do you run?"

The girl looked around stupidly. "It's—it's raining, pan."

Orrick was unmoved. "So it is. If all you run from is the rain, why look you so frightened?"

"I s'ppose anyone would if they's stopped by a horsed knight."

"She has a point," muttered Brandt.

Orrick frowned, ignoring him. "Hurry home, then ... 'less need you an escort?"

Dumbstruck, the girl lowered her arm, straw-colored hair stuck to her forehead. "Y' ain't need t' go t' that trouble, pan. My home's only there. But when me mum sees the state o' me ..."

Orrick smiled. The girl's hair dripped rainwater. Her muddy frock stopped just above scraped knees. She just returned from an adventure, it seemed. "Aye, we'll take you."

Orrick gave the girl a blanket to wear. Her nose wrinkled, but of the horse-smell she complained not. He even let her sit on Cień's back as he walked beside them.

Her house lay at the end of a row. A woman, short and thin in an apron covered in flour, shook her head as though she lost something important.

"Mum!" the girl shouted, and the thin woman turned around.

"Alma! Where were y'?" she demanded, running to them. Orrick might have thought an expression of both relief and anger impossible, but he had a mother as well.

"I's playin', an' it started rainin'—"

The mother looked at the girl sternly, which made her pause. "You went t' the pond again, looking for frogs. I can tell from the smell o' y'."

"How can y' smell anything past this horse blanket?"

"A mother can." She looked at Orrick. "Thank y', pan—"

"Pallaton. And my squire, Brandt."

"The Voivod's—" She bowed. "I'm s' sorry t' trouble y', pan—*milord*. She loves the pond an' bellfrogs is her fa-vorite—"

Orrick laughed. "'Twas no trouble. Rise, please. I saw her running and thought she was chased. There's little out today, besides."

"So, you're the new knight-errant, are y'?"

Orrick bowed, grinning. "At your service. Let me know if there's aught you need."

"This's fine, thank y', milord."

Child and mother reunited, Orrick and Brandt left to find something else.

But there was naught.

Eventually, the rain stopped. Golden air peaked down from breaks in the clouds, and even birds, hidden in trees, sang songs of relief. But still nothing for Orrick and Brandt. As more people exited their homes, the sun set. Time for them to return.

Boring. Even after a week, it was more of the same. Orrick and Brandt rode through Newtown, stopping to aid whoever asked. They even helped the same girl, whose cat had climbed into a tree.

On the eighth evening, Orrick found Nigel in his solar, bent over a desk cramped with open books and loose parchment. Danced he his quill across parchment, stopping when he noticed Orrick.

Without even looking up, Nigel said, "You've come for a task."

Orrick, on the verge of pleading, asked, "Know you of aught, Lord Father?"

Nigel closed the heavy book and pondered a moment. "Taxes are a tedious thing, Orrick. Yet they are my responsibility. So too must you think of your work as a knight-errant. Newtown pays you to aid people. You're honor-bound, truthfully. As your mother said, your time in the sun will come. Be patient until then."

Orrick nodded, remaining silent.

184

"By the way, have you written Prince Armitage?"

Orrick had sent a long letter telling of the hunt, the Oldtown ruins, and how Brandt saved him from the scimitiger. He received a letter back only yesterday but had not yet replied.

"You've the rest of the evening free. You may as well do that."

Orrick returned to his chambers and sat down at his desk with quill and parchment. He wrote about his tasks as knight-errant, the dreary days patrolling the streets of Newtown from morning to sundown. The people of Newtown lived simple lives. All he had to do was wander aimlessly around the town and stop if someone asked. He even once carried an old woman's bags back to her house. *Lordly rotter, indeed.*

Once he finished the letter, he brought it to his father, who sealed it with black wax stamped with his signet ring bearing the inverted greatsword of House Pallaton. Orrick took the letter to the tower rookery. He entered a cramped room with two beds and a single table. The next room was Orrick's destination, a wide space with a large window and long birdcages on either wall.

"Welcome to the rookery, Pan Pallaton."

Orrick jumped back. Preston Ballard, the manse's thin bird-keeper, gaunt of nose and hollow of eye. To make matters worse, he wore drab robes and kept to the shadows. Clutching Ballard's side was a small girl, no older than four, whose mother had died some time ago. How anyone could have loved

185

the man was beyond Orrick's comprehension, but perhaps he had become so cheerless because of his lost wife.

No matter, for Preston Ballard was a man of few words and Orrick wished not to ask. Instead, he held the letter out. "Another for Prince Armitage."

Preston snatched it with fingers as long and knobby as harvestmen's legs. He went to the table, the young girl trailing behind him, and scrawled on it. "You forgot to address it," he hissed. "Wouldn't wish for this to end up in the wrong hands, would you?"

"No."

Preston Ballard slunk into the room filled with cages. On the right-hand side, passenger pigeons twittered and dashed around. Thin birds with fast wings and small bones. Silver and gold feathers flashed as they darted from one end of the cage to the other in bursts of immediate speed.

The opposite wall held another group of cages, these filled with small black vultures, hooked beaks, and sharp talons, both purple, snapping. These were mar'tak, used only when delivering news of grief or death. As the passenger pigeons shot to and fro, the mar'tak remained perched, eyeing Orrick hungrily.

Ballard appeared again; the flat letter transformed into a tube. He opened one of the right-hand cages and whistled. At first glance, the passenger pigeons seemed too wild, but one of them changed direction and landed atop Preston's wrist without a moment's wait.

"These truly are well-trained birds," Orrick marveled.

Ballard tied the cylinder around her right leg and whispered something. It took off, shooting from the window and into the wild yellow skies. The birdkeeper turned to Orrick, eyes sorrowful.

"No use remaining here. Best wait in the manse proper."

Naught else to do but wait, Orrick turned 'round and left the rookery.

X: Free Folk Of The Forest

Midday, Newtown came into view. Many months had passed since she had come to Newtown, to Limehouse. Her heart pounded. Her throat tightened. Even after all these years, the city seemed bigger than ever she could imagine. But what she first noticed wasn't the *size* of the place. It was that it wasn't *green*. There were some shrubs and trees—but all the greenery she came to expect grew southward and westward. The Salt Steppe—terrible and barren. Newtown, only a little better.

Beside her strode Papa—Lasibor Budny—a tall man with deeply tan skin and blood red hair, long and matted. She had his eyes, deep green. Nervously, she wrung her overlarge tunic, green as sage. She wore her finery today—green tunic, leather belt and leather boots. She had spent an entire day braiding her dark hair, making it look as pretty as she could. But the wildflowers wilted, and it was so cold she knew she would not be able to find replacements in time.

"Stop fidgeting," growled Lasibor.

"But it's been so long. Y' think 'e remembers?"

"Don't know." Lasibor looked down at her, green eyes mysterious and untamable. "But y' may not find the time to straighten yourself. So, stop fidgeting."

Sylvia nodded and pulled her tunic's hem down, flattening the front of her garment. The two stopped at Southgate, where the guard inspected them. "Ah, the Budnys! Voivod Pallaton expects you!"

Easy as it had always been, father and daughter entered Newtown. They have been coming here for years, ever since Sylvia was a little girl ... ever since the fateful summer night she first met Orrick Pallaton. And they came frequently since. True, her visits became less common when Orrick left to the academy. Thankfully, the Pallatons continued to welcome them openly even when their son was gone.

Trees, evenly spaced, lined the paths. Lamps yet unlit stood sentinel in front of rowhouses. Further away from the town square, bigger houses appeared. Merchants, politicians, miner lords—all the people with money.

Even though she and Papa had come here for years, there was still the odd townsperson that glared or gawked. And there were parts of Brzeg they weren't allowed in unless it was a holy day. It always made her feel sad—and sometimes angry—that the townsfolks respect toward them came because they knew Nigel and Fiona and not because they were human beings.

Her mood brightened again when they turned toward the westernmost corner. Still walled within the city, and flanked by two ponds, stood Limehouse.

Sylvia always sighed relief when she saw it. She thought Turnip Marsh fine. The little cottage therein, where dwelled she and Papa, was the coziest place she knew. But Limehouse—Pallaton Manse—was so much *larger.* She remembered running through the halls with Orrick, shrieking and giggling—though now she knew not why. But now that she was grown, the halls still seemed expansive.

The sentries guarding Limehouse uncrossed their pikes. "Lasibor and Sylvia!" exclaimed the captain named Paweł. "How was your trek?"

"Fine," grunted Lasibor.

"Please come through! Know you the way?"

"Yes. Thank you."

Captain Paweł stepped aside, allowing them through. Sylvia smiled at him and said, "We named our new cockerel after you." He guffawed his approval.

Past the crimson gatehouse, they met Castellan Oger, a dark

man made darker from his time in the sun, with a face like stone: bumpy and craggy, pockmarked and scarred. Hard but never rude, Oger never smiled, and his sagging jowls made him remind Sylvia of an angry bulldog.

"Welcome to Limehouse. This way."

Sylvia and Lasibor followed him inside, down corridors to the throne room where Voivod Nigel held court. On the way, she passed a mirror and checked herself. Her fidgeting had done her tunic a disservice, so she straightened it, centered the belt, tightened it. She wished in that moment the brown leather of her belt and boots both weren't cracking.

Upon her collar, she wore a brooch of hammered copper, a triangle within a circle. It denoted her religion, her status as a freeperson. Lasibor wore the same. Some wore them as jewelry, others woven into clothing. A rare few branded it into their skin, and that always unsettled her. Around her neck she wore a silver pendant bearing a large topaz—she never took it off; it was her mama's, now hers.

Finally, she examined her face, smiling anxiously. Some pockmarks, some pimples 'round her chin, plump cheeks and wide nose. Her eyes were the prettiest thing about her, forest green and bright, if spaced too far apart. She smiled toothily, nervously. Questions. Concerns—

"Sylvia! Come!"

She squealed and followed Papa into the throne room. Black

191

carpets led from the entrance to the back, which split right and left. The small dining room lay right, a room cool and cozy. The kitchens resided in the next room over, and she could hear the stewards, sculleries, and cooks clattering pots, Mama Fields barking demands, preparing the meal.

Nigel and Fiona already sat, but they stood when Sylvia and Lasibor entered. Nigel, of black hair and black beard, wearing black and gray colors, smiled. "Lasibor, Sylvia, 'tis good to see you both."

Fiona, the hardest woman Sylvia had ever seen—which was saying something, considering she herself was a freewoman—gestured to the chairs. "Please, sit," she said. "Long was your journey and the weather is not yet comfortable."

The two did as she bade, with words of gramercy. Sylvia looked around, nervous. Her eyes widened, taking in everything. The manse itself was typically dark. Red bricks even here, black carpet, black tablecloth, red candles burning. She inhaled, smelling smoke and wax and food cooking.

"Care you for aught?" asked Nigel. "Wine? Beer? Ice-minted milk?"

"Cold goatmilk for her," said Lasibor. "I'll have whatever you have."

Nigel motioned to a steward and the butler, who both ran off. Typically, Lasibor drank milk or purified water. Only when he came to Newtown did he imbibe in drinks stronger.

"Sylvia." She turned to Fiona, who took her hands in hers. Both women's hands toughened by callouses. Sylvia gazed into Fiona's icy eyes, tracing the scar that trailed from scalp to lip. "How are you, dear?"

Sylvia smiled "I'm fine. We got new chickens in our coop. But Paweł—our rooster, we named him after your gate captain—struts 'round like 'e's a dragon. The temperament on him! 'E bit Kamień, our wolfhound, which startled Boris, our burro, who bit Papa."

"It hurt," said Lasibor.

"All survived the winter?"

"All's well," said Sylvia. "We ain't lose any animals—but came we close. Winter's when marsh turnips grow best. I can't wait until me vegetable garden again blooms. An' me herb garden—that'll make everything smell nice—oh, an' me flowerbed. Without me flowers, everything's just so brown an' muddy."

"Well certainly *something* has grown." Fiona looked to Sylvia's braids, and she lowered her head for better examination. "Beautiful, dear."

"They're dead already," she said, dismayed.

"Merely wilted," said Fiona. "Beautiful pinks and violets,

yellow daisies ... is that a coneflower?"

"They bloomed first. I thought they'd be nice."

"And they are. Truly. Happy, are we, that you're safe and well, that your coop overruns with chickens new, and that your garden has thawed and gives flowers already."

"Flowers always bloom early for me," answered Sylvia. "Don't know why."

"Well, nature must truly seem to like you," said Fiona, smiling.

"You're blessed by Driada."

Sylvia smiled back and asked, "How's it been here? Nothing seems changed."

"Limehouse stands as it has since it was first built nearly five hundred years ago."

"I know. I love it here. But I would change *one* thing ..."

Fiona chuckled. "Know I precisely what that may be."

"*Plants.*" She smiled wide. "Potted plants. Hanging near windows. Flowers in vases. Red and black are fine colors, but I need it greener."

In that moment, a steward placed a glass in front of her, sloshing creamy, frothy goatmilk. She inhaled, smelling the ice-mint that both chilled the milk and gave it a burst of flavor peppery yet cool. "Thank 'e," she said, breaking her clasp with Sylvia to take the glass.

Soon, the butler also returned, carrying a small beer barrel. "A strong beer, Your Grace; a porter of clove, firestick, and licorice."

"A choice well-made," said Nigel. "Go to work, please."

The butler set the small barrel onto a wooden barrel rest, readied a pewter pitcher, and uncorked it. The beer cascaded into the pitcher, black and foamy. Expertly, as the beer neared the lip, the butler replaced the cork and stoppered the barrel up.

The butler set the pitcher on the table and asked, "How many goblets?"

"Myself, Fiona, Lasibor, and Orrick and his squire. Five."

As the butler scurried off to fetch the goblets, Sylvia perked up and looked at Nigel. "'E comes? When?"

"When finishes he his tasks. Surprised, am I, you did not run into him not as you entered Newtown."

"We came straight here," grunted Lasibor.

"Oh ..." Sylvia saddened, wishing she had seen him.

"Y' wouldn't have wanted him t' see y' with your tunic askew."

She blushed. Lasibor spoke correct. Instead of saying aught, she gulped from her milk. The creaminess soothed her; the ice-mint refreshed her. She sighed refreshed when she put the glass down, two-thirds full.

The door opened from the throne room, and in came two more souls. One of them was long and lanky, with a large head enshrouded by bushy brown hair. The other, shorter, more muscular, bad posture. But his black hair and gray eyes reminded her of Nigel—younger, of course, and without a beard.

"Naught, naught, *naught*," complained the older man.

"'Tis getting more boring," said the younger.

"Travel we Newtown's streets from midmorning to dusk and for *what*? 'Carry my sacks.' 'Fetch my cat.' 'Find my ring.' I'm *exhausted*—"

He stopped when he noticed her, eyes curious.

Her eyes brightened when she beamed at him. "Orrick!"

Confused, he asked, "You know me?"

Dare she trust her ears? Believe she his words? Had he forgotten her? The bright smile faltered. Damn her if she didn't feel tears brimming.

To his parents, Orrick said, "Lord Father, Lady Mother, who are these distinguished gentlemen?"

Sylvia choked on her own gasp. *Gentlemen?* She thought herself ordinary, but *gentleman?* She waited fourteen years for this exact moment, and not only did he not remember her, but he thought her a *gentleman?* She knew not what else to say but, "Gentleman?"

Lasibor passed her a threadbare handkerchief. "Milk on your lip."

"Shite!" she squealed, cheeks burning, and quickly wiped away the goatmilk mustache. "Y' teased me this whole time!"

"I'm confused?" said the younger lad.

Orrick gestured. "Brandt, remember you what spoke we about? This is Sylvia and her father, Lasibor."

Brandt paled as though he saw a ghost. "*Sav*—"

"*Free folk*," intoned Orrick. "Sit."

Brandt did, nervously rubbing his knuckles, eyes darting to all in the room. "So uncouth—swore, she did—never would Ozella—never would my sister—"

"What's his problem?" asked Sylvia.

"Rhabdolian," answered Orrick. She bristled—Rhabdolians,

especially those devout, would see her tried for heresy. But Orrick sat beside her, and she felt warm. "He's not accustomed to free folk. But glad am I to see you."

"I'm surprised y' remember me. I was s' sure y' forgot."

Orrick rubbed the back of his head, grinning. "I nearly did."

She could not hide her dismay.

"Look not so dour! 'Twas a busy fourteen years for me. Paging and squiring; learning and fighting. But I promise, my memories cleared as roamed I through Limehouse."

"All 'em?" she asked.

"Sylvia," warned Papa.

But Orrick answered, "All of them? Remember I ... we demanded sweets from the kitchens. Remember I—*ah*! When brought we that sand-rat into Limehouse from the Steppe!"

"—but it escaped—"

"—and the hounds chased it—"

"—and we chased the hounds—"

"—and the sentries chased us all!"

Sylvia brightened again. "All through the manse, into the

kitchens and the downstairs in the servants' quarters. We were in so much trouble!"

"But laughed we for hours."

They both laughed again now, and she felt as though only the two of them sat in the small dining room. She asked, "Remember y' nothing before that?"

Orrick shook his head. "Naught. Should I?"

"Sylvia," warned Lasibor again.

"I guess not," she said.

"So," said Orrick, grinning, "what brings mine old friend here?"

"Ah, y' know, this is a *special* occasion."

"Special?"

"Oh, aye, 'coz we only come t' Newtown 'round the winter an' summer solstices."

"Śńeg Czas and Słońçem," answered Orrick.

"We remember Mama on Śńeg Czas—that and some chickens we lost, sometimes. Papa brings pelts an' makes the wine o' the damned."

Orrick looked ponderous. Wine of the damned is bitter herbs and marsh turnips fermented together, a thick tarry liqueur only drank during the night of mourning.

"It has been a while since I attended Śnieg Czas," said Orrick. "This year I'm old enough to drink the doomed wine."

"Happier, we always come t' Słońcem. The suckling pigs, the dancing, the music—Papa always brings chickens. An' also the fire-jumping. Remember the fire-jumping, Orrick?"

"No more questions," said Lasibor. "Not about that." He turned to Nigel. "We need t' speak about private matters."

Nigel nodded. "Tonight, when sleeps Limehouse. Come to my solar."

Sylvia eyed them curious. Orrick sighed, contented, did not seem to notice. He asked, "What makes this so special?"

"Ah!" Sylvia blushed. "You're 'ere. I mean, you're returned. You're *back*."

"Stop stammering," said Papa, and Sylvia quieted. "We came t' see y', Orrick, as congratulations."

"Well—" he smiled at Sylvia, then Lasibor "—certainly, do I feel congratulated. I Smell already the roast and am famished after a long day of boredom. Aren't we, Brandt?"

Brandt the squire looked 'round, still nervous. "Y-yeah ..."

It's like 'e never saw free folk before, she thought. But she knew the tragedy; Rhabdolians—and indeed most of Tourm outside Brzeg—mistrusted and disliked free folk. *Why's 'e Orrick's squire, then?*

"An odd choice, I know," said Orrick, almost reading her mind. "He's a good lad with good skills. Already he grows accustomed to life in Brzeg, though knew I 'twould be difficult to deal with the cultural differences."

"Ah, so I see."

"Saved my life, though. I've chosen well."

"Thank 'e, Brandt," she said.

"Y-yeah," he sputtered.

Stewards soon served supper. As Orrick surmised, a roast came, and various other dishes, with it. Mashed turnips—not marsh turnips, thankfully—and stewed cabbage and a sauce of black peppercorns that was a little too spicy for her. The goatmilk helped with that, though.

All the while, she and Orrick spoke. Her face reddened, and she felt insecure that her life was so boring compared to his. She tended chickens and grew flowers while he caught pirates and rode horses. But if he seemed to notice or care, he made no mention of it. He listened raptly when she told him of Paweł and Gloria and Kamień and Boris. And as they talked, she beamed at him like the sun.

"By the way," said Orrick, "beautiful flowers. Why didn't I notice them before?"

Sylvia gasped, blushed, reached to her braids. "No. Don' tease! They were the first t' bloom but they're already wilted ..."

"Are they?" Orrick plucked a pink dianthus from her hair. Indeed, it appeared vibrant and lively.

Sylvia marveled, blushed, and said, "You've become quite a gentleman."

"As had you, for a time."

She stuck her tongue at him and they both laughed.

"How long will you be staying?" asked Orrick.

Forever, she wanted to say.

But Papa answered, "A couple nights. We must get back to tend our chickens. Kamień can only do so much against thieves and foxes."

Evening carried on into night, guided by laughter and stories, until Brandt—still nervous and silent—yawned. Fiona bade them all to sleep as servants lit sconces.

Later, Sylvia sprawled out in her bed. Massive Limehouse meant massive rooms, which meant massive beds. She loved sleeping here. The linens felt smooth as velvet on her skin. And Fiona doted on her, giving her a nightgown of green silk to sleep in. She lavished in it. All she owned came threadbare. But one day, she promised herself, she would sleep on fine linens every night.

Yet as comfortable as the linens were, she could not find sleep. Curiosity tickled her brain. She slipped from her linens, lit a candle, and took it with her as she crept 'round the manse.

The corridors, blood red brick in the daylight, now all looked black. Sylvia avoided patrolling guards at every turn, ducking into privies, concealing the candle flame to hide behind antique suits of armor. At last, and though it took a small while to find, came she upon Nigel's solar. It must be—it was the only room still lit, and two voices mumbled behind the closed door.

She peeked in through the keyhole and saw Nigel and Papa talking. They each held a tumbler of clear liquid—probably white whiskey. Careful not to make a sound, Sylvia set the candle down and pressed her ear against the door.

"Too eager she is, asking him such questions," said Nigel.

"She's been patient," replied Papa. "We've waited sixteen years. I can't blame her for being eager. Orrick's grown finely."

Sylvia widened her eyes. *So they* are *talking about us*!

"Remember our deal," said Nigel. "We've too traditions to

uphold. Orrick is not ready for such knowledge."

"He's of marrying age—"

"He's newly knighted and a boy of one-and-twenty," said Nigel, interrupting. "Not yet has he proven himself a responsible leader, and that is what I need of him. One day he will be voivod. The people will look to him for protection and guidance. Brzeg must trust him."

"Is that why he roams the streets from day t' dusk?"

"The people *must* trust him," repeated Nigel. "Knight-errant is an important tradition amongst House Pallaton. His subjects will come to him with problems small. But when he is voivod, and sits he the throne and holds he court, they will trust him with problems larger."

Both men fell silent. Then Papa asked, "How long y' think it'll take?"

"Five years."

Sylvia almost gasped but covered her mouth.

Papa voiced her concerns for her. "That's too long."

"Understand, Lasibor, the people must come first. 'Tis not only her I must appease, but everyone living in Steppe, Hills, Forest, and Marsh. A woman will only be a distraction. He must lose not his head over a pretty face."

"He's riding around town. What if he meets a gentlewoman, or a merchant's daughter?"

"Then have I the unfortunate task of telling him. Besides, their joining was foretold by the summer spirits."

"But they were burned," said Lasibor. "Y' know what that means."

"I know …"

"Y' don't think it's a problem?"

"I don't. We have instilled a sense of responsibility in Orrick, a sense of duty. He goes not around seeking women's company. In fact, the only female he has talked about since returning home—" Sylvia held her breath "—is an alewife's daughter of eight springs, who keeps losing her cat and skinning her knees."

Papa grew silent. Sylvia peeked through the keyhole and saw him sip from the tumbler.

Nigel said, "Sense I your concern. Fine—we shall tell him."

Sylvia beamed, biting her lip to stifle her excitement.

"But not right now," said Nigel. "'Tis still too soon to consider marriage but … he will know."

"When?"

"Let us give him a few more moons carefree. Come Słońcem, return to Newtown as you usually do. We shall tell him then, with you and Sylvia present both."

"Then he will know he's promised?" asked Papa.

"Yes, but their marriage must needs wait a few years more. Is this well with you?"

"It is."

Sylvia leaned against the door and sighed. She knew. Papa had told her right away that she and Orrick would be married because they, as children and convinced it was a game, jumped the fires and came out hands still clasped. But Orrick must not know—not until he becomes a leader of the people. Still, it looked as though he would soon know—in three moons.

Papa and Nigel would converse about more boring things now, if they hadn't already. The Emperor of Brigands and all that. She only cared about the information she already got.

Happily, Sylvia collected the candle and wandered back to bed, this time to sleep comfortably.

XI: The Royal Writ

The next few days went by quickly. Quicker than Orrick hoped, anyway. He and Brandt would finish their patrol or their training, and—still in the day's sweat and armor—he would head directly to the small dining room. Red walls, oaken table, black cloth, red candelabrum … and her.

Today, he returned from a patrol. Once inside the dining room, he beamed when he saw her. Sylvia—with eyes as green as the nature she so enjoyed, and often in a matching frock—smiled back, just as enthusiastic to see him. He sat next to her, waiting for the stewards to bring the meal. Tonight, however, sadness touched her smile. Orrick knew why: 'Twas her last night before returning.

"How was it?" she asked.

"Little to speak of, truly."

"How's Alma, the alewife's girl?"

Orrick chuckled, sighed. "Fell she from a tree two nights past, trying to get her damned cat. Poor girl broke her arm. Alas, 'twas even duller without her."

"How could it have gotten even *duller*?" whined Brandt.

Brandt, initially mistrusting of Sylvia and Lasibor, had these three days warmed up to them. No longer did he warily eye them, trembling like he may flee the room.

"Your father runs y' all 'round town," she said. "Do Brandt an' y' only train once a sennight?"

"Wish I we could train more ..." said Orrick.

"Me, too," said Brandt.

"I saw y' two nights ago. You're good ... I think. Honestly, I don' know much about swords. But I know when someone's showing off."

Orrick guffawed and rubbed his brow. *Dammit, she knew*! "Aye, I admit, the training was supposed to be for Brandt. But you came to watch and—"

"And you took me down," said Brandt. "We were practicing footwork and you tackled me."

"Aye," said Orrick, "and the lesson is, keep your footing."

"And then," continued Brandt, "demanded you other knights to come. Fought you four in sequence!"

"And none hit me once," said Orrick. He looked at Sylvia. "I became a competent duelist in Nin, and I hope to enter the mêlée come next tournament."

Sylvia giggled.

Orrick cleared his throat and looked back to Brandt. "Mine apologies. Merely, I became swept away—"

"Aye, aye," said Brandt dismissively. "Know I perfectly well why you did it, pan." He gave Orrick a sly grin.

"Wipe 'way that smirk or I'll have your scouring mail."

Brandt did and Sylvia laughed heartily. "Y' two 're such good friends!"

"Ah, no, Lady Sylvia," said Brandt sheepishly. "I am but his humble squire."

"I am no lady," said Sylvia.

"One day you will be, the way Orrick looks at y—"

Orrick threw a napkin at him and he silenced, but Sylvia continued laughing. Soon, Lasibor, Nigel and Fiona joined them.

Lasibor was much harder to read than his daughter. Both their eyes were green, but hers were radiant and resplendent as a sunlit grove, and his as deep and foreboding as the wildest forest. A man of few words, Lasibor's sinewy muscles, deeply tanned skin, and height perfectly encapsulated what the rest of Tourm's people feared ... but that is based on appearances alone. He cared for his daughter and his land, and Orrick respected him. But the way he sometimes looked at Orrick made him feel the respect was not mutual, as if he mistrusted Orrick somehow. But Orrick could not think of any reason he might have given to earn that mistrust.

"We've asked Mama Fields to prepare a Brzegu specialty," said Nigel. "And we've a special beer, an ale brewed with ginger and honey."

"'Tis a gift from Alma's mother," said Fiona. "She thanks you for looking after her daughter."

Orrick felt the blush keep up his neck. "She needn't have ..."

"Perfect is her selection," said Nigel, "for tonight we have honey-braised bearpaw with horseradish salad."

The meal was one of the best Orrick had ever eaten. Redder than beef, sweeter than venison, grainer than pork, the braising and the honey sauce melted in his mouth. The salad, with lettuce and beets, paired perfectly when topped with horseradish dressing. The heat hit not on the tongue, but in the nose. The honey and ginger ale enhanced the flavors of the meal, but also refreshed the palate.

All the while, he and Sylvia looked at each other, sometimes smiling, sometimes sadder. During dessert of gingerbread, Orrick asked, "When will you return?"

"Słońcem," she replied quickly. Nigel and Lasibor looked at one another, but said nothing, so Orrick cared not.

Orrick smiled at the thought. "Summer Solstice. I look forward to it."

"An' I—I mean, an' we."

Next morn, Orrick met Sylvia and Lasibor outside the gate-house. He bowed and said, "I come to escort you to Southgate, my lady."

"No need," she said. "It's still early."

"This is not because of duties," said Orrick. "I want to."

She blushed and he walked them to Southgate, making small talk. Lasibor loomed behind them like a tree, silent as ever. Orrick only now realized how little they came with. Nigel and Fiona at least packed horses when they traveled. Lasibor and Sylvia carried only ragged rucksacks.

"A question if I may," asked Orrick. "What are your brooches?"

"They mean we're free folk," Sylvia answered. "The circle means forever, an' the triangle means creation, life, an' destruction."

"And all free folk wear these?"

"All do—some have jewelry, some have it on clothing, an' others. Well—"

"Brandings," said Lasibor.

"I see"

"It symbolizes our religion," answered Lasibor.

Orrick blinked confused. "I thought we were of the same beliefs: The overgods connect all?"

"Free folk practice magic Tourm-men ban," explained Lasibor. "Sometimes the magic is dangerous. We never hurt others intentionally, but—"

"But the Church of the Branch tries us," said Sylvia.

"Yes. For heresy."

"That I knew," said Orrick, "but never *why*."

"We believe magic will come back," said Sylvia. "The same

magic the overgods gave people so long ago—an' some of us try t' awaken that power again."

Orrick thought about Nib. But his thirteen-pointed star was much more complex than the free folks' encircled triangle. And he, himself, mentioned that the Order of the Grand Star existed not to *revive* the old magic, but study it and learn the unabashed history of the world. If Nib could do that, why couldn't the free folk have their beliefs also?

"Brzeg is built upon Aileron's religion, which came from the elves and free folk," said Orrick. "Did we not fight against the Church of the Branch centuries ago for religious freedom?"

Lasibor shook his head, wagging his bloodred tangles. "Brzeg and the free folk may share the same beliefs, but Brzeg still abides by Tourm's magic laws."

"Free folk prefer t' be free," said Sylvia. "Living in Tourm means we can't practice that magic."

Orrick looked sadly at Sylvia. "I did not know."

"It's something we'd die for," she said, "and *have*. But just because we *would* don' mean we *want to*. Y' know?"

Orrick nodded. "Aye, lady mine, I know."

"Oh, hush with the 'lady mine!'" But she giggled and blushed, which made him smile.

Coming to Southgate, Orrick said, "Here we are. Fare you well. Good tidings on your journey. Pray I your chickens remained well."

"If Kamień did his job, ain't nothing t' worry about," said Lasibor. Surprisingly, he extended his hand. Orrick hesitated, but clasped his wrist. "Thank you, Pan Orrick."

Even more surprising, Sylvia threw her arms around him and embraced him. Years of forest-living made her stronger than he realized. She squeezed, and he squeezed back. "It was *so good* to see you."

"Enough o' that." Lasibor, even stronger, pulled her away.

"Fourteen years an' now you're back. I can't wait 'til Słońçem."

"Nor I," said Orrick. "Farewell, Sylvia, Lasibor."

After the Budnys left, Orrick grew restless.

During the days, he and Brandt traveled around Newtown or sparred in the yard. The evenings were different, however. No longer did he have his childhood friend to placate his nerves. Instead, he hid in his room and counted his money, again and again, making sure all the coins were still present. And they were, twenty-five pecks and two dashes. On more than one occasion, he found books in his father's library, but nothing held his attention.

He looked up from the open pages and out of his window. *I*

should be out there. There were places to explore, glories to win, wicked men to fell. Yet here was he, talents and skills wasted roaming barren streets.

What were the odds? As Pan Callows had put it, he was a green knight—a knight without experience. *Yet how might I earn experience if I remain doing naught? Would that I was named a guardsman.* He remembered when the idea seemed appalling to him. If he were a guardsman, he would have a job to do. He realized how foolish the thought was—at least now he could ride about town. A guardsman just stood in one place. Hopeless, he closed the book.

Days passed without any change. Orrick started worrying about the pigeon. Was it taken by a hawk? Or perhaps it was shot down—by whom? A Kendalan archer? A treacherous rotter? Such thinking was futile. After all, he reminded himself, Tourm had not seen war for fifty years.

That thought took him back to the Black Horseman, the night the rogues had laughed and chided and died. "War's a-comin'." But where was the evidence? Rumors, and he remembered something after that ... a conversation, but not one that he was having. What was it?

Orrick sighed. Even if rotters and freemen *did* plan a revolt, what could he do? He could not kill them as a squire. Being a knight would not magically make it easier.

That night, Orrick and Brandt sparred together. Brandt's skill continued to grow, but so did Orrick's. He coached the lad as they went, reminding Brandt of balance and never to drop his guard. When they both grew tired and sweaty, Orrick adjourned to his chambers and stared again at the window instead of the book in front of him. He closed it and shut his curtains, banishing his room to darkness.

There is naught for me this night, he thought. *Would that more jadwilki came down. Or a vampire cat, or even a scimitiger—aught at all!* As he opened the blankets and stepped into bed, he groaned, "I'd even fight polterfurniture should the undergods be mad enough to make them."

Blue and breezy, the next morning came. Seven days since he sent the letter and no response. As he dressed, the back of his mind flared. What if something had befallen the Prince?

A knock interrupted his thoughts. Orrick scowled and pulled his tunic over his head. "Who comes?"

His eyes widened when Brandt entered out of breath. Orrick briefly feared that Newtown was under siege.

The news was happier. "A whitetail hawk arrived!"

Orrick blinked, momentarily confused. All the sovereigns of Tourm—from dukes to knights—sent their messages with passenger pigeons. The royal family, however, used whitetail hawks. He wondered if this had aught to do with the letter he sent to Armitage.

"Who else knows?"

216

"You, me, and the Ballards."

Brandt led him to the rookery. Indeed, a beautiful whitetail hawk had arrived, massive compared to the other birds. Her entire body was dust-gray, save for her tail, which was a fan of long, white feathers. Preston had put it in a cage separate from the passenger pigeons, which was well because they were the hawks' main prey. Yet the iron bars deterred her not; she cast golden eyes at them, watching them dart.

Preston handed the parchment to Orrick. The wax had a silvery sheen, the gyrfalcon of House Pardwy, wings spread wide, on the center. Orrick broke the seal and unfurled the letter.

"'Tis the Prince's hand," Orrick exclaimed. He read the message hastily, then again slower.

"What does it say, Pan Pallaton?" asked Brandt.

"Armitage has regained his taste for Flavès whites, although fears spring water might be white whiskey instead. And he mentions a conversation we overheard in the Plaintive Hound. I remember none of it, yet he knows the entire tale by heart."

"Never mind *that*," Brandt whined. "What does it *say*?"

"The King is to send an envoy to Kendala. An ambassador from Tourm is to meet with King Archibald and his council. For what, it mentions not—but I might fathom a guess." His eyes met Brandt's. "Kendala seeks war, and the envoy means to prevent it. Armitage has vouched for me to go with them."

Brandt's eyes widened. "That means I'm to go as well! I've never been to another kingdom."

"Nor I," said Orrick, pondering the parchment. "Lord Father and Lady Mother ought know of this. Follow me."

They thanked Preston Ballard and rushed from the rookery. After asking several guardsmen, Orrick ultimately found his parents in the parlor. Brandt respectfully bent his knee, but Orrick remained standing. Nigel first read the parchment, then passed it to his wife.

"'Tis a royal writ disguised as a friendly letter," said Nigel, sounding like he wanted to spit.

"I want to go," said Orrick.

Nigel folded his arms. "I think it unwise for King Biel to take his son's word. You're a knight yet green. Sending you to a country as ambitious as Kendala is folly. What's more, neither do we know the ambassador's identity, nor how many knights travel with him. I dislike this, Orrick."

"'Tis a job, and one decreed by House Pardwy," argued Orrick. "A novice I may be, but I'm no mewling babe. Fought I pirates squiring for Count Atrax."

Nigel frowned. "Smugglers are not—"

"If I'm to be a great knight worthy of the Pallaton name, I'll need experience in matters such as these, and experience shan't be gained remaining here. We cannot know when such a chance again comes."

Nigel's glare darkened. He formed his argument. Orrick could practically see Lord Father's mind whirring like drawbridge gears.

"Nay," said Nigel. "'Tis too risky."

"Why?" asked Orrick. "Why do you stay me?"

"*This* is your home, Orrick," said Nigel. "*This* is where you belong. We cannot send you knowingly into fire. Your duty first comes to Brzeg."

"I understand not why you stay me," said Orrick. "A voivod *is* a warlord—at least that's what it once meant."

"Why so willing are you to get yourself killed?" asked Nigel. "Help me understand that."

"You treat me as a child."

"Because you yet are! At least 'tis how you act."

"I'm a child no longer but a knight—"

"A knight *green*. But even if you are, you still my son—grown or little, that matters not. Further yet, you are a knight in *mine* employ."

Orrick pointed to the letter. "According to that, I'm a knight in *King Biel*'s employ."

Nigel paused, glowering, thinking of his counterargument. This time, it appeared Orrick had snuck through his defenses.

He growled, "As you like it, then."

"Nigel—" Fiona snapped, but he shook his head.

"Speaks he sooth, my lady," said Nigel through teeth gritted. "I forget Orrick is a man now. Too harsh have I with him been."

"You'd send him off?" asked Fiona. "Even after ... your promise?"

"I mislike it as much as you, but I cannot deter him. A voivod does more than govern his lands: he protects the realm by guarding the kingdom against enemies. If Kendala is fool enough to make war, then he *needs* to know how to do his duty."

Fiona glowered. "I cannot argue ... but I'd like to."

Orrick looked confused. "Wait, what promise?"

"Never you mind. For should ever you hope to be House Pallaton's worthy lord, you must needs take this journey." He handed the letter back to Orrick. "It says to report to Albicant in four days' time. We'll leave you to it."

Guilt crept into Orrick's stomach as his parents left the parlor. But there was no time to confront it. "Come," he told Brandt, though with a voice hoarser than he wished it to be.

XII: The Procession Prepares

Orrick and Brandt dressed in their armor and equipped their sword-belts. They stopped by the kitchens on their way to the stable. As Orrick reached them, he found Ramona Fields standing in the entranceway. She was perhaps a year or two older than him, but bulkier—bulky enough to fill the entire doorway. Her apron was a collage of colors: juices from vegetables, blood from animals. Stringy black hair jutted every-which-way from the cap plastered to her scalp. One moment with her was enough to know why the scullions knew her as Mama Fields.

"What bid'ness got ye in the kitchens?" she demanded.

"Brandt and I leave for Albion. Seek we provisions to see ourselves fed."

The large woman thrust her fists to her waist, eyeing him crookedly. Though merely the manse's chef, Mama Fields took her job with more honor than any knight. Her scrupulous gaze unnerved Orrick. He wondered if she had somehow turned to stone when she barked, "No!" and slammed the door shut.

"You command little respect around your own manse," said Brandt.

Orrick smiled bitterly. "Her tune shall change when I become voivod. Come. We need naught from her."

"We don't?" asked Brandt.

"We'll find berries and game."

Foodless, they went to their horses. Not long thereafter, they again wandered the Homey Hills as they had two weeks past, this time heading east, returning to Castle Albicant. Orrick was sure Brandt was thinking it, but he was kind enough not to say that he longed for greener pastures, the grassy vales, and the River Milkmoon. Truthfully, Orrick longed for the same. The only way they differed, is Orrick thought Brandt also wished for a church.

"You're quiet, Orrick," said Brandt.

That is true. The last thing Orrick had said was that he would hunt sand-rats in the Salt Steppe. Upon his return, he carried a slack, round body, slung over his shoulders by a long, wormlike tail. He promised they would eat it when they made camp for the night. That was hours ago.

Orrick looked to the sky. "May I confide my feelings with you?"

"Of course, pan."

Orrick smiled. *At least Brandt becomes more accustomed to the correct honorific.* "I feel I've disappointed my parents. They've acted like this since we left Nib's cottage."

"Why do you think that is, pan?"

Orrick sighed. "Mayhap they worry, as parents are wont to do."

Brandt nodded. "Mayhap ..."

He seemed aloof, as though something also troubled him. Orrick bit. "Speak your troubles to me. It does no good to hide them."

Brandt nodded. "Well, I've seldom seen my parents since I began the academy seven years past. Now I travel further away from them. I miss them as much as your parents must have missed you."

Orrick turned his attention to the Homey Hills, how they rose and fell like waves in the sea. Brandt's words gave him much to think about.

"Pan Pallaton?"

"Yes?"

"I'll not be a squire forever. I'll be knighted, and I hope to father children and have squires as well." He gave Orrick a sheepish glance. "You don't suppose I could have *both*?"

"Child and squires? I don't see why not. Lord Father has—"

"No, I mean my child who is also my squire. Of course, I'd treat them as I would any other squire. 'Tis a happy thought of mine, if odd."

"'Tis a gesture fine, methinks, so long as the child learns his duties. Tourm needs strong knights, not suckling cravens so attached to their families. Perhaps when I've sired a son of my own, I'll make him my squire."

"Perhaps our children would enter the academy the same year," said Brandt, turning his smile to the heavens.

"Think you of Wąda?"

Brandt snorted. "You guessed. And ... you, of Sylvia?"

Orrick blushed. "These are good thoughts indeed." And together, the two watched the stars.

The following morning, their trek continued anew. Roaming hummocks flattened into verdant grasslands. River Milkmoon slushed and slurped in their ears long before it entered their sights, a promise of thirsts quenched. They reached the banks by nightfall and made camp, and traveled along with them the next morning, stopping to drink handfuls from the shallows

225

as their horses grazed.

From there went they north and crossed Butterbean Bridge, which connected the banks of Brzeg and Domoż. Once they crossed the river, they saw the plush, soft meadows, groves of trees, and gentle hillocks of Ostromys Vale. From there, the Domoż Highroad would take them to Albion City.

Eventually, the greenery of the highlands faded, replaced by a dusty platform stretching for miles. Great red buttes rose into the air, atop which roosted fat, crooked silhouettes of grim mar'tak. Those same dark birds picked at the remains of some animal long dead.

Past Pallaton Plateau—named for Aileron and rending the Fangaard continent in half—were the rounded tops of Starter Mountains. Mist flowed between their peaks, reminding Orrick of something unnatural in the star-spangled dusk. He knew the stories that goblins once existed within. But there were other tales that the mines were not the deepest parts.

Ahead of them spread Albion, the great white city. Ivory towers reached to the heavens like the pleading fingers of broken men. Thus, had it become a haven for such. Men without trades came there hoping to learn. Desperate families brought their children to Akademia Magia to test them for any innate abilities.

Orrick had seen it from the distance of the plateau many times. He even remembered the first time, when he was seven and new to the academy. He had returned several times since becoming Count Atrax's squire. Every time he saw it again, rising from the red plains, he was breathless. This time was no different, even though it was not that long since he last left.

Orrick and Brandt rode to Whitegate, the largest and foremost gate used for visitors. Two knights guarded it from the gatehouse, faces reflecting both valor and fatigue. A quick look at the ramparts showed fifteen crossbowmen kept silent watches as well.

"State your business," the left guard demanded. Orrick handed Armitage's letter. He looked at it and called to raise the gate.

King's Street was the centermost path that led from Whitegate to Albicant's gatehouse. Two grooms helped Orrick and Brandt from their mounts. One said, "We'll get your horses properly fed."

Brandt put a hand over his stomach.

"Are you well?" asked Orrick.

"I could do with a proper feeding, myself."

They ate the sand-rat when they made camp the first night, but they survived the second night only by picking from the passing orchards.

A steward appeared and led them to Whitehall. Seated at the lords' table were King Biel, great and blonde and unruly, and his wife, the prim and haughty Queen Jeneve. She smiled

227

politely when they entered, which did not surprise Orrick. She was a daughter of House Berwyn, therefore Brzegka. Behind them was Ladd pan Winchell, dressed in white plate armor and cloak, underlings in silver scales.

"I'll rouse the others," the steward announced. "Supper shortly arrives."

Orrick and Brandt approached the table and dropped to their knees. "Your Majesties," muttered Orrick. As a squire, Brandt kept silent.

"Orrick!" someone shouted from the back of the hall. Even with his head down and eyes averted, Orrick knew it was Armitage. He could also tell that he grinned from ear to ear.

"You received the letter, then," said Armitage, closer now. But Orrick still knelt, unsure of what to do. Armitage clicked his teeth. "Rise and answer your prince! Honestly, your piety is absurd!"

Orrick's face grew hot, although he was unsure why he felt embarrassed. Nonetheless, he stood and faced his friend, bowing at the waist. "I have—rather, I did."

As always, Armitage was impeccably dressed, this time in a doublet of white velvet that shimmered like steel. About his neck was a pendant that held a single amethyst, a droplet of purple against a snowfield.

Suddenly, he remembered who sat behind him and choked,

"*Your Highness.* I hope we're not come too late."

"On the contrary," said King Biel, "we're just ready to start."

Orrick turned back to him. "Your Majesties, I apologize for speaking out of turn, but I came not without concerns—rather, my Lord Father's concerns. How many shall come in this envoy, and who leads?"

Bushy eyebrows furrowed. King Biel peered down at Orrick from atop the risen platform. "Voivod Pallaton had these concerns? We'd no word when the hawk returned."

"Had I awaited your reply, my place in the host would have been forfeit," answer Orrick. "I left Newtown before the hawk was sent back. Mayhap Lord Father thought it of no import."

Orrick felt Armitage's hands over his shoulders, a sign that he would cajole this conversation in another direction—or at least attempt to. "My lad must be famished after such a ride. 'Tis three or four days from Newtown, you know."

"Worry not for us, Your Highness. We ate sand-rats from the Steppe and apples from Ostromys's orchards. Came we not to desperate measures."

Even as he said it, Orrick knew it was a lie. His very words betrayed him, and his rumbling stomach immediately after.

"Would that your lord father allowed us food from the—"

"*Silence*, Brandt," Orrick hissed. His squire averted his eyes. Orrick looked at the Prince, then the king and queen. "Mine apologies. 'Twas not the easiest of trips, but we managed."

Armitage smiled politely. "Mayhap I think differently than a knight, but I'd call eating sand-rats desperate. And it matters not now. Look."

From the doorway leading to the chambers came several figures, some of them familiar and others not. The steward led them passed the golden-veined tables, up to the dais. The King invited all parties to sit at the lords' table, knights and squires both.

To Orrick's surprise, Chelsea pani Wingate entered and sat. She smiled at him, and Orrick nodded politely. With her came a girl of dark skin and black ringlets. She spotted Brandt and smiled briefly. Brandt, on the other hand, looked shocked.

Wqda, must be, thought Orrick.

More servants came from the kitchens, bringing a simple yet enchanting meal. Six peafowls glistened in a bright red sauce of dragonbell peppers; bowls of mashed carrots and sliced yams saturated with butter and honey; salads of vinegary cabbage, beets, and fava beans. As a gift, the knights from Astoria had brought two casks filled with a beer called barleywine. Though it had the same viscosity and color as mud, Orrick thought it sweet as candied fruit when it entered his mouth, but it left an aftertaste as sour as bile.

When the meal commenced, King Biel stood. All eyes went to him as he spoke. "Members of the peerage and esteemed knights, my thanks for coming this most dire hour. On the morrow shall you start for Kendala to meet with King Archibald. It shall be no small task, but I bid you remember, 'tis your hands stay the oncoming war."

Armitage tensed in his seat beside Orrick. Next to Armitage sat his younger brother, Alabaster. He, too, wore a doublet of white, but not so fine. His warmer complex allowed for matte white instead of something as metallic as his brother's.

When the King sat again, Pan Winchell cleared his throat, drawing the attention to himself. He recited the names of all those that sat around the table, listing their ranking, station, domain. There were a few Orrick recognized, such as the giant knight Erasmus pan Altgeld, and Chelsea pani Wingate. She beamed at Orrick once more, but he did not meet her gaze. Most everyone else at the table hailed from Rhabdolia. The very thought made Orrick want to shrink away. Brandt, however, almost looked at home.

Winchell continued. "His Majesty, King Biel, has asked these three lord commanders to come with their finest soldiers. Pans Seabolt and Volker come with three knights and squires each, Pan Pallaton with his squire, and lastly, our ambassador, Count Draque, with five of his best archers and their squires."

As Pan Winchell named them, Orrick counted in his head. Twenty-seven in all, which seemed extensive for a peaceful mission. *And among them, the finest knights in the kingdom. Is there truly a need for that many?*

He silenced his thoughts when King Biel spoke again.

"This journey comes with great peril. Mayhap you've heard the rumors. I'll hide them no longer. King Archibald of Kendala seeks to reclaim West Nin, which Tourm had won two-hundred years past—and we know not why."

Oscar pan Draque, Count of Waldsee spoke next. He was Lord Commander of the White Falcons, a knightly order that employed only the finest archers in Tourm. Not yet thirty, his bright blond hair, straight back, strong chin, and crystal blue eyes made Orrick think of something more than a knight—a hero. Pinned upon his breast was a brooch in the shape of a diving falcon and made entirely of mother-of-pearl.

"We thought those feudal times behind us," he said. "Border wars things of the past, fodder for history books. Mayhap our nations aren't on the best of terms, but there's no need for these ... skirmishes."

"These 'skirmishes,' as you call them, are acts of war if ever I've seen one," growled Pan Seabolt, lord commander of Tourm's light cavalry, the Golden Bulls. A lion's mane of silver hair shrouded his head, a royal blue doublet stretched across his broad chest, too tight for the muscle underneath. He was the oldest at the table, old enough to remember Rhabdolia's Revolt, but not to have fought in it.

He leaned forward. A golden bull's-head badge shined on his

breast. "Kendalan soldiers have attempted—perhaps even managed—to sneak past Tourm's Gate and into Nin. One such *skirmish* saw three Black Dogs and five armsmen dead."

King Biel's face reddened. "Attempted or managed, which is it?"

Draque answered, "We believe the small few who've gotten through our defenses most likely made it through the Sea of Trees."

A collective gasp rose like a brandy thrown on flames. The Sea of Trees was a hinterland separating Kendala from Nin and was nothing but hundreds of miles of forest. To find one's way across such a strain of uncharted fathoms was unheard of.

"Worry not," Seabolt continued. "I only mentioned the worst of them."

"And their casualties?" asked Biel.

"Most were felled, according to Duke Belmont's accounts. Some escaped through the Sea of Trees but were not pursued."

"Why seek they Nin? To what end will it serve them?" asked Duff pan Volker. His smooth olive skin and shiny black hair oiled with the exotic spices of Mielle, a free city in the lower reaches of Rhabdolia and high seat of the Church of the Branch. To convey his position, a wolf's-head brooch, wrought of silver, gleamed upon his violet doublet.

Draque leaned forward. "We know not. They've Bugross Bay, which is larger than both Newport and Southport, so they're not without ports and oversea trades."

"Mayhap the Elder Mountains then?" Volker suggested, reclining. Orrick saw the pattern on his doublet, a cloth-of-silver wolf baying at a moon made of pearls. It looked expensive, but Volker seemed neither to notice nor care about the butter stains.

The Count waved his hand. "They've many mountains in Kendala, including the Ironfangs, rich with ore."

Volker smirked. "Then mayhap the famed lemon groves of Landon Valley?"

The laughter around the table was small and polite but ended tersely.

"*Why* is of no import," said Draque. "Kendala attacks without provocation; and received we no declaration of war."

"Quite right," said Biel. "Precisely why I've gathered you. Go to them in the name of peace. Above all else, Kendala is a country loyal to their throne. I'll keep no truths from you: this excursion may send you to your deaths."

Orrick drank from his tankard, feigning indifference, the same as every other soldier present. Next to him, both Brandt and Armitage tensed in their seats. Alabaster, on the other hand, seemed delighted.

"This is why Father chose you," said the younger prince. "Not only do you stand the bravest man in Tourm, but the fiercest as well."

"You've Pan Seabolt and me," said Erasmus. "The Silver Wolves have their cunning, the White Falcons their marks-manship, but why a knight so *green*?" Heir to the Rhabdolian Duchy or not—eight-feet-tall or not—Orrick wanted to smack the sneer from his lips.

Volker said, "Forgiveness should I speak out of turn, but I quite agree, Your Majesty. If I understand correctly, Orrick has not even been knighted a moon."

"Neither has my cousin," countered Armitage. "They were knighted together. Does she not come?"

"Pani Wingate's skills are uncanny, and she is under the di-rection of her lord commander," stated Volker. "Pan Pallaton comes as a green knight-errant."

Armitage put his hand on the table. "I'd take caution were I you, Duff."

Raised eyebrows, he asked, "And why is that, Your Highness?"

"Because—" chuckled the Prince "—Orrick is known for killing wolves."

Volker shifted his guileful gaze to Orrick's, who felt he had no other choice but to smile.

"'Tis scimitigers I wish not to meet again," Orrick said meekly.

"Are you skilled with the spear, lad?"

Orrick turned his attention to Seabolt. "Aye, pan."

"And the bow and arrow?"

Orrick wondered where this was leading. "Not enough to impress the White Falcons, pan."

Seabolt frowned. "That's a no. How are you on horseback?"

"Raise not his hopes, Lord Commander!" cried Altgeld. "He may think you recruit him—"

"Shut up, Altgeld!" He looked back at Orrick. "Horseback, lad. How are you with it?"

"Well enough—"

"Well enough?" spat Armitage. "He rides the wind as though Wróżka carries him!"

Orrick swallowed hard, trying not to blush.

Seabolt appeared not to notice. "What of the blade?"

"He's better with the sword than all else," said Armitage.

"'Tis how he felled the jadwilki, my lords," said Brandt. Everyone at the table turned their attention to him. Shamefaced, he averted his eyes.

"Remember your place, Brandt, and speak not out of turn," Orrick reprimanded. Then he addressed the table. "I'm a knight green, I won't deny. Sooth, I feel privileged, even out of place, sitting amongst men as you. So, ask I, take me to learn. I'll want not for much food, nor ask you to lay your lives down for mine. Put me with the squires if you must. All I ask—humbly, of course—is that I have my chance."

Volker fell quiet. So did Altgeld, though he frowned. Seabolt, on the other hand, cracked a sagacious grin.

King Biel took advantage of the silence. "I trust we'll have no more arguments regarding my selected knights. Now if I may, I'd prefer to speak about the future."

"Yes, Your Majesty," the table sounded. Orrick and Brandt tried to stifle their smiles, but Armitage did nothing to hide his.

"Good, then. I've sent a whitetail hawk to Czerny Wideleç, the capital of Kendala. Archibald knows an envoy comes, and that means it no harm."

"This is confirmed?" asked Draque.

"It is. As for the course of action, you'll ride south in a group. Belmont knows you come and will share his hall with you for the night."

237

"Newport?" asked Draque. "Wouldn't Southport be quicker?"

"Belmont shall have testimony for you, Draque. From Newport you'll ride for Durwyn's Pass and remain in Tourm's Gate. Slake there your thirsts and mayhap even find another bed. Three miles westward is Kendala's Gate. The guards shall let you through, though I doubt you'll find the same hospitality."

"I doubt we'll find *any* hospitality," muttered Volker.

"Pray tell," said Draque, "is that why we use Durwyn's Pass? Were we unable to secure safe passage into Bugross?"

King Biel frowned. "Aye, 'tis."

"A royal envoy that must take the long way," said Draque. "Such a pity ..."

"It matters not. After that, you'll find yourselves in Kendala's vast countryside. Camping makes more sense than finding inns or castles. You'll have a sennight's march from Kendala's Gate to Czerny Wideleç. There shall you meet Archibald."

"He shan't be happy with us for slaughtering his men," said Volker. "Nor his soldiers for the deaths of their brothers."

"Alas, we shan't find surcease should this turn to be an ambush," said Seabolt.

"Which is why you go with such a large party," said Biel. "Kendalan loyalty be damned, one Tourmian knight is worth ten of theirs."

"Is this why you've requested fifteen knights and their squires?" asked Orrick.

King Biel nodded.

"Forgive my saying so, Your Majesty," said Volker, pausing to dab red sauce from his lips, "but I doubt we'll meet only three hundred soldiers. Our deaths seem more and more likely."

Eyes full of worry, King Biel looked at each commander. "I cannot know what that old fool thinks. Trying has only disrupted my sleep. All I can do is pray for your safe and swift return. Should Wróżka ever have existed, she'll hear and answer."

Orrick found himself praying for the same thing. He doubted not that Brandt felt the same, nor anyone else for that matter. He had wanted something more exciting than Newtown, adventure in faraway lands. It seemed he would get that, with promises of certain doom. He would need to fight, and that reminded him of the alleyway in Newport and the Black Horseman tavern in Albion. Fighting meant death, and after pleading with the military leaders, he expected no help.

So worried, Orrick barely touched the sunberry tartlet presented for dessert. With it, the servants also brought a flute of Flavès white, but his head and stomach reeled from the barleywine. Thinking back to the white whiskey, he only sipped from the flute once out of politeness, unable to stomach more. He wished for sleep.

The meal finished. Servants led the guests from Whitehall to their quarters. Albicant was large enough that each knight and squire had rooms of his or her own. Orrick found his spacious enough for a single person staying a single night: No pictures upon the drab walls, no armoire or closets for clothes, nothing remotely ornate besides. The room did have a bed, and a nightstand on which the servants set a pewter pitcher and glass should Orrick feel thirsty. In one corner stood a mannequin to hang his armor on. In another, a brazier unlit.

At the steward's leave, Orrick changed into his bedclothes. As he pulled the blankets from the small bed, there came a knock on his door. Tired and hoping to find solace from his worries, he answered not. Louder knocking followed. Orrick swore under his breath and bade the visitor enter.

"You seemed ill," said Armitage, slipping inside. "Thought I to check on you."

He still wore his evening attire. The amethyst at his chest gleamed in the wan candlelight.

"The barleywine was stronger than I like," Orrick answered. That was half the truth. The bile-like aftertaste lingered in the back of his throat even now, burning as though he had vomited. He feared he yet might.

Armitage eyed him pointedly. "'Tis not meet to lie to your prince."

Orrick sighed. "No, 'tis not. Fear I the errand."

"I'll not speak false, my lad. I fear it as well."

"You do?"

Armitage sat on the edge of the bed, depressing the mattress under his slight frame. He looked to heave a sigh, but instead said, "Would that I might take up the sword! Alas, my place is in court. Besides, Alabaster is the one skilled with weapons, but Father would never bid him go. Good, because I prefer him to stay. I prefer you to stay too."

"Swore I knightly oaths before king and court," said Orrick. "My solemn promise is to defend Tourm. I must go."

"This could be war!" Armitage croaked, eyes fearful. "There have been skirmishes here and there, but never *war*. I'd thought—hoped—Fangaard was behind all that."

"True, Tourm has seen fifty years of peace. But calms seldom last. 'Tis why we still have knights, armsmen, and smithies."

"You misunderstand! They say old Archibald is *tetched*. They say he counts himself amongst the ancient conquerors that forged Kendala into the kingdom it is today."

Orrick folded his arms. "Who are *they*, precisely?"

Armitage waggled his fingers dismissively. "It matters not *who*. What matters is the *subject*. Tourm and Kendala are

241

neighbors—"

"We're separated by the Ironfangs and Sea of Trees."

"Fine! True! I acquiesce! Leagues of hinterland stand between them and us, but we *are* neighbors nonetheless."

Orrick thought back to rogues in the Black Horseman, the words he and Armitage had shared at Lamplighter Inn before he graduated, the conversation overheard in the Plaintive Hound, and the royal writ Armitage had sent him.

It all began to make sense.

"You ... brought me here not to send me away. You knew of this! You—"

"I brought you here that we might escape together," he admitted. "Let us flee in the night! I know a secret way out of the castle! We may not go horsed, but we could be on our way—"

"To where?" snapped Orrick. His expression softened. He had not meant to be harsh, but the Prince ...

"Pinberry," answered Armitage. "We'll find a nice chalet on the Crèmeal mountainside, or perhaps a small house in Dactidé. You prefer the country, I know, and I, the city—"

"*No.*"

The Prince stopped. Good. Armitage's words cycled through Orrick's head. *It is unmeet to be angry with your prince. But acts he the fool, speaking of fleeing his kingdom and his responsibilities.*

"All knights have a duty to uphold the realm. But the king, which one day you'll become, must also adhere to the realm's interests. Please understand, we go *preventing* war. If one day it comes, we'll be both ready."

Armitage sighed heavily. His shoulders, usually back and narrow with proper posture, slumped forward as his eyes remained downcast. Orrick wished he had more comforting words, wished he could promise safety. He thought Armitage might enjoy a glass of wine at that moment, as well. Alas, he could offer none of those things.

"You are ... good in your beliefs. A good king stands by his people through peace and war."

"Worry not." Orrick forced a smile and placed his hand on Armitage's back, callouses poking the fine velvet. "A knight stands by his realm and his king. Be brave, Armitage. Crisis—not calmness—is when people watch their leaders most."

"Would that you were in my guard," he said, hoisting himself from Orrick's bed. "'Tis not mine own men that trouble me, but oft—"

"I know."

"You do, eh?" He offered a wan smile. "Best that you rest, my lad. You're required in the gatehouse at dawn." Then he left the guestroom, much to Orrick's relief.

Despite his worry, Orrick slept throughout the night, waking only once with a throat so dry it felt as though his mouth was stuffed with linen. *Damn the barleywine*, he thought, drinking large gulps of water straight from the pitcher.

Morning came with swift rapping upon Orrick's door, followed by the immediate entrance of Brandt, Tartus, Callows, and Grimm, each flanking Armitage himself.

"Rise and shine, my faithful knight!" bellowed the Prince.

Orrick woke with a start, eyes darting about the room. For a small moment, he was certain that Kendala had come to him. Seeing it was only his friend, he relaxed.

"You seem in better spirits."

"Indeed, and I've you to thank for that! And you?"

In truth, Orrick felt groggy. The dry mouth lingered despite draining an entire pitcher. "Well," he lied.

"Well, well is well!" said Armitage. He looked sideways at the guards. They backed out of earshot. "My thanks," Armitage whispered. "You returned me to my senses."

"Did you truly think I'd flee with you?"

Armitage chuckled. "I—ah—it was worth an attempt, at least. As you may know, I've taken rather hard to the bottle—well, more like the cellar, wouldn't you say?"

He smiled at Orrick, who raised his eyebrows.

"No," Armitage said, dejected. "No, I suppose you wouldn't say so—well, you *might,* were it not for the whole ... *treason* ... thing ..."

Orrick still said nothing, and Armitage continued without a care. "Anyway, 'tis unmeet for a king or prince to carry himself in such a manner. You've mine apologies as well as my thanks."

Orrick smiled. "Glad to hear we've the sensible Armitage returned. Now, I dislike offending His Majesty's envoy, so—"

"Ah," Armitage gasped and exited. Brandt entered and shut the door behind him. Orrick stripped from his bedclothes and donned his armor. Brandt affixed his baldric, which contained the iron longsword on his left side, a dagger at his left thigh, and a dirk behind his back.

This is how noblemen ought to dress, he thought briefly before opening the door. Armitage, along with his sworn guardsmen, waited outside his chambers.

"Return to me, will you? I—*Tourm* needs kind, strong knights that befriend princes and defend peasants. Tourm needs knights like you."

245

"I know not what waits beyond our borders, but I'll do my utmost for Tourm's safety."

Orrick and Brandt bowed respectfully. Armitage bowed in turn and led his knights away.

Orrick led Brand to the gatehouse's portcullis. Count Draque awaited them, wearing silver armor and a milk-white cloak. Mounted and prepared, as well, were the lord commanders: Duff pan Volker in bronze plate mail and violet surcoat, and Elton pan Seabolt in golden plate mail and white surcoat. A bucking gold-cloth bull emblazoned its front. House Seabolt's sigil—a bolt of forked, blue lightning striking a green sea—was on the back.

Eramus pan Altgeld stood in line with the other Golden Bulls. Heads taller than all the others, he still wore the huge plate mail. At his left side was an arming sword, but he leaned against a halberd of frightening size. Orrick saw the light cavalrymen did not wear plates like Altgeld and Seabolt. Instead, they wore armor made of red leather toughened to look like stone. Over the strange armor, they wore plain surcoats of white linen, golden bull's-head brooches upon their breasts.

Next to them, the White Falcons dressed in white linen tunics over leather armor, milk-colored capelets to match their lord commander. Chelsea lined with them.

Count Draque eyed Orrick contemptuously. "Fall in line."

"Honestly, what're we to do with a knight so green?" asked

Volker. "He cannot fall in line because he hasn't a proper commander."

"I'm my own commander," Orrick countered, "and here we stand."

Seabolt smiled, seeming to like that response.

Orrick stood at the end, next to the Golden Bulls with their strange armor. He felt more comfortable at that end than the opposite, which contained the Silver Wolves.

Draque cleared his throat. "The lads in the stables will soon bring our horses. We've an arduous journey ahead and our rations shan't hold the length. Find we little solace but for the Seakeep and Tourm's Gate. Until then, we must need live off the land. When we cross the Twin Gates—"

"That's where the trouble begins," said Seabolt, nodding wisely.

"Correct, Elton. As His Majesty mentioned last night, we'll find no hospitality beyond Tourm's Gate. Make we camp in the grasslands and rice paddies of the Wideleç province, never to leave the enemy's hands. No doubt they shall turn us away from their towers and subject us to the poorest of inns and alehouses. We'll keep watches as we sleep. 'Twill only be the lord commanders that counsel with Archibald, and 'twill be only I that speaks lest otherwise questioned. A handful of knights and their squires shall remain as guards for the treaty. All others shall remain ready to flee. Am I understood?"

247

Shouts of "Aye, Lord Commander!" and "Yes, my lord!"

Grooms soon came with the men's horses—all but Seabolt, who went to obtain his himself: a destrier of notable size, all black except stark white shins, and eyes red as fire. Many of the other knights rode chargers draped in coats of their order and their houses' sigils. Even Altgeld rode a great beast of a warhorse, crème-colored, purple-eyed, and bred large enough to hold his bulk. Orrick nearly felt ashamed when silver-eyed Cień, much smaller and less fearsome, trotted up to him, led by a stable boy.

Brandt aided Orrick onto his horse and then climbed upon his own brown sumpter. Orrick watched the other knights. Most knights needed the aid of a squire to mount their horses, but Altgeld required two. The rest of the Golden Bulls climbed atop their drákoń coursers without any assistance.

"What do you make of that?" Orrick asked Brandt, who only stared, mouth agape.

All mounted, the portcullis opened, and they followed Count Draque into Albion's streets and beyond.

XIII: On The Road To Nin

Most of the host's time was spent on horseback. The dusty plains set before Albion City led to a brown, pebbly road. Ostromys Vale sprawled out before them, named for the House which reigned before Pardwy.

The rations they took with them from Castle Albicant were gone by the third day, as they passed Butterbean Bridge. They had replenished their stores with apples from Ianth's Orchards, their wineskins from the Flavès Vineyards.

On the fourth night, the procession made camp upon the Domoż Highroad. Orrick and Brandt sat near a small campfire. Each ate an apple, listening to the indistinct chatter from the soldiers nearby. The orders all sat in separate groups, receiving instructions from their lord commanders. Orrick and Brandt were of their own order and thus sat alone.

As Orrick threw his apple core behind him, a shadow appeared over the flames. He looked up, unsurprised to see Chelsea smiling down at him. He had noticed her glances as they traveled, and when they sat around the fires at night. She would always turn her head away, smile at the conversation, but Orrick knew she stared. *Was she going to continue staring despite her engagement?* he wondered.

Flatly he asked, "Yes?"

"Spoke I with Pan Malloy," she said, uncertain of herself.

"Another White Falcon?"

"Aye, and he says he could see Turnip Marsh before sunset. We should arrive at the border by noon tomorrow."

Orrick was jealous of the archers' keen eyesight. He said nothing, only stared at her, mouth clenched. He saw the way the shadows played with her face, how the firelight made her thick curly hair shine like molten gold. She looked pretty, skin pale and clear, eyes as green as the sea. Brandt thought so too, his mouth gaped. Or perhaps he was just not used to a knight orderly speaking with them. How foolish, for Orrick then realized Wąda Tuttle stood behind her, nervously shuffling.

Despite his feelings, all Orrick said was, "You've mentioned this to Count Draque?"

"We have. And now—"

"You mention it to me. Why?"

Chelsea looked taken aback. He maintained evenness in his tone, but she was unprepared for that question. Seconds passed and, when no utterance came, she turned and went back to her campfire.

Orrick remembered her as the gangly girl keen with any weapon that required aiming, but so poor with the sword. For a moment, he felt like they were together again that rainy morning they separated, remembered her pink lips puckered—

"Pan Pallaton!"

One of the leather-mailed Golden Bulls, Kevin pan Scritchfield, offered a curt bow. "Lord Commander Seabolt requests your presence." Orrick looked to Brandt, but the knight said, "*Your* presence."

Orrick stood and followed him, leaving Brandt alone. The knights of the Golden Bull sat around the roaring fire. Sounds of the oncoming night filled Orrick's ears. River Milkmoon babbled like an almsman, crickets tuned their fiddles in the tall grass, birds in nearby trees rattled like lovers.

"Have a seat," said Seabolt.

Orrick took the seat upon a log across from him, next to the giant Altgeld.

Seabolt smiled. "We're discussing war, lad. Do you know what Virgil xu Lac likened war to?"

Orrick blinked, surprised, and not only because he was being questioned about the famed poet, but because it was an odd request after days of being ignored. Still, it would not do keeping a commander waiting, so he thought about the question.

Virgil xu Lac was a soldier during the goblin wars. He was the youngest son of a lake lord and was never its heir. During a feudal battle, he was captured and, whilst imprisoned, turned to writing poetry, mainly his philosophies on war. After his execution, his poetry garnered many prints and many more quotes. Akademia Palatæ taught his writings, namely his wartime pieces, *Wolves of War*.

With that in mind, Orrick answered, "Wolves, pan."

Seabolt raised his eyebrows, hazel eyes dancing in the firelight. "Indeed, he did. Fought he in the goblin wars, most likely battled jadwilki. Now, what did he liken to rabbits?"

Despite having been taught many of his works, Orrick remembered not. He guessed, "Peasants? Or knights, perhaps ... soldiers?"

"Life," Seabolt corrected. He took another swig of wine. A golden rivulet trailed its way down his white-stubble chin. "The wolves of war come hungry. Life is like a rabbit, small, defenseless, cunning, apt to flee. Peasants, soldiers, clergy, royalty, all live, and thus all are ravaged. Fire destroys lives, homes, forests. Blades rend fathers from their children ..."

"Forgiveness, Lord Commander, but what has this to do with aught?" asked Altgeld. He looked neither frightened nor interested by Seabolt's words.

"Virgil xu Lac, a poet, fought many battles and helped shape Tourm into this mighty nation. Forever shall there be wolves, just as there shall forever be war." Seabolt drew again from the wineskin, then tied it off. "That's enough of that," he said, before looking Orrick in the eyes. "Have you ever *read* Virgil xu Lac?"

"Wolves of War, pan," Orrick answered, afraid this hoary man could set his words afire in his mouth if he were displeased with the answer. "I'll admit I've not retained it."

Seabolt grunted, aiming a fat, crooked thumb at the Golden Bulls around the campfire. "Neither have they. Funny thing is, Virgil's origin is unclear. Some say he was Rhabdolian—a lake lord's second son that would never inherit. Others say he was from Oldtown, which stood before Newtown."

"Yes, pan. Oldtown stood in the north, near the Homey Hills. Newtown was built where the Hills meet the Steppe."

"Newtown again?" asked Altgeld, glowering. "When will the prestigious nation of Tourm be rid of that awful place?"

"Shut it, Altgeld!" Seabolt snapped. He looked back at Orrick, eyes crinkling with kindness. "At least you know your history. I'll bet your lord father has some of his books. Ask him; you shan't be disappointed. Neither would he, and nor would I."

Orrick was unsure what to say, so he stood to leave.

Seabolt stopped him with a hand. "You like cavalry?"

Taken aback, Orrick sputtered, "I—"

"I've seen you ride. Sit back down, lad."

Orrick did, confused but curious. "Something wrong, pan?"

"Wear you long your horse's stirrups." Seabolt grinned as he had in Whitehall, sagaciously yet mischievously. "Atrax wouldn't've taught you that, lad."

"No, 'twas something I did on my own. Less swith ride I, but with better control, as if mine horse and I are one."

"Aye," grunted Seabolt, "same as the Golden Bulls and Golden Dragons."

At the mention of Seabolt's own order, Orrick mustered the courage to ask about the Golden Bull's strange armor. Their mobile leather mails held Orrick's attention for days. Now was his opportunity to learn more.

"Riding armor, 'tis called." He snorted. "More like *fleeing* armor."

"What mean you, pan?"

Instead of answering, Seabolt barked, "Dowd, demonstrate

riding armor's flexibility!"

Dowd stood with feet spread, knees bent, and arms outheld. "Riding armor is made of two layers of toughened leather with steel plates sewn between them," he explained. "The joints are made in a way that movement is likened to a simple tunic, and yet looks it like plate armor. Overall 'tis light, durable, and resistant to strong winds."

Dowd put his arms to his side and bent his knees; up and down and up again. He flexed his elbows in and out, moved his arms up and down at the shoulders, bent his waist, leaned far on either leg, dropped to one knee, leaped up, turned his neck all without a hitch, flaw, or hindrance. Orrick smiled, impressed.

"Down with you, Dowd! Stop showing off!" Dowd bowed to Orrick, then to his lord commander before taking his seat. "Riding armor was specifically designed for light cavalry."

"But you and Altgeld wear it not."

"We're *heavy* cavalry," answered Altgeld.

"But you ride not with the Golden Dragons?"

"I once did, but the Golden Bulls needed a lord commander, and I refused to change my ways," said Seabolt.

Orrick nodded. "The men are able to mount their horses without the aid of their squires. How are they in combat?"

"We've used them in the yard with swords blunted, but never in combat true."

"Naught feels as good as true steel plate," Altgeld interrupted. "The others may keep and damn their mobility. I am well protected in a shell of metal. But at least they're not in rusted hauberk."

Orrick folded his arms over his chest, ashamed by his chainmail shirt. He was aware fully that his equipment was embarrassing compared to Seabolt's scalemail, Altgeld's plates, and the riding armor worn by Dowd and Scritchfield.

"I'd like riding armor of my own," he answered. "'Twould certainly offer better protection than these steel rings."

Seabolt looked Orrick up and down, scrutinizing him as he stroked his stubbly chin. "Perhaps one day you shall."

Whether by luck or skill, Malloy the White Falcon had presumed correctly. They reached Turnip Marsh by noon the next day. The forested hinterland was made dark by the River Black. Mostly uncharted, it separated Domoż and Brzeg from Nin to the south.

Everyone rode down the stony path in a single line, surrounded by birches, cottonwoods, basswoods, maples, and tulip trees. The path soon declined into a swamp. Hooves sloshed through thickets and wetlands. Willows dipped their tendrils into murky waters. Islands of soft ground patched with wild onion breached the surface.

The further they wandered, the wilder the undergrowth became. Waters ran thicker and darker than the night. Steam rose. Tall reeds yellow as saffron shot from the inky pool and climbed over the party's heads. Grey-and-black bubbles floated in the dead marshes. *There is something beautiful about this place*, Orrick thought, *secluded and harsh though it may be.*

Seabolt ordered Scritchfield to bring him one of the black bubbles on the end of his pike. The Golden Bull stabbed one and pulled it to him.

"Marsh turnips," Seabolt said with a lopsided grin, "which only grow in Turnip Marsh. Ever see one, Lord Pallaton?"

Orrick wanted to spit at the title but remained polite. Large and flaccid, the marsh turnip reminded him a great deal of a cow's liver. "No, pan, I've not."

Seabolt pulled the black bubble from the spear and weighed it in his hands. Initially round and puffy, pulling it from its skewer caused it to deflate. Blacker than death, the oil inside spilled from the gash and washed over Seabolt's gauntlet.

Distrusting, Orrick eyed the marsh turnip. "It looks a turnip not at all."

"None know if they're vegetable, tuber, or fungus. Some even call them fruit. They're edible, you know, though they offer a foul taste eaten raw, and only slightly better cooked. Surviving off them, Brzeg once held out against a Ninnish siege."

"Durnas Midway," Orrick said, awed. Seabolt hailed from Rhabdolia. Unable to help himself, Orrick asked, "You know Brzeg history?"

"We are all of Tourm," Seabolt answered. "Prejudice against your fellow countryman offers little value in wartime."

Orrick nodded, Brandt smiled, and Draque rode to them and examined the marsh turnip.

"These are what we'll eat tonight," their leader decided. "White is Tourm's color. 'Tis the name of our high seat, our castle, and towers, the knights that guard it, even our steel—yet there would be no Tourm were it not for these black morsels."

"Why suffer ourselves to eat these when we've packs of apples and wine?" complained Dowd.

"Food comes scarcer in Landon Valley, and we have a long way yet until Newport," said Draque. "Our stores will keep until we're gone from these forsaken fenlands."

Not wanting to get off their horses, Dowd and Scritchfield used their pikes to stab through the marsh turnips. Without spare bags, they carried the marsh turnips skewered upon their spears' shafts. Oil leaked from the gashes as they traveled. When Scritchfield dropped his spear into the black water with a *splash*, he sent his squire into the muck to fetch it whilst the other knights—excluding Orrick and Seabolt—laughed.

"You seem not to find that funny," Seabolt whispered.

"Nor do you," he replied.

Spear and marsh turnips collected, the party continued riding into the night. Darkness devoured the clouds. Here, away from any lights, the sky looked as though some celestial scribe had spilled his ink over the world. The weary soldiers ceased their gossips and japes until there was no sound but horses' hooves sloshing through water thick with oil.

But the marshlands lasted not forever. A collective sigh of relief went up when Draque's charger stomped upon semisolid earth. To their dismay, the soil was still too moist to make camp. Drier, harder soil came an hour later.

Several campfires lined the glade. White Falcons sat with Count Draque, Silver Wolves with Duff pan Volker, and lastly, Golden Bulls flanked Seabolt. With neither a commanding officer nor subordinate soldiers, Orrick and Brandt again sat alone—until Seabolt bade them both sit with him.

The squires took out the pots they kept packed onto their sumpter horses and used the leftover bacon grease to fry the marsh turnips, sizzling, snapping, spattering black oil as they cooked. As before, the marsh turnips deflated, black slime oozing from the wounds.

What Orrick and Brandt finally received were two shriveled discs the color of burnt bacon and the texture of over-boiled mushrooms. Orrick bit into his marsh turnip and chewed.

Rubbery and slick, it reminded him even more of undercooked liver. The only way he could describe the taste was burnt water.

Altgeld and Scritchfield hemmed and hawed. Seabolt, however, ate somberly. The other commanders around the other campfires did the same, biting and chewing without a word of complaint. On the other hand, knights and squires frowned and spat, gagged, and grumbled, much like those within the Order of the Golden Bull.

"How did people eat these?" carped Dowd.

"'Twas a siege!" Seabolt exclaimed, drawing all attention to him. "You know what happens during a siege?"

Around the campfire, knights and squires shook their heads.

"Virgil xu Lac wrote, 'War is a wolf whose teeth are swords and whose mouth is death.' *That's* what happens. Death surrounds you on all sides: enemies, traitors, nature, hunger, thirst, rot, disease! Farmers cannot grow food, folwarks are burned by scouting parties, livestock slaughtered or stolen! There was naught else to eat but these!" He cocked his head in Orrick's direction. "What do *you* think of them, knighted errand boy? The marsh turnips, I mean?"

Orrick tried to show no embarrassment or anger to the slight. Instead, he answered, "Doubtless, these are the strangest plants I've tasted. I mind them not. Though lacking crunch, I liken their flavor to water chestnuts."

"There's a good lad," Seabolt said, smiling. "In battle, being fickle gets you killed." He aimed his thumb to his knights, the same as he did the previous even. "You know, you make *them* look green, but I'd expect no less from a Pallaton."

Orrick smiled at the compliment.

The first time he ever saw the lord commander was during the feast. Quiet and composed, he spoke with hoary wisdom, as though he were a grandfather. Since then, he had divulged more of himself, and Orrick saw the hardened scars beneath his kind wrinkles.

Daybreak saw them begin their descent into Landon Valley. Mountains laden with forests of green pines climbed high on either side of them. The wide and mighty River Lachlan cut across the valley right down the middle. It would lead them to Nin Bay, where they would find a haven in Newport. The knights camped once more in a grove near the river. Szalet, a mountainside village east of the Lachlan, became more visible by moonrise. Stone-colored houses mingled with the trees, an illusion of camouflage. The illusion vanished when, at night, the townspeople lit their hearths. Windows gleamed through thick pines even from a distance.

"Why did we not just go there for the night?" asked Dowd.

"Far too displaced," Seabolt answered. They would have to climb the cliffs and navigate the forests before reaching that village. Even though they camped on the eastern banks of the Lachlan, the glowing windows were miles out of the way. However, the next night, they did find solace in Statek, Chelsea's hometown. Called the Village of Vessels, it had been constructed from the remains of riverboats ruined in the Lachlan. Chelsea, Wąda, Count Draque, and the other White Falcons stayed with Chelsea's family.

Other knights sought shelter in inns, and others yet in Statek's single, crumbling church. Brandt wished to sleep there, and Orrick acquiesced.

"The church?" laughed Altgeld, heading to the inn. "They'll turn you away for a savage!"

Orrick grumbled, but Brandt said, "They won't." But he sounded uncertain. "At least, I *think* they won't—not if it's a Ninnish church."

The outside was the same as every other building, built from boats. Inside, however, Orrick saw high arched rafters and stained glass much the same as Limehouse's shrine. However, instead of depicting the overgods, the stained glass was simply beautifully colored. In between each window, a small picture showed parts of Sibilia's life—from her talking at birth, the river, teaching her disciples and the clerics twelve.

Excited, Brandt led Orrick to the alter, behind which stood the statue of a crooked tree with twelve crooked branches. Over this display, a circular window of yellow glass, so that even the moonlight shined golden upon it.

"The tree is Sibilia," Brandt explained, "and the twelve

branches are the overgods. And the twelve roots—" he pointed to them, which Orrick missed at first "—are her clerics twelve."

Orrick folded his arms. "I admit, I knew not the church was so steeped in tradition. Never have I been inside a House of the Branch."

"The same with me and Brzeg," said Brandt. "Knew I 'twas different, but never did I think how wondrous it might be."

"Brzeg and Rhabdolia are different, but similar."

"As your lord father said, Brzeg and Rhabdolia need not be friends but allies. But when my squiring is done, I'd like for us to be friends."

"You needn't worry about that," said Orrick, smiling. "I'll agree that Sibilia played a role important during the Days of Devils. But I shan't, at the tree, kneel and pray."

Brandt looked dismayed, then thoughtful. Orrick wondered how he may next rebuff his squire's attempts to convert him. Instead, Brandt asked, "Where comes Brzeg's beliefs?"

"Aileron was elf-friend. His companion was Elsu Jolon Ellard, a wood elf. But methinks their beliefs coincided—not that he gained from the elves." Orrick shook his head. "Truly, know I not. I must needs ask Lord Father."

"Is it not possible Aileron was a disciple of Sibilia, a knight arborescent?"

"Methinks not, for Aileron felled goblins for coin."

"Then ... how came he to fell undergods?"

Orrick smiled. "From what I remember, one got in his way."

Brandt looked awed.

"Mayhap 'twas luck, mayhap skill, but certainly 'twasn't because of devotion to the Branch. Now let us sleep; we must need rise early if we're to make Newport by evenfall."

The abbess, middle-aged and shaved bald, offered only hard pews to lay upon and a few sackcloth blankets. Orrick used his rucksack for a pillow but rejected the blanket so it might be given to another sleeper.

They reached Nin's Newport by the next evenfall. The bay's green and foamy waters stretched out to them like a deep dragon's maw. Behind buildings of black brick and salt-tinged wood were masts as far as the eye could see, sails furled and hulls rocking in the waves.

Meeting them at the gates was a gaunt man with creased skin and oil-black hair pulled into a tight tail. His lamellar was enameled navy blue, over which he wore a cloak made entirely of mar'tak feathers. Knights wearing grey scalemail and thick cloaks of black leather surrounded him, the onyx brooches on their breasts carved to look like black hounds.

Draque dismounted and gripped his wrist. "Well met, Duke Belmont."

"Welcome, Draque," growled the Duke. "I trust Newport finds y' well."

"Rode we a long way, my friend. May we trouble you for the use of your hall?"

"I thought he knew we were coming?" whispered Brandt.

Orrick shushed him. Perhaps Brandt forgot that counts must relate to dukes with courtesy. House Belmont would see the throne before House Draque, after all.

"Ye may spend the night, as per our agreement," said Belmont, voice thick with the salty accent of Nin. "The cooks prepare the meal now. Barrels o' cider be brought up from the cellars."

Belmont and his protectors led them to the edge of the bay, past the wooden wharves to a platform of stone. The Seakeep loomed a half-mile out to sea, a blazing beacon on the highest tier. A bridge of matching stone connected Seakeep to the rest of Nin.

The led their horses to its stables on the mainland, then crossed the stony bridge on foot. Its sides, much like Orrick suspected of the castle's, were plagued with salt, seaweed, barnacles. Every now and again a great wind would stir the green waters and spray Orrick's face, salting his tongue and stinging his eyes. He looked back and saw Brandt's face spritzed with droplets, his eyes wide with wonder.

"Impressive, is it not?"

Brandt smiled wearily. "I'm glad the bridge is sturdy."

Inside the Seakeep, stone walls were the same gray as those on the outside. The floor was tiled the same color as seaweed. A carpet of black velvet ran from the entrance hall, up a staircase in the foyer, and then split in twain to carpet the second level. Stone-faced, black cloaked knights guarded entrances.

The dukes of Nin were called the Lords of Valerav Sea, River Lachlan's estuary. Orrick could see why, for not only did Belmont command the Order of the Black Dogs, Tourm's knights specializing in maritime combat, but everything within the castle reminded Orrick of a murky death: newel posts fashioned like spiraling mollusk shells, narwhal tusks framed portholes, and wainscoting depicted fish swimming in jagged lines.

The oil paintings upon the walls portrayed great warships colliding with each other as the men onboard struggled for life. The boneless fingers of giant krakens reached from the sea to pull down whaling ships as great cliffs white with salt dropped into a roiling unknown of green foam. Lastly, laden on the Seakeep's walls were banners portraying House Belmont's sigil: a dark green deep dragon, its tail rising and falling from a blue sea like three pitted hills.

Though footed on solid ground, Orrick felt seasick. Or perhaps the bridge still affected him. In either case, he dared not speak a word of it for the risk of insulting their host.

At last, the party reached the great hall which was large enough to hold twenty times their number. Orrick could still hear the sea rolling outside. The knights and squires sat at the long tables, everyone glad to be under a roof of wood and stone. Draque, Seabolt, Volker, and Belmont all sat at the lords' table at the end of the hall. Altgeld joined them and they did not complain. Orrick wondered if he could expect the same lax treatment, but knew that if he went up, Brandt would stay behind. He stole a look at his squire, who sat next to him still excited despite the long journey through the vale, lowlands, forest, fen, and valley.

No, he decided. *This is best.*

The feast itself consisted of roasted seabird, hot lamprey pies, steamy and creamy crab-claw pies, butter-drenched snails, raw oysters, salads of blueberries, fireberries, and sunberries, and charred frogs' legs. It was all extraordinarily rich, and the sea-salt cider did nothing to wash it down. Indeed, the saltiest apple cider Orrick had ever tasted, he had it oft with Count Atrax. "The apples are fermented in brine," he told Brandt, who wrinkled his nose.

Laughter rang out from the tables. No one guessed—but many feared—that after their solace in the Seakeep ended, laughter would become rarer and more precious than gold.

267

XIV: The Twin Gates

Westward they rode, following nin's shores. The path had become pebbly with great cliffs rising to northward. Southward bluffs tumbled into the Valerav Sea. Durwyn's Pass, a narrow stretch of bedrock between Nin and Kendala, overlooked a sheer two-hundred-foot drop. Rain buffeted them as they crossed, doing little for their spirits.

The twenty-seven travelers stayed the course, winding with the path, taking care not to look over the side of the cliff to the churning sea below. Orrick did once and immediately regretted it. Thereafter, he could feel every stone Cień stepped on, every shudder from the breeze. His face remained passive, but he squeezed the reigns as tight as he could, praying his rouncey would not slip on the wet rocks and send them both tumbling over.

Ahead, a stone-gray castle nestled between two craggy walls, looking like part of the mountain itself. The illusion broke when the pointed towers came into sight. The stony battlements, banded with bronze, loomed overhead. Archers' metal caps peeked from behind the merlons above.

From the towers, two banners. Against the earthen walls and sparse pines flapped the gold-and-blue squares of House Pardwy. Below it was a gray tower on a stark-white field. He could not have been more relieved.

A dozen knights awaited them, scowling under the dark clouds. There was something familiar about the knight that stood at the fore, the silky sheen of his chestnut hair, his defined jawline. He smiled, his teeth straight and white.

"Anton!" called Orrick.

"Orrick? But why are *you* come?"

"Because rides he with us," answered Draque.

"Ah!" Anton turned to him, clapping his fist over his heart. "How punctual is my lord."

Draque offered the smallest of smirks. "I trust Pan Jarl is prepared to receive us. I fear we shan't continue on this day."

"Of course, my lord."

While the guardsmen led everyone inside the fortress, Orrick remained with Brandt and the other squires. Seabolt, reins in hand, led them to the small stables. Inside, sour with the smell of damp hay and rotted wood, Orrick understood just how minuscule Tourm's Gate truly was. With barely enough room for all twenty-seven horses, a few sumpters had to share a stall.

As they watered their horses and fed them with barely dry hay, Orrick watched the Lord Commander. He saw how fierce Seabolt could be, capitalized by his vicious-looking, red-eyed drákoń. At times on the journey, another horse would step too near, and Widdershins would snap at them. Stranger, whenever the horses went to or were retrieved from the stables, Seabolt always collected his himself, instead of Scritchfield, his lieutenant. Seabolt oft whispered to the beast, stroking his black nose down, smooth and straight. Everything about their interactions piqued Orrick's curiosity.

"Why care you for your horse and not Pan Scritchfield?"

"I bred Widdershins from mine own horses and trained him from a foal. I'm the only one he obeys."

"Widdershins is purebred, isn't he?"

"Aye, and you'll never find a horse more durable."

"Is it true about drákonie?" asked Orrick. "That they were created by elves?"

Seabolt stroked his chin. "You know the legend?"

"I do, pan. The elves imbued them with magics long forgotten. When expanded the realms of man, several drákonie escaped from the elves' domain."

Seabolt eyed Orrick queerly. "You remember this and not Virgil xu Lac?"

Orrick tried not to blush. "Ah—er—well, always have I liked horses—"

"So," said Seabolt thoughtfully, "style you your stirrups longways, and you're interested in horses. Your rouncey—?"

"Cień."

"Cień is of drákoń descent—and nicely cared for." He pattered Widdershins's neck. "Widdershins was an experiment, you know. I wanted to see if the horses would respond better to their knights if said knights bred and raised them, themselves. Do you think it's worked?"

"I do."

Seabolt laughed and clapped Orrick on the back and the left the stables. The gesture confused Orrick. He had difficulty reading Seabolt. Sometimes he acted gruff, even insulting. Yet knew he some Brzeg history, invited Orrick to dine with him, inquired after Orrick's thoughts.

Orrick decided it was best not to dwell on it. He and the squires followed Seabolt from the stables, briefly back into the chilly storm before heading inside, which was the same as the outside: floors, walls, ceilings, drab stone all. No carpets underfoot, nor any decorations save the occasional sconce. In the great hall—which was unworthy of the name—most of the knights already sat, but a few of them stood. It was meant to seat a party only half their size.

"This'll be where you'll eat for the night," said Anton, "and where you'll sleep."

A collective gasp rose from the visitors. Many asked, "Why?"

A new voice, rickety as rust, answered, "'Coz we only got spare beds for the commanders, 'at's why."

Everyone looked to the doorway where stood a hunchbacked old man. Arms and legs like pale sticks, his face was a gnarled canvas of scars and wrinkles. A single, bulbous blue eye set within a visage that made Orrick think of alabaster tree bark. The other eye was gone, replaced by a pink lid that flapped and stretched with every expression. Aside from his thick white eyebrows, he bore hair on neither head nor chin.

"Well met, Robyn pan Jarl!" Count Draque extended his hand.

The old man took it, and Orrick saw his two middle fingers had been cut off at the first knuckle long ago. He also saw that his left arm ended at the elbow. There was no doubt the man had seen more than one battle in his day. Now, he spent his final days as Lord of Tourm's Gate, captain of thirty men.

Altgeld stepped forward. "As heir to Rhabdolia, demand I room in a tower as well!"

Jarl raised his bushy brows. "Y' don' see Pan Pallaton complainin', do y'? 'E's heir o' Brzeg!"

"Bugger Brzeg," spat the giant knight. Orrick and Brandt recoiled, offended. "Orrick is no duke."

"Nor ye," growled the Gate Lord.

Altgeld stood up from the bench, drawing himself to his full eight-foot height. Wide as two men abreast, he was a terrifying sight for all in the room, except for Jarl. He merely remained scowling, looking up with his one shaky eye, blue as a summer morn.

"You're getting old," Altgeld said. "Should you not retire? It looks as though some of your parts have thought the same—they've gone already."

"Threatenin' me was a damn fool thing t' do." His one eye remained fixed on Altgeld's, but he spat at the giant's feet.

"How *dare* y—"

"What? Y' think I'm 'fraid o' your *size*? I popped maidenheads bigger'n y'!" His eye snapped to Seabolt. "Get o'er 'ere *now*, y' lout! This 'ow your soldiers speak t' those o' higher office 'at open their gates t' guests?"

273

Altgeld scoffed. "Why ask him—?"

"Shut up!" he snapped, eye rolling back, reminding Orrick of a tumbling jester. "One more word outta y' an' we'll see if the *Kendalans*'d offer y' a bed—for your body, at least. No doubt your *head*'ll rest 'pon their gates."

"You *dare*—"

"Aye, I dare! Listen t' yer commander!"

Seabolt had enough. "Dammit, Altgeld, *sit down*! Already you tread thin ice."

Fuming, Altgeld did as his commander bade.

The Tourm's Gate squires served supper not long thereafter. Wooden bowls filled with a thick beef roux, carrots, and turnips congealing in swampy gravy. Sadly, it lacked any strips of meat.

Still, it tastes better than rotting apples and a handful of berries, Orrick told himself. He, along with a small group, stood in the hall just outside the door. As he thought, the 'great hall' was far too small for all of them.

Orrick lowered his spoon as Anton approached, now considerably drier, and clasped wrists with him. "So," Orrick said, smiling, "this is where they put you?"

"Would that I had something more boring," said Anton.

"We've had Kendalan smugglers trying to get past our gates every three nights. None made it, though."

The shine in his eyes faltered, concerning Orrick. Before he could ask, Anton queried, "How's the life of a knight-errant?"

"Uneasy," he answered. "There was naught with which to prove myself in Brzeg. The men I ride with think me green." He sighed. "I've yet to earn their trust."

"I admit my surprise when I saw you. You travel with many seasoned knights, most of them highborn. You *are* green compared to them." He paused a moment to spoon some of his own roux into his mouth. He swallowed and said, "Tell me of aught you killed."

"Five jadwilki and a scimitiger—well, *Brandt* killed the 'tiger."

Appraising the squire, Anton raised his brow. "Did you now?"

Brandt bowed his head. "My victory is my master's, Pan Dasher."

"Speaking of killing," he whispered to Orrick, "What make you of Pan Altgeld's outburst?"

"I'd sooner not speak of Pan Altgeld, all things considered."

Anton's eyes fluttered, confused. "Why not?"

"He has not been the kindest."

"Were I more than a baronet's son, I'd be entitled as well."

Orrick raised an eyebrow. "Careful, Anton. You speak of Brandt's future liege lord and the future king's law-brother."

"Perhaps he'll be your squire's liege, but he's naught to Brzegu. And 'king's law-brother' is no title true. Even if it were, he is not just yet, as Gate Lord Jarl so kindly reminded us."

Orrick shook his head. "I'd rather not speak of it." He shoveled the rest of his roux into his mouth.

"As you like it," Anton answered, resigned. He no longer whispered when he said, "I do wish you luck in Kendala. I've not the foggiest why King Archibald attacks Tourm."

"Mayhap vengeance," Orrick answered.

"Vengeance for victories cleanly won centuries past?"

Orrick stroked his chin. "Perhaps he fancies himself a war-lord?"

"In his old age?" Anton questioned, shaking his head. "He's been a peaceful king all his seventy years—at least until late. Something changed his mind—but what?"

"That matters not," sighed Orrick. "No longer does he have a claim to Tourm's lands."

"Mayhap he's mad," offered Brandt.

Anton's pleasant, handsome face grew hard as iron. His eyes met Brandt's again, this time unpleased. Anton looked the squire up and down, judging him. And that meant he judged Orrick. "Remind your squire he speaks not lest spoken to." His tone was flat, and he did not look at Orrick when he said it.

"Remember your place," said Orrick sternly.

"*My* place?" the lad hissed. "I *know* my place. Forgive me if House Hargrove isn't as fine as Pallaton or Dasher." He turned to Anton. "Remind me again, pan, what you'll inherit?"

"You *wretch*!" His hand went to the dagger at his hip. "I should carve out your tongue for such insolence … or perhaps your mentor ought do it instead?"

"Enough," said Orrick. "Brandt is a good squire. I've too many liberties given him, and he forgets his place. There shall be no tongue-carving." To Brandt, "Remember your *position*. Squires address knights when only firstly addressed. None asked of you."

"Forgiveness, my lord," said Brandt slowly, deliberately, "but what good is speculation unless all possibilities are examined?"

"A thought wise enough, but none asked of you."

"Was it a thought you would've come to? I only wanted to—"

"*Brandt*," snapped Orrick. The chatter closest to them faltered and, as he became aware that those around them stared, he tried to keep the blush from rising. "A squire's place is the service of those knighted. Until you feel Szczerbieç's touch, you'll not know such kindness from other knights. Until you receive such grace, I'll hear no more, either."

"But—"

Anton lashed out with his mailed fist and cuffed Brandt's ear. Orrick watched his squire tumble to the floor. His plate shattered. Runny brown roux seeped into the floor's cracks. The murmur within the crowded dining hall ceased. All eyes fell upon them.

"Back t' your meal, y' scumpin' louts!" barked Jarl from the lords' table. At once the conversation and chewing continued until the great hall buzzed anew.

Orrick closed his eyes, turned away. *I must need be firmer in disciplining my squires.* As much as it pained him, he admitted, "Pan Dasher was right to cuff you."

Dammit, he could *feel* Anton sneering. Brandt stood without assistance, glowering at them both. His cheek reddened, an angry welt building. "Then take I my leave."

Orrick's squire left to be with the others. He turned his gaze to his empty plate. *I wish not to see Brandt treated so roughly but speaks he so frequently out of turn. I was too liberal, and 'twas only a matter of time ...*

Anton leaned against the wall, seemingly unbothered by Brandt's outburst. "What make you of the whelk's comment? Could Archibald have, in his old age, maddened?"

"I cannot know. None of us can. The only way of knowing is speaking with him. Doubtless, we'll dislike the answer, whatever it may be."

Anton might have been unbothered, but Orrick was not so cold. "As for Brandt, I'll discipline my own squires from now on, if you don't mind."

Anton licked his lips, unable to bring himself to meet Orrick's eyes.

After the meal, the Tourm's Gate squires cleared and scoured the mess from the floors. When it was time to sleep, the soldiers vied for the tabletops. Blankets and pillows were scarce as well, and the first knights and squires to receive them were the first ones served. All others had to take the hard floor, clothes, and rucksacks for pillows. Some of the squires attempted to sleep with their backs to the wall, others slept in the corridor which no one had swept. Despite his outburst, Altgeld went without a room, but was first to claim a tabletop.

Orrick and Brandt shivered on the floor in the dining hall, separate from one another. Orrick was unable to sleep. Throughout the night, he wished for the outdoors over these stone tiles.

In the dim candlelight, a brown spider tickled its way across the floor, unbothered by the sleeping bodies. He sighed, knowing

279

the true reason he found no rest. Brandt lay on the other side of the room, huddled with the other squires. He had tried to speak with the lad several times, to no avail. Brandt ignored him and went away.

Orrick was angry, but not at Brandt. He did this himself. He remembered the House of the Branch. Orrick taught Brandt, but Brandt taught Orrick, as well.

A hand roused his shoulder. Tired, he looked up and saw Anton. "Come with me."

Orrick took care not to wake the sleepers around him. Stiff-necked, the side of his face stung. *Chainmail makes for a terrible pillow.* To save space, he had rolled it under his rucksack, but as he slept it shifted and dug into his face. He felt better now that he wore it correctly.

Outside the dining hall, Anton thrust a steel cup at Orrick, filled to the brim with hot tea. Bitter, though he was glad for the warmth.

Gingerly stepping over the scarce few soldiers sleeping, Orrick followed Anton up battlement's stairwell. Fresh, chilly air was just past a crumbling wooden door.

Eastward, the sun rose. Golden light spilled onto the world like a dying lord's tarnished ring. Mist, silver as spiders' silk, crept along the rolling green vale. Westward, across the narrow path, more raised walls of stone. Kendala's Gate. It looked identical Tourm's Gate, and from this height, three miles seemed not so far. A breeze swept over them, rustling their hair, chilling their necks. Orrick felt glad for the tea steaming in its steel cup.

"Beautiful, isn't it?" asked Anton. "You'd never think that just across the way lay screaming plunderers."

"I'd believe anything," said Orrick. He remembered the thought that gave him the courage to accept Szczerbieç's grace. "Always shall there be evil men. That's why knights exist."

"Knights exist to kill and die, in that order," Anton countered.

"Knights exist to protect," Orrick argued.

"Yes. Protect," said Anton, eying Orrick curiously. "Remember you when Rupert killed those deserters?"

"How could I forget? They screamed, but never once begged mercy." Orrick held his hand out to Kendala's Gate. "They claimed war comes. I no longer doubt this is what was meant."

Anton silently turned to face the sunrise, giving Orrick time to sip thoughtfully. Finally, and without looking at him, he asked, "Have you killed anyone—any *people*?"

"No." Orrick shook his head. "I told you, only the jadwilki."

"Palatæ's instructors don't tell you how we're all just walking bags of meat and blood. Even after the deserters, I didn't believe it until ..."

281

"Until what?"

Anton turned a remorseful gaze to the heavens. "I killed someone."

"Have you?" He tried not to sound as surprised as he felt.

"Some Kendalans tried to get past Tourm's Gate. 'Twas past midnight, I on third watch. I saw them come but I'd no time to ring the bell. I—" He looked Orrick full in the face, eyes shining with the mysticism of some lost magic. "My blade went right through him, Orrick. He only wore a tunic—*right through him*. I watched him, shivering, bleeding, curled up on the dirty floor like a babe, sweet blood mingling with sour offal …"

Orrick remembered the putrescent stench that rankled the air in the Homey Hills. He and Anton looked toward the horizon again. The golden rays crept across the bruise-colored sky like vines on an old wall.

"I'd like to do that," Anton said after another silence.

"Do what?" Orrick asked. *Makes he no sense. Is he drunk?*

"Be an Akademia instructor. War's not for me. What's for me is teaching children how to hold a sword, scour mail and whet blades, how to saddle, pack, and mount a horse. None of my squires would speak so freely to their knights as yours does. You mark me that."

"'Tis a good dream," Orrick concurred, insult aside.

"Would that it was come true," he whispered. Then he sighed. "War may not be for me, but it appears I'm for it."

Orrick watched the sky, still bereft of life in the early hours. "War is a wolf and rabbits are life itself."

"What?"

"Virgil xu Lac. We read him in the academy. Seabolt reminded me."

"I remember, I suppose. We were not at war then, and I thought his poems of no consequence. And Didact Nudny bored me to sleep, too."

Orrick chuckled. The doting old man could ramble on for hours without asking a single question. "Aye, he was boring. Still, I should like to read Virgil xu Lac if I survive Kendala. Mayhap I'll have a greater appreciation for his work."

"That's also a good dream," said Anton solemnly. And the two watched the sun come up.

Orrick rejoined the procession after the sun had fully emerged from its earthly reservoir. Tourm's Gate's soldiers awaited them at the postern.

"I mislike this," said Jarl to Draque. "The enemy's too scumpin' cheeky."

283

"Must we so soon call them *enemy*?"

"See if they ain't," growled Jarl. "'Sides that point, your goal's Zachwalaç City, known by its black tower wit' two prongs scrapin' the sky."

"Thank you for your assistance, Pan Jarl. We hope to remain the night here again, and shortly."

"Y' ain' leaving yet," spat Jarl.

"What—?"

His glassy blue eye rolled over to Altgeld. "Him."

"Me?" Altgeld asked, both prideful and concerned.

"Yeah, *you*. You're lucky t' be 'live, y' know."

"I was unaware my life was in danger."

"'Twill be now more'n ever," Jarl growled. "I oughta gut y' righ' 'ere on the Pass o' Brother'ood!"

"Pan—"

"Don't *pan* me! What's your rank?"

Altgeld looked abashed, and Orrick tried not to gawk. He answered, "Cornet."

"Cornet. A sub-lieutenant. What? Y' ain't good 'nough t' be a *real* lieutenant?"

"Initially, but I—"

Jarl's eye rolled to Seabolt before tumbling back to Altgeld. "But you're foulmouthed, insubordinate, and entitled. Heir or not, that shite don't cut it in a military order." Jarl sneered and made his face look like a rotting turnip. "So, my successor had t' dock y'."

Altgeld nodded.

"Listen, lad. I don't care how big y' are, never speak 'at way t' a cap'n—'specially not t' me. Now off wit' y', y' scumpin' louts!"

"It appears squires aren't the only ones who know not their place," said Anton, flashing his white, straight teeth.

Brandt scowled. Remained he near Orrick but gone was his prideful step. Averted he his eyes and slumped his shoulders, ashamed. Silent throughout, Brandt did his duties, but wanted not to further incur a knight's wrath.

Damn you, Anton.

"Farewell, Pan Pallaton. Try not to get killed."

"Nor you, Pan Dasher."

Then, for the first time in centuries, Tourmians entered Kendala.

XV: Beyond The Borders

K endala's Gate stood only three miles west, but it seemed much further. The grass, shiny with dew, was lush and springy beneath Cień's hooves. As they approached the gate, five spearmen stepped forward.

Draque bade the company halt. Orrick frowned when he saw them, so similar to Tourmians and yet so different. Their armor was not at all like plate or scales. Instead, the cuirass was barrel-shaped, lacquered shiny black like a beetle, with a hood that rose above the scalp. Bright silk of different colors filigreed the armor. Each of them held a long spear, the shafts enameled scarlet with horsehair tassels under the blades.

"Why stay you our ride?" demanded Draque.

"Why indeed?" asked a Kendalan soldier. He came from behind the line of spearmen, wearing a cape of yellow silk over his carapace armor. Unlike the pikemen, his armor seemed less bulky, without the hood. Beady eyes, sallow skin, and thinning hair did little to garner trust. More than that was the weapon he held: a blade straight and short, seeming to emerge from a golden scimitiger's mouth.

"Who halts us so violently?"

"Edün an'Dréll, the Gate Lord of Kendala's Gate."

"Well, Pan an'Dréll—"

"No *pan*, Tourm-man. Just an'Dréll. *An'* means I'm a Grand Knight, a master amongst Earth Dancers."

"Well, an'Dréll, know you why we're come?"

The Gate Lord sneered. "Tourm-men are bigger fools than we thought. At least we've the good sense to sneak into Tourm by night. You ride up all a-clamor!"

Draque stiffened. "We're come to see King Archibald on behalf of King Biel, in hopes of quelling whatever drives him to war. We come in peace."

Kendala's Gate Lord stroked his thin, black beard. "You come in peace?"

"In peace," repeated Draque. "We assure you."

"A funny thing," said an'Dréll, smiling. "I've never known men of peace to come with such arms."

"All we desire is a peaceful resolution."

"Feh," he scoffed. "You'll have no such thing."

"No such—? Our king sent a hawk telling your king of our arrival. King Archibald knows we come. He expects us."

Small and dark, an'Dréll sneered all the while. He bellowed, "Open both gates!"

Jangling chains and grinding gears met their ears. The wrought iron gate opened before them, but the five spearmen remained in place, weapons forward. An'Dréll still wore his sneer, as though he knew something the envoy did not. Orrick moved his hand to his sword.

Curious, Draque bit. "The gates have risen, why don't your men aside?"

"Kendala's Gate was built to keep Tourm-men from entering our noble land after you wrested Nin from our hands. The King may have granted a pardon, but I have not. Men, attack!"

The spearmen spread out, aiming their spears at the horses, which nickered and backed away from the points.

"Should we be so diplomatic now?" growled Altgeld. It seemed his ire had returned.

"Whatever evils you mean to do, reconsider them!" the Count snapped. To the White Falcons, he said, "Ready your arrows."

Chelsea blinked, confused. "Pan—?"

"Our mission may be one of peace, but we must fight if threatened."

"I mislike this," muttered Seabolt, drawing his sword. "This treachery goes deeper than it appears."

Orrick's eyes went to the archers on the ramparts. They watched, arrows neither drawn nor nocked. *Pan Seabolt speaks true—something's afoot.*

"Lay down your arms and stand aside!" shouted Seabolt.

Surprisingly, an'Dréll did. He waved his tiger-hilt sword, and the spears lowered. "Very well, Tourm-men. You may pass."

One of the spearmen moved. "Are you certain—?"

Mail rang against flesh as an'Dréll slapped the soldier's face. With a clatter, the spearmen stumbled. "They'll pass, I said!" His eyes again found Draque's. "The Tourm-man speaks true. The King shall decide their fates."

With a swish of his citreous cape, an'Dréll stepped aside, unblocking their way to the stony tower.

The narrow gateway forced the entire company to go through in a slow-moving single line. More spearmen stood watch inside the gatehouse. Though the few yards from one end of the gatehouse to the other, the Kendalan's shifty eyes bade little confidence.

In dismal torchlight, spears of differing lengths, adorned with strange heads, smiled like highwaymen. Unmoved, the soldiers only stared as Cień clomped past. Orrick kept one hand on the rein and the other on the hilt, ready to draw at any danger.

Yet danger never came.

The other side gave way to miles of verdant radiance, with hills and mountains spiraling downward. Circular terraces spilled over with the greenest, cleanest water Orrick ever saw. Jellyfish willows, tendrils shining like gems, dripped their branches off the sides, rolling down unto the terrace below. Certainly, Orrick could not liken the view to anything east of Durwyn's Pass.

"What?!" someone shouted from behind.

"Hold—*hold*, I said!" It was Seabolt.

Orrick looked behind him and saw one of the stationary spearmen, stationary no longer, poking his spear at a squire's horse with a horrible, gravelly chuckle. The sumpter nickered and backed into a knight's horse, which threatened to lose its balance.

Seabolt lashed out and cut the head from the spear. Orrick held his breath as the other spearmen advanced, weapons pointed. All around him, White Falcons nocked their arrows.

Orrick became aware he had drawn his own sword but could not remember doing so.

"Stand down, men!" cried an'Dréll from the ramparts. Flanked by motionless archers, his wispy beard and yellow tassels blew in the breeze. "Your fun is had! Let them on!"

The spearheads pointed skyward once more, but the Kendalans still sneered. Seabolt lowered his sword but sheathed it not.

At Draque's gesture, the peaceful host continued down another narrow pass of roughhewn stone. This time, instead of bluffs dropping into the sea, the path cut across rows of terraces, leading to a valley below. Each terrace, a cliff unto itself, held a basin, green and overflowing with clean water. Ragged people sifted through the mud, gathering rice into hip-mounted baskets.

"What damn fool puts six soldiers against thirty?" demanded Seabolt.

"They had more," argued Volker.

"They *used* six!" said Altgeld. "Six outside, six in—and we could've taken them!"

"You cavalrymen forget yourself," said Draque. "Seek we peace with Kendala. Attacking them would have—"

"They attacked us first," snapped Seabolt.

"They didn't," said Orrick, drawing their attention.

"What mean you?"

"The archers never nocked their bows."

The three commanders eyed him, along with Altgeld.

"They *did* have archers," Volker reasoned. "At an'Dréll's word, we'd be plunged into fire."

"Yet gave he no such command," Draque deduced. "Why?"

Seabolt spat and Widdershins quickened his trot. Before leaving them, he muttered, "'Your fun is had,' said an'Dréll ... "

Come twilight, the host reached the bottom of the terrace path. Moorlands spread before them. Hills and valleys green with moisture. Brown swamps budding with tiny plants. Overhead, the sky cold, gray, hard as steel. Farmhouses made broken rings at the swamp's edge, windows alive with yellow light.

"We'll find no succor there," said Draque, noticing the younger knights eying them. Instead, they remained outdoors with thin sheets of burlap between them and the ground.

Days went on as they traveled through the moorlands, treading muddy paths crisscrossed between the shallow paddy waters. As they went, rice farmers continued cultivating. It was the children, drenched and filthy, who stopped to stare at them, fear in their eyes. Orrick tried not to stare back but seeing them worried his heart.

"We've done no wrong and already they mistrust us," Chelsea whispered. She rode nearer to him now that Brandt, still hurt after Anton struck him, cowered away with the rest of the squires. He still came when Orrick called him, helped him mount and dismount, took his baldric, sharpened his swords, all without a single word.

Orrick admitted, if only to himself, that Brandt acted somewhere between a spoiled child and a frightened animal. And it wasn't as if he hadn't tried making amends. He saved him seats near the campfire—spurned for a place with the other squires. He offered light, even humorous conversation—received halfhearted shrugs and silence. *He acts the child, indeed. I could demand he talk to me, but then who would the child be?*

The knights did naught to aid the situation. Altgeld continually insisted Orrick and Brandt were having a lovers' quarrel.

"Spurned you for another woman," Altgeld would say.

Indeed, Brandt spent more time around Chelsea's squire, Wąda. In his sadness, he seemed to have lost his awkwardness. *He at least smiles around her.*

"Orrick!" Chelsea hissed, nudging him. "Did you not hear me?"

"I ... mine apologies, I did not."

She nodded her head toward the townsfolk, golden ringlets shaking. "I said, we've done no wrong and already they mistrust us."

"Should men foreign, horsed, and armed ride into Albion, would *you* trust *them*?"

"No," she admitted. "I'd not."

Continuing northwest, they reached drier land, the muddy trail becoming a road well-worn. Forests sprawled on either side, though the one to the east stretched further and spread wider. Mountains rose from a haze, rounded, snowcapped peaks that Orrick recognized.

"The Sea of Trees," Chelsea confirmed.

The hinterland on the western side of the River Lachlan created a several-hundred league border between Tourm and Kendala. Rumored to be home to highwaymen and savages, none dared enter it. That was well, for no maps told of a clear path. Since boyhood, Orrick had heard stories about men that entered it never to return. Then again, the same was said of Domoż's Whitewoods, Brzeg's Turnip Marsh, and Rhabdolia's Forest Maze.

In groves, they found trees bearing purple fruit shaped like spin tops. Dowd had spotted a squirrel eating one, which made Count Draque deem them safe to consume. The skin was bitter, meat tart and crumbly, but it was better than wild mushrooms and stale rations. Chelsea fired an arrow, taking the squirrel through the eye. She and Draque shared it that night.

It rained the second day. The knights brought their horses under the canopy of the forest, but that did little to appease them.

On the third day, the sun again shone, and the horses were happy to slake their thirsts on the dewy grass. The host passed the village on the way. Cowherds, shepherds, and swineherds watched them fearfully. A mother came to speak to her husband and drew her daughter close as they passed. However, the villager's reception no longer mattered to Orrick or anyone else. They could see the twin spires of Czerny Widoleç in the distance, foreboding as a black dragon.

For supper that day, the White Falcons went into the woods and returned with squab, each expertly shot. The squires plucked the feathers from the unfledged pigeons and roasted them over a small fire. Small, the tender meat glistened with fat. Delicious though they were, each person received only half a bird.

The more Orrick saw, the more impressed with the White Falcons he became. Since their march began, he noted their tracking abilities and their dexterity with their weapons. When the spearmen inside Kendala's Gate turned to attack, they nocked their arrows faster than most men could draw a sword. He understood why. In the morning, first thing after dressing, they strung their bows and fletched a dozen arrows. Kept they their bowstrings all day taut, undoing them only before sleep. And their quivers they wore at their hips, not upon their backs.

As Orrick saw when he and Malloy shared the third watch, he strung his bow first thing and fletched after everyone else had woken. Orrick remembered the Blood Knights, the finest swordsmen in Fangaard, and wondered if they treated their blades similarly.

The envoy prepared to begin anew their trek. Brandt remained near Wąda, aiding her to pack her sumpter horse. Orrick approached, smiling apologetically. Brandt affixed the saddle-bags and without facing him said, "I'll help you to your horse in a moment, Lord Pallaton."

"My thanks, Brandt." He sighed. Despite Brandt's coldness, Orrick had something to say. "Every day come we closer to Zachwalaç. I want you near me when we arrive—for your protection."

"As you like, my lord."

"*Brandt*—" Orrick meant not to sound so harsh. For a moment, fear shone in Brandt's eyes but then returned they to their cold, placid look. "I just want your safety."

"Forgiveness, my lord, but for the nonce I'm quite busy. I'll see to you shortly."

Naught else to say, Orrick nodded and turned away. He heard Wąda say, "You needn't be so hard on him. 'Twas not he who

297

cuffed you."

"We're all of us but squires to them. One day we're laughing and the next ... 'tis like I'm a stranger."

Damn you, Anton, thought Orrick as he returned to Cień. *And damn me, too.*

He did want Brandt to be safe—and safety would not be guaranteed once reached they Kendala's high seat.

XVI: Into Fire

Soon, the black spires of Zachwalaç were no longer faceless monsters on the horizon. They arrived at the royal capital of Kendala, a barrier of black stone between them and the city. And though they were not surprised to see the portcullis shut to them, they gasped when the longbowmen walking the ramparts aimed their weapons at them. They all wore barrel-shaped armor, similarly to the soldiers from the gate. However, as archers, it appeared the armor had relief around the shoulders to better accommodate bows.

"Stand down," called Draque, and brought his charger to the fore.

"What business have Tourm-men here?"

"Our business is with King Archibald. He expects this emissary."

The longbowmen chuckled. "*Does* he?"

Before Count Draque could ask the question's meaning, a young man joined the soldiers atop the walkway. His long face was buttery as tallow, framed by overlong hair as black and greasy as tar. His ashen eyes were cold and pink with sleeplessness. Under them were weeping bags of puffy skin. Yet as Orrick stared, the more saw there was something regal beneath the listlessness. After all, he wore a velvet doublet of forest-green, and upon his back was a sable-trimmed maroon cloak.

The young man eyed them all, going from one knight to the next. "Why are Tourm-men come to Zachwalaç?"

A wave of confusion rumbled through the knights and squires. Orrick kept his teeth clamped shut.

Draque called up, "Who addresses me?"

"Archibald Hŭdàshī the Second," the young man proclaimed.

Orrick's breath caught in his throat. *The Second? Something's amiss.* He edged closer to Brandt and whispered, "Remain close to me."

The squire scoffed.

"You must need trust me, Brandt. I cannot—"

"Do you conspire down there, Tourm-man?"

Orrick snapped his gaze back to the young man, uncertain of what to say.

"No conspiring occurs, Your Highness," answered Draque. "King Biel had sent a whitetail hawk proclaiming a herald. *We* are that herald, and I am he who leads it. Might I speak with your father, Prince Archibald?"

"*King* Archibald," he scoffed, sounding proud and annoyed. "Foreigners may address me as Your Royal Majesty. Wodniça's Moon saw my father dead."

No doubt Draque was as surprised as Orrick, as well as the rest of them. That was nearly four months ago. Happily, Brandt moved closer to Orrick.

After a moment of consternation, Draque collected himself and pressed onward. "Well, we bid Your Royal Majesty good noon and add that you've Tourm's condolences for the loss of your father. Surely the people of Kendala mourn their king, just as they are glad for their new one—"

"Enough pomp," said the new king. "Why are you come?"

Silenced, perhaps offended, Draque looked at the men flanking him. The twenty-seven Tourmians whispered to one another, some muddled whilst others cowed.

Draque returned his attention to Kendala's new young king. "King Biel confirmed the whitetail hawk. Is there some misunderstanding?"

"No misunderstanding," answered Archibald. "I received no whitetail hawk."

"'Twas for your father, the late King Arch—"

"I did not ask who my father was!" the young king snapped. "I *know* who my father was! He was a simpering craven who forgot his ancestors. I asked about *you*. Why stand *you* before me?"

"We seek you—"

"*Doubtless you seek me*," Archibald shouted, eyes smoldering.

Draque winced, along with many others, Orrick amongst them. As someone who struggled regularly with patience, he felt glad not to be in the Count's place.

"I know that as well. What I know not is *why* Tourm-men, bearing arms and riding warhorses, seek me. You are simple. I'll ask plainly: What is the meaning of this sortie?"

"'Tis no sortie but a peaceful excursion," Draque answered. "In these trying times, we'd think ourselves foolish if an emissary from Tourm traveled not with a host of knights, and what are knights without squires?"

"What are any of those without weapons and warhorses, you'd next ask me. Why does that oaf-king send emissaries prepared for war?"

"We are *not* prepared for war, Your Royal Majesty. Behold, our host is small and we've no herbalists or illusionists amongst us. Pray, tell how a gathering of seven-and-twenty can hope to besiege the mighty Zachwalaç?"

"I never said you were *good* at making war, only that you're come to make it."

Draque fell silent. So did Archibald. Orrick disliked him speaking ill of Biel, yet the young king appeared adamant.

Archibald exhaled, eyes returning to impassive pools. "*Why* are you come if not for war?"

"The opposite—seek we peace," Draque answered, with a tone suggesting he was tired of explaining himself. This was the third time he mentioned it. "King Biel sent a whitetail hawk to convey our coming."

"Yes. You've mentioned that—a lot."

"Because speak we sooth, Your Royal Majesty. And now we're come because we wish to know why your father attacked Nin."

But he didn't, thought Orrick.

"I must question if you *are* come in peace. Did you not attack the guardsmen at Kendala's Gate?"

"What lies—?"

"Stay yourself, Elton," said Draque. To Archibald: "Mine apologies, but you were misinformed. 'Twas *they* attacked *us* as we rode through. Granted, we drew our weapons as it happened, but would you not expect us to defend ourselves?"

"Perhaps they would've felt safer came you unarmed."

"Regardless, our clash was short and bloodless. Now, Your Royal Majesty, why would your father attempt Nin?"

Archibald smiled devilishly. If but momentarily, the look made Orrick fear undergods had returned to Fangaard.

"Look at you, filthy mongrels come sniffing from the moors. You've the sniveling look of Tourm-men, and their lack of wits besides!"

Draque, struggling to remain tactful, asked, "Of what do you speak?"

"Are you that nescient still? 'Twas not my father's command that saw Nin attacked, but mine!"

"Why? Your father was a gentle king."

"My weakling father was a disgrace to the ancestors of House Hŭdàshī, the greatest dynasty Fangaard as ever seen! Thus, did he no justice to all the other Kendalan Houses, great or small, ancient or new. He couldn't be allowed to live any longer, not whilst my ancestors were upset with him so!"

"Your Majesty—?"

"'Twas not only Father that disgraced House Hŭdàshī, but the Tourm-men as well! With Father finally dead, able am I to do as mine ancestors bid. Reclaim, shall I, their lands stolen by Tourm! More than that, an empire I shall make of all Fangaard! I'll ask you now, Tourm-men: Has your oaf-king sent you to surrender?"

"We'll not surrender ... Your Royal Majesty." The Count was losing his patience. A longer second had passed before he used the honorific. "And we ask you speak no ill of our king."

"Why not? After all, it seems I'm the better choice: young, handsome, thin. He seems an utter lackwit besides."

He is indeed young, thought Orrick. *But his thinness comes from malnourishment rather than fitness. As for being handsome, perhaps that would be true if he did not look as though he hadn't slept in a fortnight ...*

"You dare call our king lackwit? At least he was not possessed to choose the ill-fated actions you have!"

"*Ill-fated*?! I am not the one that makes war with an army of seven-and-twenty. Unless—" he squinted to the distance "—you're but a scouting party?"

305

"No men follow us, and none hide in the wings. Come, are we, to keep peace and prosperity in Fangaard. Beseech we you to cease your attacks on Nin. Those feudal times are gone. We are more civilized than our ancestors, and our borders are unlike to change."

"Funny you should say that." Archibald smiled. "We Kendalans place more into our ancestors than wearing their symbols and forgetting the songs written about them. We *are* our ancestors. Their blood flows through us as surely ours flowed through them."

"We implore you heed our words!"

"I'll hear no more words but declarations of fealty. Plan I in one moon to descend upon Tourm. You'll be spared should you here and now bend your knees."

Draque fell silent, crystal-blue eyes wide with indecision and fright. King Archibald played the fool. With his father dead, he sent soldiers to attack Nin to appease his ancestors.

With his father dead, the whitetail hawk came to him …

The new king knew they were coming, knew to wait for them at the gate, and then he would demand fealty or death. Whether 'twas Archibald's luck or request that Biel sent military leaders, Orrick knew not. Regardless, it was as Seabolt thought—as they all feared.

This is an ambush.

"Well?"

"We'll not betray our kingdom!" shouted Drague.

Archibald's smile lessened. "A pity, that. Tourm shall become Kendala, and Kendala shall become Fangaard."

He turned on his heel. Brandt gasped and Orrick's eyes went wide. Emblazoned on his cloak was a gold-cloth scimitiger.

"Kill them all," he said, loud enough for them to hear, before disappearing from the walkway.

"This means war, you know!" shouted Draque, face scoured by rage. He faced his archers and spat, "Fire, dammit!"

"Fall back!" commanded Seabolt. "Fall back and make a line!"

Atop the battlements, archers loosed their arrows. The White Falcons returned fire in kind. Plumes of white down sprouted from the Kendalan's faces like flowers in a magic garden.

Orrick reared Cień, bade Brandt follow him. "Our lives are forfeit if we remain!"

Indeed, they were.

He tried not to look at Dowd, who had already taken two arrows, one to the neck and one right between his fearful eyes, which rolled into the back of his head. Away from him now, Orrick could not shake the sight of the fallen knight's legs helplessly kicking, blood spurting from his throat as he fought for breath.

Brandt did as Orrick bade. Cień' silver eyes grew wild at the scent of blood. Orrick struggled just to keep a straight gallop. An arrow soared overhead by a foot, another stuck in the ground nearby, a third clattered against Orrick's roundel. At last, they were away from the crossfire between the tower archers and the White Falcons.

Behind, Brandt drove Nash with all his might. Unencumbered by supplies and a drákoń besides, Cień was faster. Arrows followed them from the ramparts. At last, he pulled his sword free. But what good was a sword against archers on a wall?

No choice but to keep his distance, Orrick came up the line made by the White Falcons. He went beside Chelsea just as she loosed an arrow in unison with the others, peppering the archers black and white.

"Siege tactics are good," said Chelsea, smiling and drawing another shaft, "but win they no archery contests."

With a sound like a cracked whip, her arrow whizzed through the air and caught a bowman in his left eye. He slumped over.

Orrick looked at her surprised, but she chuckled and took up a new arrow.

"Would that I could help."

"You brought not your bow. Haven't you been practicing?"

"I—" He wanted to say he had not, but the words caught in his throat. His mind glimpsed the academy, remembering as she taught him proper stance, how to use his back. The vision vanished when Altgeld rode to them.

"'Tis futile here!" he bellowed. "We must retreat!"

"And go where?" argued Orrick.

"Pan Pallaton has a point. Retreat and they'll pursue," Seabolt shouted over slapping bowstrings and whistling arrows. "The Twin Gates are a sennight away, and the guards will notice our injured men. No doubt they'll be alerted, besides."

"Bugger Kendala's Gate!" Altgeld exclaimed. "They've but thirty men. Stand we a better chance there than here!"

Orrick shook his head. "No, the Sea of Trees is the only way!"

"The hinterlands?" The giant knight looked livid, as if he wanted to strangle him.

"We'll come to the borders, through the Sea of Trees, then cut north. We must need live off the land, but eventually we'll find Turnip Marsh."

"I've never heard a plan more terrible," spat Altgeld.

"But it might be the best hope we've got," said Seabolt. "Tell the men to fall back. We shan't lose any more Tourmian blood this day!"

But as he said it, the sound of grinding metal-filled their ears. Malloy the White Falcon shouted, "They open the gates!"

All eyes went to the drawbridge as it opened before them. Soldiers horsed upon coursers and chargers galloped from Zachwalaç's walls. The warriors spilling forth held wide, curved swords and the strangest spears Orrick had ever seen, like tridents but with so many more prongs. The horses they rode were black-eyed and dull-hooved.

White Falcons flew their arrows, bringing down both horse and horseman. The beasts screamed as their legs gave out and their weight crushed the soldiers atop.

More and more soldiers poured from the gates, too many for even the White Falcons to keep up with.

"We must need hold them off," said Seabolt, wrenching free his sword. "White Falcons maintain the line. Silver Wolves will catch any that get past us. Though we haven't the men for our full formation, go we to the fore! Golden Bulls, *charge*!"

Orrick joined the Golden Bulls. Eyes narrowed, Brandt sat atop Nash.

"No," said Orrick, "remain behind—"

Shouts of "Tourm!" filled the air, as well as cries for "Astoria!" "Albion!" and "Rhabdolia!" The Golden Bulls charged, horses snorting.

Brandt shouted "Maycoast!" and bade his horse charge.

Orrick followed closely behind. "Brzeg!"

In the fray, Orrick lost sight of Brandt. There was no time to look for him. Tourm knights and Kendalan soldiers clashed all around.

Orrick swiftly learned that slashing at any approaching soldier was not enough. His sword scarred the lacquer, but otherwise glanced ineffectively off the rounded armor. The idea struck him that the potbellied cuirasses were designed to catch arrows and spearheads. But if they could not be pieced, then perhaps like a beetle's carapace they could be—

Orrick fell backward, unhorsed, chest afire, grass cold and wet beneath him. An enemy arrow struck him in the right breast. He hissed at every motion that twisted where it had bitten him.

Get up! he told himself. This is what Lord Father feared, the warnings he gave. He did not want Orrick to die here, in a land foreign. Thinking of his family, his mind went to Sylvia, her green eyes bright, her smile broad.

You'll see her again, he thought, teeth gritted, *just get up*!

Orrick stood and examined himself. Thankfully, his hauberk, leather jerkin and woolen tunic, protected him from most of the damage. With a reckless tug, the arrow came free. Painful though it felt, the blood upon the arrowhead told him the wound was not deep.

Orrick collected his longsword and stood, searching for Cień. The black rouncey ran confusedly, blood streaming from his flank, silver eyes wide.

"Cień!" he called to no avail.

More arrows rained from above. Orrick ducked, rolled away from them, heard his drákoń's pained nickers. Cień—Armitage's gift upon his knighthood—lay on the ground, riddled with cyan shafts.

No time to mourn. Alas, no time even to put the poor beast from his misery.

Grunting, Orrick narrowly avoided a charging courser, whose rider swung something like a morning-star.

Anger burned within him. He had felt fear when he saw Dowd struggling for life, but no longer. At the sight of Cień, rage coursed through him like wildfire. His horse—these men had killed his horse!

Orrick faced the courser again, ducking under the whipping flail and slashing at the mount's front leg. The horse screamed and bucked, and the soldier tumbled over. Within that same moment, Orrick gripped his blade near the cross-guard and plunged the point into the Kendalan's chest.

If the armor cannot be pierced, he thought, *then perhaps like a beetle's carapace, it can be crushed.*

With a sickening crunch, the lacquer splintered, along with the wood and hide underneath. Blood spattered over Orrick's face as the soldier groaned and died.

He pulled his sword from the corpse. Blood and meat stuck to its fuller. At that moment, time seemed to stop.

I ... killed a man ...

"Orrick!"

He knew not who shouted his name, but another second into his reverie would have seen him without a head. Orrick ducked a sword-swipe. Drunk on screams and blood, Orrick crossed blades with his attacker. They rounded each other and Orrick used his longer sword to his advantage. He leapt over the corpse and found Brandt fighting soldiers. It was he that had called his name, Orrick was sure.

Knights fought and died all around. Most of the rampart's longbowmen had been felled. Their arrows came fewer. The true danger was the foot soldiers and cavalrymen charging from the gates.

Altgeld was among those still fighting. He looked more a warrior than Orrick had ever seen. Over eight feet tall, destrier and crème-colored surcoat both awash with blood, he swung his mighty halberd wide and hard, chopping through lacquered hoods, taking off three men's heads with a single stroke. Orrick watched in awe and horror as the giant knight cleaved through a soldier's helm, spattering blood, bone, brains.

The White Falcons did well, too. Shortly after forming a line, they used the distance to pick off their foes with ease. Draque remained protected behind his archers, shouting for them to continue their barrage as he added his own.

The commanders' fighting was something to behold. Volker moved fluidly despite his plate armor. He preferred to stab men in their backs, using his shield to keep foes at bay until he created an opening. He had taught his Silver Wolves the same.

As for Seabolt, that was a sight unlike any Orrick had never seen. Widdershins crossed the field like lightning, running Kendalans down, biting and trampling them as his rider slew foes with the master-forged broadsword, Almace.

Orrick put his sword through another Kendalan, the sounds of battle and death distant to him. All the while, his eyes flickered to Brandt, who slashed gracelessly. To make matters worse, Nash backed away, panicked.

Orrick fought his way over to him, plowing through the men surrounding his squire. They lashed out with their spears, but Orrick found his way around, parrying, slashing, until all were dead or injured.

"My thanks—"

"Save them!" he shouted. "Disobey me never again! Now come! We must regroup!"

Brandt's shame become fear.

Behind him, Orrick heard the tightening of metal, the sound of a hammer breaking the air. He turned just in time to see the chain serpentine and then *snap* straight and taut. Orrick moved to avoid being brained but tripped over a felled soldier—Tourmian or Kendalan, he saw not.

The flail-wielder stood over him, his weapon raised, but Brandt took the leather-gripped blade and put the point of his sword into the soldier's back. Blood sprayed from his mouth as he keeled over, coughing, dying.

Another Kendalan raised his spear to skewer Brandt whilst the lad fought another foot soldier. Orrick removed the foe's hand with a swipe and then thrust, leaving a jagged red ruin of the knight's throat.

Brandt asked, "Are you well, my lo—*pan*?"

Orrick's mouth pulled into a small smile as he looked into his squire's eyes, happy to once again be on speaking terms.

Trumpet blasts aroused his senses. *A clarion call!*

Swiftly, Orrick leapt onto Nash's back. "Get behind the line!"

As they escaped, a Kendalan soldier tried to intercept them. He died from a white-fletched arrow. They dodged swordsmen and spearmen, as well as arrows loosed from the battlements. The White Falcons' soared the opposite way.

"We must away," said Seabolt as Orrick and Brandt reached

315

the line.

Altgeld rode up as well. He and his destrier, Thrythgar, suffered no damaged, but they dripped with blood. "More soldiers come."

The land between the line and the castle was laden with bodies, blood, and beautiful tassels. The wind stank of raw meat, hot blood, offal. Maimed soldiers screamed and cried, but there was no way to end their misery.

Frightened, Orrick looked toward Seabolt. "We must away indeed."

"Duff!" shouted Draque. The olive-skinned knight turned to him. "Take your men to Tourm's Gate." To Seabolt, "Take Orrick and Erasmus to the Sea of Trees and make for Albion."

"And you?"

"The White Falcons have sustained no casualties but four squires. Half my archers ride with the Silver Wolves, the rest join you. We'll hold them off whilst you retreat. Worry not—we'll soon depart!"

Galloping hooves filled their ears. The two remaining Silver Wolves and their lord commander were already black ants nearing the horizon. With them were three other mounts, white capelets billowing.

"Come off there," said Seabolt. "We'll be faster if you've a horse of your own." He gestured to a spare horse reigned by Mandel Lunt, Altgeld's squire. Altgeld, himself, already charged to the forest beyond.

Orrick nodded his thanks and climbed upon Tort, Dowd's blue-eyed, skewbald courser. Chelsea and Wąda continued firing.

"Chelsea, you've my thanks!" said Orrick.

"We'll hold them off," she replied. "We'll be right behind you."

"Be well, Wąda," said Brandt. "Don't be long ..."

The girl, who shot slowly and sporadically compared to the other archers, smiled. "You, too, Brandt."

Sad and frightened, visions of bloodshed fresh in his mind, Orrick reared Tort. He and Brandt followed Seabolt into the forest.

CONTINUED IN WOLVES OF WAR, ACT II:
STORM AND SIEGE

Thank you for reading.

Thank you for reading. If you would like to comment on this book, we would love to read it. Swipe to a new page at the end of the book if you are reading digital to let us know what you think.

If this is a physical copy or you want to say hi visit the team at:

https://privatedragon.com/

If you want a review to matter for the future of the world! Leave a review on Amazon.

Our team is busy making more books and games. Find another outstanding book or game and what Adam is working on at our website.

Hope to see you there!

About the Author

Adam has loved fantasy since he was a kid, and medieval Eastern Europe enthralls him. He lives in Chicago, where he sings in a band called "Sacred Monster" and practices Japanese swordsmanship. He enjoys playing guitar and is a devout follower of rock and metal music. He hopes to add his own twists to the world of fantasy with his first novel, turned series, "Wolves of War."

You can connect with me on:

🐦 https://twitter.com/adamtsconlonsff